LORD APACHE

Stranded in the middle of the ... :ompromis-
... rritory, an
... st suddenly
— and his
l, armed as
id a rather
io entry in
to the Far
besieged by
tiful young
ive. But he
im well: an

SPECIAL MESSAGE TO READERS

THE ULVERSCROFT FOUNDATION
(registered UK charity number 264873)
was established in 1972 to provide funds for
research, diagnosis and treatment of eye diseases.
Examples of major projects funded by
the Ulverscroft Foundation are:-

- The Children's Eye Unit at Moorfields Eye Hospital, London
- The Ulverscroft Children's Eye Unit at Great Ormond Street Hospital for Sick Children
- Funding research into eye diseases and treatment at the Department of Ophthalmology, University of Leicester
- The Ulverscroft Vision Research Group, Institute of Child Health
- Twin operating theatres at the Western Ophthalmic Hospital, London
- The Chair of Ophthalmology at the Royal Australian College of Ophthalmologists

You can help further the work of the Foundation
by making a donation or leaving a legacy.
Every contribution is gratefully received. If you
would like to help support the Foundation or
require further information, please contact:

THE ULVERSCROFT FOUNDATION
The Green, Bradgate Road, Anstey
Leicester LE7 7FU, England
Tel: (0116) 236 4325

website: www.foundation.ulverscroft.com

LORD APACHE

ROBERT J. STEELMAN

SAGEBRUSH
Large Print Westerns

First published in the United States by Doubleday

First Isis Edition
published 2016
by arrangement with
Golden West Literary Agency

A catalogue record for this book is available
from the British Library.

ISBN 978-1-78541-019-2 (pb)

Published by
F. A. Thorpe (Publishing)
Anstey, Leicestershire

Set by Words & Graphics Ltd.
Anstey, Leicestershire
Printed and bound in Great Britain by
T. J. International Ltd., Padstow, Cornwall

This book is printed on acid-free paper

"Darrel Duppa was one of the queerest specimens of humanity, as his ranch was one of the queerest examples to be found in Arizona, and I might add in New Mexico and Sonora as well. There was nothing superfluous about Duppa in the way of flesh, neither was there anything about the 'station' that could be regarded as superfluous, either in furniture or ornament. Duppa was credited with being the wild harum-scarum son of an English family of respectability, his father having occupied a position in the diplomatic or consular service of Great Britain, and the son having been born in Marseilles. Rumor had it that Duppa spoke several languages — French, Spanish, Italian, German — that he understood the classics, and that, when sober, he used faultless English. I can certify to his employment of excellent French and Spanish, and what to my ears had the sound of pretty good Italian, and I know too that he was hospitable to a fault, and not afraid of man or devil. Three bullet wounds, received in three different fights with the Apaches, attested to his grit, although they might not be accepted as equally conclusive evidence of good judgment. The site of his 'location' was in the midst of the most uncompromising piece of desert in a region which boasts of possessing more desert land than any other territory in the Union.

"What caused me most to wonder was why Duppa ever concluded to live in such a forlorn spot; the best answer I could get to my queries was that the Apaches had attacked him at the moment of approaching the banks of the Agua Fria at this point, and after he had repulsed them he thought he would stay there merely to let them know he could do it. This explanation was satisfactory to everyone else, and I had to accept it."

On the Border with Crook,
Capt. John G. Bourke,
Third Cavalry, USA;
Charles Scribner's Sons,
New York, N.Y., 1891

Oh, that the desert were my dwelling place
With one fair spirit for the minister
That I might forget the human race
And, hating no one, love but only her!

Childe Harold

Byron, George Gordon
(Lord Byron)

CHAPTER
ONE

At ten in the morning the Fahrenheit thermometer stood at one hundred degrees. September sun glittered on the harsh mirror of the desert. Mirages shimmered around the pack train. Even the mules were deceived, straying from the rutted wagon road to reach the beckoning lakes, tree-rimmed islands. But there were no lakes, no islands, not even human beings; the caravan might have been traveling through a lunar landscape.

It was three days since they had left the village of Phoenix, at the junction of the Salt and Gila rivers. Under the shade of his Bombay *topi*, Jack Drumm's wind-reddened eyes stared at his man Eggleston.

"Are you all right, Eggie?"

The valet smiled wanly, holding the umbrella over his bald head. Incongruous in the heat, he wore a wilted collar and nankeen coat in spite of his master's kindly permission to remove them.

"I am well, Mr. Jack," he murmured, "except for a slight ringing in my ears, and a touch of giddiness."

Drumm handed him a canteen. "In Marrakesh, in Morocco, you remember they warned us to beware of the desiccating effect of the desert. This Arizona

1

Territory heat is certainly worse." The plump young man scanned the horizon through a brassbound telescope, his straw-colored mustache twitching in distaste. "A sun-baked inferno! I don't know what possessed me to route my Grand Tour through this wasteland! We should have taken the steam cars direct from San Francisco to New York, and thus home to Hampshire."

Eggleston handed back the canteen. "I am refreshed now, sir. Please do not worry about my welfare! I am a coper, as you well know, and will handle anything that comes my way, even the very fires of hell!"

Drumm clapped him on the back. "Spoken like a true Briton, Eggie! I am proud of you. Anyway, this is certainly the hottest part of the day, and it can only become cooler." He pointed to a tracery of green in the distance. "That must be the Agua Fria River. According to my map, it is a tributary of the Salt. After we negotiate the pass ahead, the river is only a few miles farther. We will camp along its banks tonight."

In spite of Drumm's prediction, the day grew hotter. The playa, as the early Spanish explorers named the desert, sweltered in the sun as the heavily laden train toiled toward the pass. Whorls of dust arose, swirling like dancers across the plain. The wind blew with the hot breath of a forge. Far to the north, beyond the new territorial capital of Prescott, the Aquarius Mountains were a jagged brown scar on the horizon. The Mazatzal range, to the east beyond the meandering Agua Fria, loomed high above the desert, a few trees greening its high ridges. For a moment there was a wink of light

2

from its wooded slopes, perhaps a ray of sunlight reflected from snow-water; then it was gone. On Mazatzal, Drumm reflected, it would be cooler. According to his map the peak was over nine thousand feet in elevation. But on the playa there was no relief. Like insects trapped on a gigantic baking dish the party inched northward toward the river.

Late in the afternoon they turned aside from the deserted road to rest in the shade of a scraggly bush. From his *Traveler's Guide to the Far West* Drumm identified it as the desert ironwood. He was preparing to sit beneath it with his pad to make a quick sketch when Eggleston cried out in alarm:

"Careful, sir! Don't sit there!"

Drumm watched the dusty gray coils as the snake writhed from its lair, tail buzzing, undulating body making diagonal marks in the sand.

"*Crotalus cerastes*," he murmured. "What they call the side-winder, Eggie. Very common out here! Good Lord, look at it travel, will you?"

While Eggleston brewed tea over a fire of mesquite twigs, his master took out his sextant and sighted the elevation of the sun. "We are very near my dead-reckoning position," he announced. "Perhaps another two days to the town of Prescott." He consulted the map, and pointed. "Over there is a small settlement called Weaver's Ranch. Can you imagine, Eggie — human beings actually *choosing* to live in this desolation?"

The valet fingered a strip of rawhide dangling from the branches of the ironwood tree. "I wonder what this is, Mr. Jack."

Together they examined it, a leather thong knotted along its length in a way that seemed to indicate a message.

"This too," Eggleston muttered apprehensively, pointing to cabalistic figures freshly scratched on a boulder. "And over there also — a pile of rounded stones."

"Well, they are manmade, that is sure," Drumm said. "No desert tortoise or Gila monster is likely to have manufactured them."

Eggleston swallowed. "Perhaps — Indians?"

Drumm shrugged. "If there are Indians about, they are probably Pimas, or Papagos; docile farmers, as they informed us in Yuma, who do not molest travelers. The Apaches, of course, are warlike, but I understand General Crook has pacified them. They are living peacefully on the government's reservations."

The valet was still doubtful. He pointed to the tracks in the wagon road. "None of those traces appear to be very new. Where, then, are the wagons?"

Drumm put away his navigation instruments and took the cup of tea and the biscuit Eggleston offered.

"What do you mean?"

"In Phoenix, old Mr. Coogan, who sold us our mules, said there would be frequent wagon trains carrying goods to Prescott and Fort Whipple and the Army camps — stagecoaches, also, on regular routes to the north. But we have not seen a vehicle since we left Phoenix."

Drumm rubbed a sunburned nose. "That is so," he admitted. "Something *is* odd about the situation!"

4

Together they squatted in the scanty shade of the ironwood tree, feeling the immensity of the deserted land, their smallness in it. Unlike the beneficent orb so welcome in Hampshire after a damp and chill winter, the sun here was brassy and impersonal. Here, also, the wind blew steadily; dust devils swirled, the horizon stretched to infinity.

Drumm cleared his throat. "I am quite sure, Eggie," he said, "that there is no danger to us."

Still, the scrap of leather with its ominous knotted message danced in the wind, the scratches on the boulder confronted them with an arcane message, the geometrical pattern of stones somehow menacing.

"Besides," Drumm added, "we are well armed." Taking the Belgian fowling piece from his saddle, he examined the load. "In any case, there is nothing to fear from the tribesmen who inhabit this area. They are poor ignorant brutes, like the fellahin we saw last year in Egypt. They would probably break and run at the first volley from modern weapons."

They got again into the saddle and advanced toward the pass. Anxious to reach the Agua Fria, Jack Drumm rode along the column, whipping up the sullen mules. The valet galloped after a stray and whacked it soundly on the rump.

"Ho, there, sirrah — back on the road! Mr. Jack, was there ever anything so stubborn as a mule?"

"I fear," Jack Drumm said, "that my own stubbornness is evident also, Eggie. I know you did not wish to embark on this desert journey. Instead, when we landed at San Francisco from Japan, you preferred to go directly east. Well, I am now of the same mind. I understand there is a military telegraph at Fort Whipple, near Prescott. When we reach there I will arrange to have a cable forwarded to my brother Andrew at Clarendon Hall, advising him I have abandoned this foolish journey through the wilds of America, and plan to return home directly without seeing the Grand Canyon of the Colorado or the famous Painted Desert. Surely the Grand Tour has been grand enough without this bleak and inhospitable wasteland!"

The Prescott wagon road soon pinched in to a narrow canyon, walls steep and abrupt. At the entrance they looked at each other with misgiving.

"Hallo!" Drumm called, cupping his hands.

His shout died away in the depths of the canyon, to return a moment later in an eerie diminishing echo. The air was hot, stifling, somehow taut.

"Well," Drumm shrugged, "there is no other way to go but through the canyon!"

They herded the mules before them through the cactus-studded defile. The beasts plodded unwillingly, heads down and ears laid back, braying protests as they slipped and scrambled on the rocks. Drumm kept the fowling piece across his lap, ready for action, and Eggleston gripped his pistol tightly. As they rode, both watched the rocky heights; it was patent that hostile Indians could ambush them from above. Even if the Pimas and Papagos were amicable, and the Apaches confined to reservations, the pair was not too far from the country of the Navahos.

A few hundred yards into the canyon Eggleston raised a hand. "*Hsst*, Mr. Jack! Did you hear that?"

When they paused, the weary mules paused also.

"Hear what, Eggie?"

Borne faintly on the wind, there came to them the far-off rattle of hoofs and a shrill neigh. The mules pricked up their ears. Old Mr. Coogan said the mules could smell Indians. If they acted uneasy, as they were now certainly doing, hostile tribesmen might be about. One animal rolled eyes whitely and started to back down the canyon.

"The Indians," Drumm said in a tight voice, "may be friendly after all, Eggie. But be ready to fire when I give the command. First, however, I will attempt to 'palaver' with them, as they say on the frontier."

Tense and expectant, they waited. Above, a hawk wheeled on a rising current of air. The bird could see whatever peril awaited them, but they could only watch and listen. The clatter of hoofs grew louder, and a curl of dust rose from the cleft of the canyon above them. Someone shouted, a cry that might have been a war whoop. Jack Drumm paled, but spoke firmly.

"Steady, Eggie! Remember the hollow square at Lucknow!"

Suddenly a banner wavered above the rocks, high on a staff. A moment later a trooper cantered down toward them. The rest of the column picked its way down the narrow defile — lank, angular men, in corduroy and buckskin breeches and sweat-soaked flannel shirts.

"Thank God!" Eggleston breathed a heartfelt relief. "Look, Mr. Jack, it is the cavalry — the U. S. Army!"

7

To Drumm, familiar with the Royal Horse Guards in their blue tunics, white helmets with horsehair plumes, and polished steel cuirasses, the oncoming soldiers were a nondescript lot with little discipline and even poorer appearance. The lieutenant, a young man in a felt hat, sporting a ragged black beard, was slouched in the saddle as if it were an easy chair.

"Dunaway," he drawled, extending a hand to Jack Drumm. "B Company, Sixth Cavalry, from Fort Whipple." He jerked his head toward the ridge above them. "Saw you from on top. Had our eye on you for a long ways. See any hostile sign on the playa?"

Drumm took off the sun helmet and wiped the sweatband with a fresh handkerchief.

"Any what?"

Dunaway was impatient. "Hostile sign! Indians! Apaches!"

"Actually, no." Drumm put on the topi again. "No Indians, that is. But there *were* peculiar things in the road. Knotted rawhide strings, piles of rocks, hieroglyphics scratched on boulders."

Dunaway nodded. "Apache messages; that's the way they keep in touch with each other."

"But I thought —"

"All hell broke loose two days ago!" The lieutenant slapped the battered hat against his thigh; a cloud of dust arose. "Agustín burned Weaver's Ranch to the ground — killed Weaver's boy Sam and some Mexicans, set fire to the hay, butchered a steer, and ran off the stock they couldn't eat. It's up to us to put him back in the bottle and ram home the cork."

8

"Agustín? Who is Agustín?"

Dunaway gave Jack Drumm a pitying look. "You never heard of him?"

"No."

"Agustín is just chief of the Tonto Apaches, that's all! Took his braves and ran away from the Verde River reservation after a fuss with the Indian agent about bad beef his people were issued. You fellows were probably on the road when it happened, and didn't get the word. But everyone between Phoenix and Prescott knows! We've alerted all posts by telegraph. Things have come to a standstill — nothing moving on the wagon road, everyone scared. Territorial Legislature even wants General Crook removed unless we cut Agustín's trail mighty quick and dehorn him."

Eggleston looked puzzled, turning to his master for enlightenment.

"I think," Jack Drumm said, "it is meant that the cavalry must find Mr. Agustín quickly, and — well, render him harmless, one might say."

Dunaway regarded him with amusement. "I guess you might say that." He grinned, fondling his beard. "You're English, aren't you?"

"John Peter Christian Drumm, from Clarendon Hall, in Hampshire. My father is — was — Lord Fifield, the ambassador. Before he died, he insisted I see something of the world. But I must admit I was not prepared for Arizona."

Dunaway blew his nose with a handkerchief of the kind called a bandanna and stuffed it into a hip pocket. "Few folks are," he said, condescension in his voice. He watched his men milling about Drumm's pack train, exclaiming at the quantity and variety of equipment. "Look!" a brigandish-looking corporal cried. "God damn me, if it ain't a commode — a — a mechanical slop jar!"

Drumm's tone was sharp. "Don't touch that! It's a delicate machine!"

In his rolling cavalryman's gait, Dunaway strolled over and inspected it. "I swear!" he muttered, touching one of the metal tubes that entwined the device.

"There's a tank for water," Drumm explained. "You pull the chain, then the water —"

Someone guffawed. One grizzled trooper slapped his thigh, two others fell speechless with merriment into each other's arms. Lieutenant Dunaway stared unbelievingly at the loaded mules with their burdens of paraphernalia.

"Tents, cookstoves, imported biscuits, liquor, camp chairs —" He jammed the shapeless hat back on and motioned to the trumpeter. "You limeys!"

"I beg pardon?" Drumm asked.

Dunaway continued to stare at the impedimenta of the caravan while the brassy throat of the bugle shattered the silence.

"I swear!" he muttered again, and shook his head.

"What do you mean?"

"I'm a simple soldier, Mr. Drumm," the lieutenant snapped. He waved to his men. "We're all simple soldiers! We eat sour bacon, mostly, and rusty beans out of a can. We make water on the nearest bush — when we can get out of the saddle long enough, that is. So it's sand in our craw when the Sixth has got its hands full protecting legitimate citizens of the Territory, and then comes up on a circus like you got here!" Dunaway's voice had been condescending; now it turned contemptuous. "I'd advise *you*, Mr. Drumm, or whatever your name is, to shuck off all this junk and ride as fast as you can to Prescott before you get bushwhacked!" He grinned an evil grin. "Lord, I'd like to see Agustín sitting on that throne of yours!"

"But —"

Dunaway spat. He wheeled his horse, not saying farewell. Guidon flapping in the wind, the column broke into a gallop, heading toward the playa. There was only the diminishing rattle of shod hoofs, a dissipating plume of dust. The windswept pass was silent again, and lonely, and dangerous.

"Well," Drumm muttered, mounting his gelding, "I gather the lieutenant did not think much of Englishmen, Eggie, or their traveling arrangements!"

He had heard that most officers in the modern Army were West Pointers, men with a pretense to some education in the military academy on the Hudson River. But a few uncurried roughnecks were left over from the War Between the States; Lieutenant George Dunaway with his uncouth ways was probably one of them.

At last they topped the pass and could see again the green fringes of the Agua Fria, now much nearer. The heat had abated. As they smelled water, the mules picked up their dilatory pace. The sun vanished behind a dark cloud, fringed with gold where the scattered rays emerged.

"How are you, Eggie?" Drumm asked.

The valet rolled his umbrella and tucked it into a saddlebag.

"Much better, now that the heat has lessened."

The Agua Fria was disappointing. In spite of the beckoning greenery, the watercourse was a series of brackish puddles rimmed with alkali crust. Though desert heat had dried it to a rivulet, there were, however, patches of coarse grass and stands of bamboo and carrizo reeds in the muddy bottom.

"Well," Jack Drumm sighed, "we have arrived thus far without incident, Eggie."

The valet was the first to see the man in the reed-choked river, watering a thirsty buckskin horse. Eggleston pulled at his master's sleeve. "Look, sir! Over there!"

Cautious, Jack Drumm lifted the fowling piece. But the stranger stepped from the reeds in friendly fashion, advanced toward them holding out a hand.

"Meech — Alonzo Meech, gentlemen! It's a pleasure to see white men in these parts! Where you bound for?"

Drumm slid off his horse and put his weapon in the boot. He shook hands.

"We're for Prescott," he said, "my man Eggleston here, and I."

Mr. Meech was a stocky man with a fringe of spiky gray beard and heavy burnsided wattles. He wore a flat-brimmed hat and dusty black coat, with an enormous Colt's revolver of the Navy style buckled about his waist. A bedroll was strapped to the crupper of a bony mare, and a Winchester rifle in the saddle scabbard. Meech reminded Jack Drumm of nothing so much as an English bulldog, a little gray about the muzzle and somewhat past his prime.

"Going there myself," Meech nodded. "Like to throw in with you two, if you don't mind! There's Apaches about, I hear."

Drumm noticed a shotgun strapped to the other side of the mare. "You're well prepared for them, I see."

"I am always prepared, for whatever happens." Meech put a hand on the butt of the revolver. "*Semper apparatus*, that's my motto. It's Latin, you see — means 'be prepared.'"

"We met some soldiers in the pass back there," Drumm volunteered. "They said a person called Augustine —"

"Agustín."

"Whatever. Anyway, the rascal is on the loose, terrorizing the countryside. I don't know why the authorities let such things happen! There can be no responsible government, such as we are accustomed to in England."

"Met Dunaway, too," Meech said, helping Eggleston unload the mules. "The lieutenant didn't think I'd get to Prescott with my hair on. But another day — two at the most — and I'll be attending to my business there."

"And what did you say your business was?" Drumm inquired politely.

"I didn't say," Meech answered, and volunteered no more.

While Eggleston set up the camp, Meech reclined on a boulder and watched. Finally, seeing the valet take the rubber bathtub from a mule and unfold the telescoping legs, he could not restrain himself.

"Now what in Tophet is *that* thing?"

"A necessary sanitary facility," Jack explained, pouring in the bucket of warm water Eggleston brought from the fire. "I never travel without it. Perkins' Patent India-Rubber Portable Bath — a marvelous invention."

Removing travel-stained clothing, Drumm settled gratefully into the bath. The valet brought him a packet of correspondence, a two-week-old copy of the Yuma *Sentinel*, and a gin and water in a tumbler, setting them on a collapsible table nearby.

"And what will you have, sir?" Eggleston asked Meech. "We have a wide variety. American bourbon? Scotch whiskey? Perhaps a brandy?"

Meech shook his head. "I'm a temperance man, mostly. Never drink on the job, anyway." He fumbled in a pocket. "Do miss my stogies, though."

Drumm spoke to Eggleston. "There's a fresh box of Havana *puros* on the gray mule."

Alonzo Meech regarded the proffered cigar with a dazed look. He started slightly when the valet nipped the end with a silver cutter resembling a miniature guillotine.

"I like a good cigar myself," Drumm admitted, soaping himself thoroughly. "When's dinner, Eggie?"

"Eight, sir — as always."

While Drumm scrubbed himself clean, the valet bustled about the camp, setting up the tent, shaking out sheets, plumping pillows, uncorking a bottle of Rhine wine and decanting it critically by the light of a camphene lamp. The banks of the Agua Fria took on the appearance of a small village, complete with the folding toilet commode behind a canvas screen for modesty's sake. The mules, now unladen, wandered away to munch the grasses bordering the greenish pools.

Meech pulled hard on his cigar. "I never seen anything like it!" he muttered, staring in disbelief at the Union Jack the valet ran up a pole.

"Cheers!" Drumm said, lifting his glass, and turned his attention to the *Sentinel*. The newspaper had only four pages; he had read it many times since stepping off the schooner *Sierra Nevada*, Captain Joseph Beckett, at Port Isabel, a hundred miles below Yuma. Finishing the newspaper, he turned to the packet of letters and chose the latest communication from his brother. Andrew's letter was three months old:

It is all very well to be the elder brother and succeed to the title but it is certainly a damned nuisance. I do not understand how our father managed to do at eighty years of age what I am making a botch of at forty. We must face it, Jack: I simply do not have your knack for planning, your stubbornness in pressing on to accomplish what you have decided to do. As a consequence, my account books are in a muddle, the tenant farmers dissatisfied, and bills pile up in spite of my best resolve to take care of them promptly. Of course, I

15

have my India fever to blame for it all — I do not really feel well — but at bottom I am afraid I am not cut out for a manager.

Drumm closed his eyes, shutting out the twilight bleakness of the landscape, and thought of Clarendon Hall in summer. Roses would be in bloom, white and pink and red, the garden heavy with their scent. Ancient lawns would be green, girls would come to parties in wispy summer dresses, the billiard room would be gay with banter and the click of ivory balls.

Cornelia Newton-Barrett was here yesterday with her mother, anxious for news of you. As you know, Cornelia is very fond of you, and joins me in wishing you Godspeed home.

Cornelia, Drumm thought. He recalled a winter night at Clarendon Hall, the old house creaking under the weight of snow, a fire still smoldering in the great fireplace. All had gone to bed. He and Cornelia, by arrangement, tiptoed down in nightclothes and sat for a long time holding hands. With pleasure he remembered the illicit softness of Cornelia's thigh, the depths of tender brown eyes. Then one of the servants had blundered in —

"Mr. Jack?" Eggleston coughed discreetly. "Dinner is ready."

"Right!" Drumm sprang to his feet to towel himself dry. Though the summer dusk was cool, drawing the warmth from his bath water, he felt a warm flush of passion in his loins. Cornelia Newton-Barrett would wait for him; she had promised. The prospect made this desert nearly tolerable. He got into fresh linen almost cheerfully, waxed his mustache to fierce Guardsman points before a mirror, and sat down across from Alonzo Meech.

"We are very low on food," he remarked, "but once we reach Prescott it will make no matter. Eggie and I plan to put up at a hotel for a few days rest, then I will inquire as to passage on the new Atlantic and Pacific Railroad line, which I understand we can catch on certain days of the month at Bear Spring, north of Prescott. From there we can ride the steamcars to New York City and sail home on a fast packet." Drumm turned to the valet. "Beef ragout, eh? Marvelous, simply marvelous, Eggie, what you manage to concoct with only canned meat and a few dried onions!" He poured the wine, chilled by wet cloths the valet had wrapped around the bottle, into a pair of long-stemmed glasses. "Try that, Meech! I find it a little woody, but with a nice bouquet."

Meech started to decline, then checked himself. "I don't mind a little wine with supper," he said. "Good for the digestion, I hear. It's the strong stuff that's ruined many a good man. 'In vino demitasse.' That means 'even a half a glass can start you down the road to ruin.'"

The guest had washed in the basin Eggleston furnished and combed a few strands of gray hair across his head. Attacking the ragout, he finished before Drumm had taken more than a few spoonfuls. In

17

response to a nod from his master, the valet served Meech again.

"Being out on a job always gives me a keen appetite," Meech admitted, wiping his plate clean with a biscuit the valet had baked in a tin reflector oven. Eggleston brought brandy and more cigars and the two sat finally in folding camp chairs, boots cocked on a convenient rock, watching the mantle of night suddenly prickle with stars. Swallows darted about, chasing insects, and along the river sounded a cacophony of yelps.

"What's that?" Meech asked, starting.

"Coyotes," Jack Drumm explained. "*Canis latrans*."

"I heard 'em before," Meech said, "but wasn't certain what they was."

Drumm poured him more brandy. "I say," he said, "you haven't been out here very long, have you? I mean — coyotes are all around this part of the country."

"No," Meech admitted. "I'm a city man — Philadelphia — and unaccustomed to the wilds. To tell you the truth, I figure I cut a ridiculous figure on a horse, but a man's got to go wherever his job takes him."

Drumm scratched his chin. In the morning he would require the attentions of Eggleston with basin and razor before they resumed their journey to Prescott — and home.

"My man and I," he explained, "are in the final stages of a trip around the world. Italy, Turkey, ancient Egypt, the Arab kingdoms — India, Singapore, Japan, and across the Pacific to your San Francisco, with a small side trip into the Arizona Territory, which I now regret. But you, sir, spoke of a job that requires you to visit this inhospitable place. I don't mean to pry, but —"

Meech spilled some brandy and cursed under his breath. Squinting, he attempted to focus on the lamplit countenance of his host. "Yes, I am indeed out on a job. No harm, I guess, in speaking in general terms to a pleasant gentleman like you, Mr. Drumm, though the exash — the exact nature of my mission is confidential." He winked heavily, a maneuver of such magnitude that his eye almost disappeared under the thatch of eyebrow. "I'm a Pinkerton."

"Pinkerton?"

Meech put a finger to his lips.

"Not so loud!"

Jack Drumm started to pour himself another brandy but the bottle was empty.

"It's just that I didn't know what a Pinkerton was — or is," he apologized.

Meech sprawled in his chair and lit a fresh *puro*. "I'm a private detective — trusted employee of the famous Pinkerton National Detective Agency. You've heard of *them!*"

"Can't say as I have — no."

"Catch faithless husbands 'in fragrant delicto,' nab embezzlers, put the cuffs on white slavers and dope fiends — anything that comes to hand."

"But whatever are you doing out here?"

Meech leered. "No, you don't!"

"Don't what, pray?"

"Don't get me to reveal no secrets! All I can tell you is that I'm on the track of a dangerous crin — crin — criminal. A miscreant that'd just as soon shoot you as look at you!"

"But surely there are police of some sort out here! I mean — in England we have Scotland Yard and local constables and —"

"No law out here — no law at all, except maybe the Army, and they don't concern themselves with civilian offenses! Thash — that's probably why the accused fled to the Territory. But they didn't take me into account! No, sir — Alonzo Meech don't never give up the trail!" The detective got to his feet and attempted a bow. "I got to thank you, Mr. Drumm, for your hosh — your hosh —" He abandoned the word, saying instead, "Good grub! Good company!"

Teetering, Meech walked toward his bedroll and fell soggily into a reed-bordered pool. Eggleston helped him to his feet and wiped him off. A moment later the detective was snoring an obbligato to the melodies of frogs half buried in the mud of the river.

"Thank you, Eggie." Drumm smiled. "Very good of you."

The valet finished washing the last of the dishes and pans and dried his hands.

"I've laid out your nightshirt and slippers, sir. Will there be anything else?"

Drumm yawned. "Nothing, Eggie. Turn in yourself, get a good night's sleep. It's a long way to Prescott."

CHAPTER
TWO

In spite of his growing annoyance with the Arizona Territory, Jack Drumm drowsed easily off, sleeping the sleep of the righteous Englishman. Sometime near dawn, to judge from the pallor of the eastern sky, he awoke. For a time he lay on his cot, listening to night sounds; the canvas of the tent rustling in a breeze, far-off clamor of coyotes on the hunt, an occasional *ker-chonk* from a frog in the ooze of the almost-vanished Agua Fria. To judge from their snores, Eggleston and the detective slept well in their blanket rolls on open ground. The mules, however, seemed restless. They snuffled, broke wind, moved about against the restraint of the ropes holding them to the picket line.

Yawning and scratching, Drumm padded to the door in slippers and nightshirt. A setting moon swam low in scattered clouds. The coolness of the air was laced with a faint perfume, probably from some desert plant. He was pondering this, trying to remember what the *Traveler's Guide* said about aromatic desert flora, when one of the mules, ghostly in the dawn, gave a strange whickering sound and pulled hard to the end of its rope. The rest quickly took up the odd behavior. Suddenly one burst into a chilling bray.

At first he felt, rather than saw, the intruders. Then, as his gaze sharpened, he saw the Indians slipping about the camp. One cut the picket line with a knife that flashed like quicksilver in the waning moonlight. Another rummaged through the piled packs. A third crouched over Alonzo Meech's recumbent form. Meech rose on an elbow, reaching for the Colt's revolver that lay beside him, but the Indian stepped on his wrist and brandished a hatchet.

"Stop!" Drumm called. "Halt! Eggie, where are you? Halloo the camp!"

He snatched up the fowling piece, providentially just inside the tent door, and fired as the hatchet started to descend. Howling, the savage sprang into the air, clutching an arm. Meech quickly rolled from his blankets, catching his assailant about the ankles, and caromed with him into the embers of the fire.

Though the light was not good, Drumm could see at least a dozen of the bowlegged little men dashing purposefully about the camp. Two had attacked Eggleston; one pinioned the valet from behind while the other raised a ribboned lance. Drumm fired a quick shot from the other barrel. The man with the lance dropped to his knees, holding his stomach. Just as Drumm squeezed off the shot, arms clasped him from behind; a blow on his wrist knocked the fowling piece to the ground.

Wresting free from his remaining captor, Eggleston managed to draw a pistol and discharge it into the man's face, pulling the trigger so rapidly that the several shots sounded almost as one.

"I'm coming, Mr. Jack!" he shouted. "Hold on!"

Drumm had a few wrestling tricks, learned on his passage through Persia; the Persians were great wrestlers. Dropping to his knees, he reached back to catch his assailant's ankles, and pulled hard. The Indian went over backward, breath whooshing out of him in a gasp as he landed on his back. Alonzo Meech, clothes laced with sparks from the fire he had rolled into, struck Drumm's captor over the head with the butt of his revolver. The blow glanced off; the Indian ran away toward the mules.

"They're after our animals!" Meech shouted, pulling the trigger on an empty chamber.

Horses and the mules alike were in panic. Milling and rearing, they screamed in terror. A flying hoof became entangled in the tent, dragging it down in a welter of canvas. Drumm, Meech, and the valet knelt behind an overturned table among a rubble of pots, pans, and kitchen utensils, firing at targets of opportunity. The dawn was pierced with stabs of flame, report of weapons, hoarse shouts as the bandy-legged little men rushed the defenders while others attempted to round up the animals.

Drumm clubbed his fowling piece and swung wildly as a man wearing an ornamented leather hat discharged a pistol almost in his face. Stunned by the explosion, he fell over, blinded by the flame. The Indian leaped over the table and landed astride him, searching for the throat with powerful hands. Meech, too, rolled on the

23

ground under the weight of two wiry attackers, while Eggleston snatched up a broken table leg to rain blows on their backs.

Remembering a Marseilles stratagem, Drumm drove a knee into the groin of the man in the leather hat. The grip on his throat loosened; the man grunted and rolled away. Quickly Drumm was on him with his fists. But the Indian drew a knife from a sheath at his belt. A savage slash caught Drumm across the cheek and mouth; he felt blood, tasted blood. Catching the wrist, he twisted it savagely, wanting to hear bones break. But the man heaved suddenly under him to roll free.

Meech, freed from his attackers, found time to reload. He stood behind the overturned table, Colt's revolver in one hand and Winchester rifle in the other, firing into the melee like a Gatling gun and cursing with the same copiousness.

"Oh, you bastards! You damned lousy bastards! You low-life stinking bastards!"

Shouting, "They're taking our mules!" Eggleston ran toward the milling animals. As he clung to a man's leg, trying to drag him from a mule, the Indian hit him across the face with a war club. Staggering back, the valet clutched at his nose. The man in the leather hat, sounding a wild whoop, mounted Jack Drumm's own fine gelding and snatched up the Union Jack on its staff. With a bone whistle clamped between his teeth he blew a shrill summons. The other raiders broke off the combat, vaulting onto various mounts and following their chief. In a moment, yelling and whooping like banshees, they splashed through the shallows and were gone. The last Jack Drumm saw was the despairing flutter of his Union Jack, caught by the first rays of the sun. The man in the leather hat held it high and triumphant above the reeds as he galloped away.

Alonzo Meech had run out of ammunition but not of obscenities. Cursing, he ran after the departing intruders, splashing muddily through the reeds and brandishing his useless weapons. Finally he gave up the chase and came back, wheezing a few weakened epithets.

"Well, we gave 'em as good as we got, anyway!"

"Is anyone hurt?" Drumm asked anxiously.

Eggleston, awakened in his underclothes, was nearly naked. He limped toward them, one hand holding his battered nose, blood leaking between his fingers. Alonzo Meech's black coat, which he had slept in, was torn down the back, and one sleeve dangled by a thread.

"I think one of my fingers is busted," the detective said. "And I burned my butt when I rolled into the fire with that ugly-face varmint that tried to bury his hatchet in my brains."

During the melee Drumm himself had stepped on a cactus with his bare feet; his ribs ached also where someone had hit him with a rifle butt or a war club.

Eggleston sat shakily on a rock, trying to stanch the flow of blood from his nose with a handkerchief. "But you, Mr. Jack," he said to Drumm. "We must take care of that dreadful cut on your cheek!"

Among the wreckage Drumm found a shattered mirror and inspected himself. The wound, already crusted with coagulating blood, stitched downward from his eyebrow, skirting the nose, to lose itself in the wreckage of his mustache.

"Speaking of casualties," Meech said, "*he* ain't in too good of a condition!"

In the slanting sunlight of early morning, they watched the Indian the valet had shot in the face try to prop himself on his elbows. Painfully he pushed his body up inch by inch, turning a bloody face toward them. Then he collapsed, life running from him as grain spills from a torn sack.

"Those were not Pimas, Mr. Jack!" Eggleston murmured.

They were indeed not peaceful Pimas, or Papagos; they were bloodthirsty Apaches, certainly one of Agustín's roving bands. Though the light had not been good, Drumm had seen stocky, quick-moving little men, thigh-length leggings held to waists by a leather thong. Muslin loincloths dangled to the calves behind. One wore around his neck a string of ivory-white beads — probably a rosary torn from some slaughtered Mexican. The rest had colored cloths tied around square-cut shoulder-length locks, and carried what looked like modern breech-loading rifles. The man in the leather hat, too — the one that had seemed the leader. Drumm felt gingerly at the wound on his cheek, seeing again the ferocity in the face, the conical hat ornamented with feathers and bits of glass, the animal-like glitter in black eyes. They were scarcely human, the Apaches.

26

"I ain't been in a scuffle like that for a long time," Meech said. "Not since the Cooney gang of smugglers on the Fourteenth Street docks in Manhattan in '69!" He took down his pants and inspected his scorched backside. "My butt feels like it's been barbecued!"

In the wreckage of the tent Drumm found his medical kit and roll of court-plaster to bandage Eggleston's bashed nose. But the valet objected.

"Mr. Jack, let us not waste time. Let us pack up what gear is undamaged and hurry to Prescott! There we will be safe!"

Looking about the camp, Drumm felt shaken and disoriented; in the aftermath of the quick and brutal attack, the scene was unreal. Random shots had shattered the bowl of the portable commode, which leaked its contents in a lugubrious gurgle. Looted boxes, chests, and packs lay strewn about. Scattered coals from the fire had ignited the rubber bathtub, which burned with a smoky glow. Anger began to grow in him.

"There's one mule left," Meech observed, "and my buckskin mare. They stole all the rest of the animals."

It was true; their transportation, so necessary in this desert, was badly crippled. Drumm slapped at a fly buzzing near the caked blood on his cheek. Now that the nightmare of the raid had passed, the slashed cheek began to hurt, a throb that surged with each beat of his pulse.

"Look up there," he said, pointing toward Prescott. "There — on the slopes of the mountain!"

They looked. Between them and Prescott, on the barren flanks of the mountain, winked a small bright light. It flashed steadily, repeatedly, in what could only be a manmade message of some sort.

"I remember now," Drumm said in a tight voice. "The Apaches are known to signal to each other, when they are on the warpath, with bits of mirror! Wherever the devils who attacked us have gone, carrying my Union Jack, there are even more of them on that ridge there, waiting for new prey."

Eggleston roamed sadly among the scattered utensils, the broken bottles, the wreckage of his former kitchen establishment. Listlessly he picked up a jam jar; as he held it between his fingers a crack widened. The contents slid out to plop on the ground.

"That flag," Drumm said bitterly, "belonged to my brother Andrew! It flew over his company of sepoys when he was serving in India!"

He picked up the fowling piece from the ground where it lay. The stock had broken off clean when he clubbed someone.

"I object," he cried. "I object strongly to being chivied about so! British subjects have been wantonly attacked and humiliated by foreign nationals! Good God, is there no law or order in these United States? When we reach the East Coast I intend to file such a protest that heads will roll!" Angrily he flung the broken weapon down. It had been a fine piece, costing over a hundred pounds in Brussels. For a moment he chewed angrily at a corner of his bloody mustache; his fingers worked convulsively. Then, taking a deep breath, he turned toward the valet, trying to regain his composure.

"First, Eggie," he said, "we must do the decent thing and bury this dead person. However grave has been the provocation, an Englishman has certain obligations."

Meech snarled. "Drag the bastard out in the desert and let the buzzards have him!"

Drumm shook his head. "However depraved, the fellow was a human being. He must be put into the earth in a civilized way." Finding a shovel among the litter, he started to dig. Eggleston arose with a sigh to assist his master. A cloud passed over the sun, and a chill wind sprang out of nowhere. Drumm paused for a moment in his digging, looking toward the distant mountains over which hovered a ragged scud of cloud.

"It may rain up there," he muttered. "At this season sudden and violent storms are not unusual at the higher elevations, according to the *Traveler's Guide.*"

Sullenly Meech watched as they dug.

"There!" Drumm said finally, wiping his brow. "Not so deep as it should be, perhaps, but we can pile stones on top to keep away the coyotes." In a satchel he found his Anglican Book of Prayer. While the valet stood with head appropriately bowed, he read the Service for the Dead.

"I don't believe this!" Meech grumbled, shaking his head.

Drumm took from the dead man's neck a small leather sack depending from a rawhide thong. The sack was ornamented with beads and small bits of glass, stitched in a complex pattern. Curious, he opened the sack and shook the contents into his palm: a handful of bluish grains, nothing more. Perhaps some kind of talisman, but it had not done the warrior any good. He poured the grains back into the sack. Sticking a broken Apache lance into the ground at the head of the grave, he hung the sack on it, watching it dangle in the wind while Eggleston filled the grave and piled stones atop it.

"That will do," Drumm decided. "Thank you, Eggie."

Meech regarded them both with disbelief. "I've heard of crazy Englishmen, but this beats all." He shrugged, washing his hands of the foolishness. "Well, we better get out of here! *Tempus fugits*! No telling when them varmints are likely to come back. There's three of us, and only two animals, but by riding double and changing around from time to time, we can make it to Prescott." He buckled the Colt's revolver about his waist and picked up the Winchester rifle.

Drumm pointed to the flanks of the distant mountain. The winks of reflected light were not now evident, but from the same approximate point showed a curl of smoke.

"We can hardly do that!" he objected. "The Apaches are waiting for us over there!"

After the confusion and disruption of the battle, the bony mare grazed peacefully in the reedy bottoms. Throwing his saddle over the back of the animal, Meech glanced at the distant smoke.

"Well," he said, drawing the cinch tight, "I don't know about you folks, but I've got business in Prescott, Apaches or no Apaches! My pay keeps right on going, even during an Indian war, and the home office expects me to earn it."

Incredulous, Drumm said, "But you're riding into danger!"

Pinching his nostrils together, Meech blew his nose into a nearby cactus.

"Wouldn't be the first time," he grunted. "It goes with the territory, as the drummer said." Climbing gingerly into the saddle, he let down his backside with caution. "You fellers ain't coming?"

Drumm shook his head. "I shouldn't like to risk traveling to Prescott right now, with the road swarming with Apaches. It's safer here, at least for the present. Anyway, there may be a stage passing soon, or freight wagons."

Meech shook his head and wrapped the reins around his knuckles. "I hate to leave the two of you here in such a situation, 'specially after you took me in and shared your grub. But I've got a job to do, and I mean to get about it." Raising a hand in salute, he said, "*Pax vobiscum* — that's Latin for 'good luck.'" Posting uneasily, he rode toward the distant smoke. A hundred yards down the road, he turned to call back.

"When I get to Prescott, maybe I can get a man to come out with a wagon and take you and your servant and what traps is left into the village — if you're still here, that is!"

Eggleston watched the detective go.

"I would hate," he murmured, "to be that criminal whom Detective Meech is looking for! I think he would ride through the portals of hell to bring back his quarry!"

For two days Jack Drumm and his man sweltered in a dug rifle pit behind an earthen wall, a canvas rigged on poles the only shelter from sun and wind. The clouds had vanished, and the weather turned bright and hot. During the day they saw occasional streamers of dust in the distance. Eggleston expressed a hope that they represented oncoming wagons and coaches from Phoenix, bearing news of the capture of Agustín and his roving marauders. But no wagon passed them on the Prescott Road. The bleak landscape took on an other-world quality, a painted drop in a London theater. They started at each rustle of a bush, the flight of a desert wren, a lizard skittering over a flat rock. They started, and sweated, and waited.

"I would certainly prefer," Eggleston said, "to at last be safe in Prescott, or whatever the village is called. Do you think we could possibly start off for there at night, Mr. Jack, riding double on the mule, and —"

"Much safer to wait here, at least for the time being," Drumm told him. "Perhaps Lieutenant Dunaway and his troopers will finally pass by and escort us safely there."

"I wonder," the valet said, slicing a heel of bread and spreading on it the last of the ragout, "how that Detective Meech got on?"

"Probably scalped, and lying in some lonely ditch between here and Prescott." Drumm took the proffered sandwich. Most of the food had been carried off or destroyed during the raid; this was the last. Though Drumm's prized Belgian gun was useless, they still had his .53 caliber Schroeder repeating carbine, which was a needle-gun of good design, his custom Tatham pistols in their plush-lined case, and a Sharp's .50 caliber rifle. Eggleston in addition had the six-shot revolver purchased for him by Drumm in Great Russell Street before the trip, and there was plenty of ammunition for all weapons. "But I am still hungry," Drumm muttered.

Eggleston scoured the ragout pot with the last of the bread and asked, "Why do you suppose the good Lord ever made this accursed place?"

His master washed down the crust with murky water from one of the pools of the Agua Fria. "To give good men a glimpse of Purgatory, of course, and thus make them better Christians!"

Eggleston pursed his lips, looking at the jagged wound across Jack Drumm's cheek. It was black with caked blood and bordered with a greenish-yellow stitching of pus.

"I do not like the looks of that, Mr. Jack," he said. "Will you let me wash it — there is a little of that good Charente cognac left in a broken bottle, and I understand that alcohol is beneficial to such wounds — and put some kind of a bandage on it?"

His master shook his head. "The Drumms are a hardy lot. I am sure it will soon start to heal. I fear, however, it has somewhat marred my features." He touched it tenderly. "The rascal's knife cut away some of my mustache, as I noted in the mirror this morning.

33

My chief worry is that after such bad treatment the hair will not grow again in a proper pattern."

Mopping perspiration from his bald head, the valet wandered disconsolately away among the reeds. Drumm watched him go, concerned. In a domestic way Eggleston was very capable. No one could make a better omelet, give a higher luster to the household silver, or keep such proper order below stairs at Clarendon Hall. Andrew had not wanted to give up Eggleston to serve as his younger brother's valet on the Grand Tour, but Jack Drumm in his insistent way prevailed. Now he had dragged poor Eggie over the better part of the circumference of the world. The valet had begun to look the worse for wear, though he complained little.

He was reclining on the mound of earth thrown up when they had dug the rifle pit, topi pushed over his eyes to shade them from the glare of the sunlit desert, when he heard the valet cry out.

"There!" Eggleston shouted. "That will do for you, you rascal, you!"

Snatching up the carbine, Drumm plunged through the reeds.

"What is it, Eggie? Where in the hell are you?"

Eggleston stood ankle-deep in mire. He pointed to the writhing body of a great snake, pinned to the ground by the rock he had dropped on it.

"I almost stepped on the serpent, Mr. Jack!" The valet's face was pale, and his muddy hands trembled. "I — I was reaching into the reeds when I heard this buzzing sound! The thing struck at me, but fortunately

34

I jumped back in time, though I fell headlong into the muck."

Drumm crushed the head of the serpent with the butt of his carbine.

"The diamondback," he noted. "*C. atrox*, I believe. Common from the state of Texas to the southern part of California." His eye fell on the rude structure among the waving reeds and he asked, "Whatever are you building here, Eggie?"

The valet moved gingerly past the still-wriggling coils of the snake to stand beside his handiwork. "Not knowing how long we may be stranded here, sir, I took the liberty of cutting some reeds to make us a better shelter — someplace to be out of the wind and weather." Proudly he showed his master the beginnings of a rude shack, standing on a little knoll above the general course of the river. With his knife the valet had cut the tall reeds and woven them together with strands of vine, making wall sections that he had propped together preparatory to tying them in place with further cords of the tough vines growing in the bottoms.

"My father was a weaver," he explained, "and taught me the trade at an early age. Later I will daub these reeds with mud from the river bottoms and put on a roof to shelter us from the sun."

Drumm clapped him on the back. "Capital, Eggie! You are indeed a coper, one of the best! Here — let me help you!"

While they were working on the shelter, Drumm pausing from time to time to scan the distance for signs of further attack, or possibly rescue, Eggleston came upon a stand of odd-looking plants. He pulled one up and inspected it, roots dripping mud and water.

"That is Indian corn," Drumm said. "What the Americans call 'roasting ears.' Do you remember — in the St. Francis Hotel in San Francisco they were served boiled, with butter and salt and pepper?"

"I wonder how it came to be here?" Eggleston mused.

"Probably a passing cavalry patrol once stopped to feed and water its mounts, dropping a few grains that later took root."

"Even with butter and salt and pepper," the valet said, "I remember thinking it more suited to the feeding of animals than humans. Nevertheless —" He stripped off an armful of the ears. "It is a *kind* of food, I daresay. We can not afford to be too particular!"

Drumm was plastering the roof of the hut with black clinging mud when he heard the faraway sound, a muffled popping. Running to the canvas shelter, where Eggleston was stripping the husks from the ears, he snatched up his spyglass. Focusing, he scanned the horizon. At last he made out, descending the jagged cleft of the canyon where they had first met George Dunaway and the men of B Company, a coach and team traveling at fearful speed.

"It is probably the stage from Phoenix," he told Eggleston. "From the sound of gunfire, they have encountered Agustín and his braves in the canyon."

Indian corn forgotten, they watched the distant speck, hearing the muffled rattle of gunfire borne on the wind. The coach seemed to crawl interminably toward them, though the horses were galloping hard.

"It is difficult," Drumm muttered, "to estimate distance in this ridiculous country!"

"But I am glad," the valet said, "that there is at least *some* vehicle on this lonely road, even if it be fleeing from red Indians!"

The coach reached level ground, rocking toward them in a cloud of dust. Moments later it arrived, stopping in the road with a squealing of brakes. The driver reined up the six-horse team so hard that the animals sat back on their haunches; the dusty high-wheeled coach swayed on its thoroughbraces.

"Good Lord!" Eggleston murmured. "Look at that, Mr. Jack!"

The CALIFORNIA AND ARIZONA STAGE LINE sign was riddled and splintered with bullet holes. Arrows stuck into the boot, fringed the baggage atop the coach like quills of a hedgehog. A feathered lance was driven halfway through one door.

The driver, a whiskered man in a straw hat, jumped down and opened the door. The leathery ancient in greasy buckskins who sat beside him on the high seat laid aside his rifle and assisted the passengers from the coach. Most were important-looking men in claw-hammer coats and uncomfortable-looking paper collars; all were heavily armed with rifles and pistols. There were also two ladies. One of the females was young — tall and angular, narrow-waisted, with a wealth of red hair tied in place by a China silk scarf. The other was middle-aged, gray tresses done up in a

37

bun, and carried a capacious reticule and a parasol. A powerfully built man with a square-cut black beard and gold watch chain shook hands with Jack Drumm. "Sam Valentine," he introduced himself, "from Maricopa County." He pointed to the others. "We're all elected to the new session of the Legislature. Traveling to Prescott when some of Agustín's braves jumped us in Centinela Canyon back there." He looked around at the ruins of Jack Drumm's camp. "What in hell happened to *you?*"

"Drumm," Jack said. "Jack Drumm. My valet and I were traveling through here when they attacked us also, night before last. The rascals ransacked the camp, destroyed most of our gear, and drove away our animals — except for that one mule."

The old man in buckskins grinned toothlessly at Drumm. "At first," he cackled, "I didn't recognize you, Mr. Drumm! By God, you surer 'n hell look different from the feller I sold them brutes to Saturday a week!"

It was Coogan, the mule dealer from Phoenix.

"Company hired me to take the stage through so's these gentlemen could make their Legislature session, but we got our butt shot off in the canyon back there." Coogan shaded his eyes and stared northward. "And if I ain't mistook, more of them bastards is ahead of us, between here and Prescott, just a-waitin'!" He pointed to a thin pencil of smoke in the distance. At the same time they all saw the wink of the distant mirror.

"What do we do now?" someone asked.

The young lady with the red hair and the sprinkle of freckles spoke up.

38

"Why, we go on, of course! Mrs. Glore and I have got to reach Prescott. We've got important business there!"

There was an uncomfortable shuffling of feet. An elderly man in a plug hat cleared his throat but said nothing. Another broke open the cylinder of his revolver, shucked out the empty shells, and reloaded. Sam Valentine took out a stogie and put a match to it.

"How does it look to you, Ike?"

The old man leaned on his rifle and spat tobacco juice. "Hell, I ain't afraid of Indians — never was! I fit 'em ever since me and General Dodge was up to our ass in Comanches on the Brazos back in '58! But I figger that fracas in the canyon was only the curtain raiser." He nodded toward the distant mountains. "Agustín and most of his rascals are probably up there gettin' the main show ready."

There was more shuffling of feet, scratching of heads, uncertain colloquy. One man muttered, "By God, here we are halfway to Prescott! We can't turn back now!"

"Certainly not!" the red-haired female insisted.

Valentine puffed at the cigar. "How do the rest of you feel?"

There were conferences. Finally the man in the plug hat said, "This Territory don't need no dead legislators! Anyway, I doubt half the representatives reach there by the first of the month, anyway, with Agustín running wild!"

"That's right!" said the man who had reloaded his revolver. "It ain't so much for me, but I got a Mexican wife and six kids back in Tubac. I wasn't elected just to leave Carmencita a widow and the kids orphans!"

Coogan spat a rich gout. "All right with me." He shrugged. "Stage company pays me either way." He pointed toward the shimmering playa. "Dassn't go back through Centinela Canyon, that's for sure. But we c'n cross the river and head back along the old County Road. It's longer, and rockier 'n hell — beg your pardon, ladies — but we ain't so likely to get bushwhacked."

"That makes sense," the man in the plug hat agreed. "And we might just run into George Dunaway and his men — telegraph said they was over this way. Maybe George can give us an escort and we can try to get through to Prescott again."

Valentine seemed to be the recognized leader of the group, the one they all deferred to. "All right," he sighed. "Common sense, I guess." He turned to John Drumm. "How about you, sir, and your man? We can make room for you in the coach if you'd like to go to Phoenix."

Drumm shook his head. "We're bound for Prescott and are late already. We mean to take the new Atlantic and Pacific Railroad at Bear Spring and reach New York in time to catch a fast packet, before the winter storms. No, I think we'll stay here and chance it. We are well armed, and will give Agustín a rousing welcome if he attempts to attack us again. Besides, we are hoping Lieutenant Dunaway can soon 'put the cork in the bottle and ram it home,' as he says. Then we can take the next stage and resume our journey."

The red-haired young lady was indignant. "All this gab about fleeing back to Phoenix!" she cried. "What are you — men or milk-sops? *I* am not afraid to go on!"

"That's the God's truth!" her gray-haired companion agreed, brandishing the parasol. "I ain't either!"

Valentine's tone was politic as he said, "Miss Larkin, we couldn't really risk harm to you and Mrs. Glore. The ambush in the canyon was a near thing; if we try to go on, we risk much more." He smiled. "I would never forgive myself if anything untoward happened to that glorious titian hair!"

Miss Larkin's milk-white skin flushed. Her blue eyes darkened.

"Then you won't go on?"

"I am afraid we cannot."

She looked about her. Her bosom heaved, and she clenched her fists tightly.

"Then Beulah and I will just stay *here*!"

"You can't do that!" Valentine protested.

She looked at Jack Drumm. "Beulah and I will stay here, with this gentleman, till another stage comes north and we can board it."

Drumm, who had been silently listening to the argument, could scarcely find his voice. "You — you can't be serious!" he stammered. "You can see our situation is serious here! There is no way to tell when the Apaches may mount another attack on us!"

"That's right," Coogan agreed. "Not meanin' to interfere, ma'am, but you got to come back to Phoenix with us! Maybe later —"

"We just had an uncomfortable experience in Phoenix," Miss Larkin insisted, "and I don't mean to repeat it! No, we will stay here!"

"But we have practically no food!" Drumm protested, annoyed with the arrogant female. "Most of our supplies were destroyed, and my man and I have been reduced to eating Indian corn!"

Mrs. Glore held up her bulging reticule. "Since Phoebe and I come West," she remarked, "I've found that food is an uncertain commodity. So I've got bacon in here, and eggs — a wheel of cheese — some tortugas or whatever they call 'em —"

"*Tortillas*," the man from Tubac muttered.

"Well, whatever. We'll get along all right."

"I forbid it!" Drumm insisted.

Phoebe Larkin looked at him with a hard blue eye. "You can't forbid us anything! This is part of the United States, which is a free country. A lady has a perfect right to stop and visit wherever she's a mind to." She turned to the driver. "If you will just pass down our valises —"

Coogan looked at Jack Drumm. "Short of hog-tieing her —"

"You lay a hand on her and I'll turn you inside out and stomp your giblets!" Mrs. Glore promised, holding the parasol like a weapon.

"Be quiet, Beulah," Miss Larkin instructed. "I can take care of myself. Always have, and always will." She picked up a valise. "Beulah and I will take shelter in that little shack over there until someone is brave enough to see us to Prescott!"

"Now wait a minute!" Drumm insisted, seeing the two females head toward Eggleston's reed hut. "You can't —"

Disappearing among the reeds, they paid him no attention. The company watched them go. Sam Valentine muttered, "Well, she's a strong-minded young lady, that's sure! Any Apache would be unlucky to cut *her* trail!"

There was nothing more to be done. Valentine shook hands, the legislators climbed back into the stage. Coogan spat again from his inexhaustible supply of amber juice and mounted the high seat beside the driver, long rifle across his lap. "Meant to tell you," he called down. "This is Agustín's old stamping grounds, along the river here; kind of a sacred place. His gods hang out here! Keep a sharp eye out, Mr. Drumm, for him and his coffee-colored bastards!"

Before Drumm could acknowledge the warning, the driver cracked his long whip; quickly the stage disappeared into the reeds, wheels churning in the mossy mud. A moment later it reappeared on the far side of the Agua Fria, heading toward the distant County Road, and Phoenix.

"This," Jack Drumm muttered, "is a deucedly peculiar situation, Eggie!"

The valet looked toward the two females, who were waiting impatiently, as if for a tardy innkeeper.

"That is true, sir," Eggleston agreed, rubbing his battered nose and wincing.

Jack Drumm stood in the middle of the now-deserted Prescott Road. He felt frustrated and

43

ineffectual, a feeling new to him. In sharp contrast to his gloomy mood, the setting sun painted the scene in a manner almost pastoral; a landscape by Constable, perhaps, or Joseph Turner. Eggleston's rude cabin sat on a rise surrounded by verdure, like a ruined crofter's cottage, while the solitary mule grazed along the stream. To Drumm's ear came the sound of the Agua Fria, tributary of the Salt, plashing into mossy pools, gurgling through the matted soil of the river bottom. Even the dark clouds hovering about the peaks of the distant Mazatzals were shot with gold, and a hazy mellow light enveloped all.

"Homeward the plowman wends his weary way . . ." he murmured, not remembering the exact words of Thomas Gray's *Elegy, "and leaves the world to darkness and to me."* Thinking of the annoying turn events had taken, his own mood was as dark as the coming darkness of the world.

CHAPTER
THREE

In the growing dusk they ate supper, supplied for the most part from Mrs. Glore's reticule — slices of cheese wrapped in tortillas, and an apple apiece along with ears of boiled Indian corn. They washed down the scanty fare with river water that Eggleston had poured into a pan to allow mud and ooze to settle. Miss Larkin wanted a fire to make tea, but Drumm forbade it.

"We are in Apache country, ma'am," he said curtly. "I am not about to draw their further attentions with a flame that can be seen for several miles." Inwardly he reproached himself for his coolness; Miss Larkin was a female of some status, apparently, judging from her expensive clothes, and he was hardly acting the gentleman. Still, it was unladylike of her to press herself on them, commandeer Eggleston's reed hut, and place herself and her companion under his protection without so much as a by-your-leave. But Miss Larkin was also a beautiful female. Jack Drumm was conscious of his wrecked mustache, of the ugly blood-caked scar along his cheek, of torn and dirty clothing and a need for a bath, while she smelled of clean flesh and Paris perfume.

"I — I mean —" he amended, "well, that is to say — we cannot be too careful, ma'am! We are all alone here, on a hostile desert."

Cross-legged on a blanket Eggleston had spread, she seemed not to notice but went on prattling in her quick decisive way.

"Take some more cheese, Mr. Drumm! Beulah bought it in Phoenix — it's a Mexican cheese, called *queso duro*." She got to her feet gracefully, like a deer rising, and looked at the growing sprinkle of stars. In the west there was only a faint orange flush shading off into dusky purple overhead. "I guess the desert is an unfriendly place, yes! But it is sure pretty." She took a deep breath; the fine bosom rose and fell under the lace ruching, a jeweled pin at her throat caught a last glimmer of light. "Smell that, will you? Some kind of desert plant, I'll bet! Oh, the night is so beautiful!"

At Drumm's nod, Eggleston went obediently to gather blankets and pillows and whatever conveniences he could find around the wrecked camp. Moments later, assisted by Mrs. Glore, he was working in the reed hut by the shaded light of the camphene lamp, preparing couches for the two females.

"You spoke," Drumm said grudgingly, rolling another piece of the hard cheese in a tortilla, "of a bad experience in Phoenix, ma'am."

She sat beside him again on the blanket, sipping at a cup of water.

"I don't want to talk about that! It was too scary."

Miss Larkin was certainly not like Cornelia Newton-Barrett, not like Cornelia at all. But her

46

presence, the female presence, made him think longingly of Cornelia, of home, of peace and contentment and amenities denied in this inhospitable desert.

"I suppose," she said brightly, "you're wondering who I am — how Beulah and I came to be out here, far from everything, traveling to Prescott!"

He inclined his head politely, shifting the position of the needle-gun across his knees. "You do not need to explain yourself to me, Miss Larkin."

"Just call me Phoebe," she said. With a quick gesture she took off the bonnet and China silk scarf and tossed her head, freeing the mane of red hair to flow richly about her face. "That's what I answer to back in — back in —" She paused, picked up the colorful scarf, worked it between her long fingers. After a moment she said, "My father is a wealthy judge in New York City, and Mrs. Glore is an old family friend of the Larkins. You see, I always had a lot of young fellows sparking me there —"

Drumm was puzzled. "Sparking you, ma'am?"

She giggled. "I forgot you were English! That means — well, *courting* me!"

"I see," he said, somewhat stiffly.

"I guess Papa was afraid the boys were getting too serious! So me and Beulah — Papa packed us off to travel the West, visit my wealthy Uncle Buell Larkin, who made his fortune in a gold mine at Prescott. Papa didn't want me to marry anybody but another judge, and there wasn't any in the pack that always hung around the house."

47

"That's the God's truth," Mrs. Glore called. "Every word of it!"

Drumm fumbled a hand over his damaged mustache when he looked at Miss Larkin. "I have a friend who was with me at Magdalen College. Geoffrey moved to New York City to take over his father's import business. He lived someplace in New York City near the Bronx. Tell me, do you know the Bronx?"

"The Bronks?" Phoebe shook her head. "There *was* a family of Bronsons, but they were kind of white trash. The judge never wanted me to associate with them."

Drumm was puzzled. "No, no!" he protested. "I mean the *Bronx!* It's a locality in New York City."

Phoebe pondered. "Oh, yes," she said. "The Bronx." She regarded him with asperity. "Well, I *did* live there!"

"I did not deny it, ma'am."

Her blue eyes narrowed. "But just what *are* you getting at?"

It had been a long and arduous day, and he was not in the best of moods. "I was not 'getting at' anything!" he said stiffly. "I was only wondering why you had never heard of the Bronx. Even in London we know that area!"

"And in New York," she said loftily, "we have better manners than to haze our guests so!"

He blinked. "Really, Miss Larkin —"

"I have been a perfect lady," she said. "I have shared confidences with you, told you a few details of my personal life as a proper female might, and now you are abusing me!"

Open-mouthed, he could only stare at her. The blue eyes were dark with annoyance, the lips firmly set in disapproval. Dusting her hands in a gesture of finality, she got to her feet. "It really is not nice to be so suspicious, Mr. Drumm. I wonder you have any friends!"

"Look out!" he called after her. "Ma'am, be careful! You're walking right into a barrel cactus — *Echinocactus grusoni*, I think!"

Pausing in flight, she drew her skirts aside from the menacing spines.

"Thank you," she said curtly, "but I don't need your help, Mr. Drumm. I saw the cactus myself and I don't need *any* man's help! I can take care of myself — always have, and always will!"

While Eggleston slept, Jack Drumm took the first watch. He squatted for a long time, chill and uncomfortable in the single burr-covered blanket remaining to him after the valet had fitted out the reed hut for the females' occupancy. Moodily he stared into the darkness. Along the river the coyotes started their music, and a night bird tuned up in a nearby bush.

Miss Larkin was certainly an odd person; he suspected she was not even a proper lady. As for that story of living in New York City, it was an obvious fabrication. But there had been no need to lie to him; what did he care about her past?

Near one in the morning, to judge from the position of Orion's belt, he woke the weary Eggleston and lay down himself, hands clasped behind his head. Around the distant Mazatzals forked lightning played, shimmering silently against the dark clouds. Long moments later he heard a cannonading of thunder. But she *was* beautiful! Not the patrician handsomeness of Cornelia Newton-Barrett, but instead a kind of coltish attractiveness, a careless charm that seemed unaware of its own beauty. Closing tired eyes, he finally slept, exhausted by the events of the day.

In the first flush of dawn he awoke. A single ray of sunlight crept through a notch in the sierra, lighting the disorder and confusion of the camp. Eggleston lay propped against a boulder, Sharp's rifle across his knees, sleeping. Poor Eggie — the valet was done in too! But soon they would be on the cars at Bear Spring and out of this infernal wasteland. Drumm yawned and stretched his arms. In spite of cramps in his legs and an aching back, he felt almost cheerful. Home, soon — the green hills of Hampshire!

The morning was yet chill, and he did not care to leave the scanty warmth of his blanket. As he lay there, he was puzzled by a faint rumbling, so faint he seemed almost to feel it rather than hear. He raised himself on an elbow and looked around.

Miss Phoebe Larkin had also heard the strange noise. In the gray of dawn she hurried from the reed hut with a blanket about her shoulders, otherwise dressed only in camisole and lacy petticoats. Her feet were bare.

"What was that?" she called to Drumm.

"I don't know," he said, and sat up — looking, listening.

50

Phoebe stood in the shaft of sunlight, tumbled red hair falling about her shoulders and glistening sleekly, like the brush of a fox in autumn. "There! I heard it again!" She raised a slender finger. "Listen!" She wore a lot of rings; though Drumm was no expert, many of them were heavy with what appeared to be diamonds.

He got up quickly in his drawers, his own blanket held modestly about naked legs. Now there was no doubt of the queer sensation. Under his feet the hard-baked earth quivered, trembled, rolling slightly so that he felt giddy. It was almost like his attack of mal de mer on the stormy passage from Marseilles to Alexandria.

Eggleston woke up and stared at them. "What is it?" he called. Then he felt the rumble and jumped to his feet.

"In my guidebook," Drumm said thoughtfully, "there is an account of a dreadful earthquake that occurred near the city of Los Angeles, west of here, in the year seventeen hundred and —"

The rumbling grew; the earth shook.

"Seventeen hundred," Drumm repeated, "and —"

Hair done up in curl-papers, Mrs. Glore rushed from the reed hut. "Lordy, Lordy, Lordy!" she quavered. "What's happening?"

"Mr. Jack!" Eggleston shouted. "Look!"

Down the valley of the Agua Fria, rolling like a steam locomotive, came a wall of water as high as their heads. Boulders, trees, and uprooted bushes caromed in the muddy torrent. The last thing Drumm saw as the great tide reached them was Eggleston's reed hut, riding high on the crest.

He opened his mouth to cry a warning but there was no time. The waters reached him, bowled him over, filled his mouth with sand and mud. The world turned, the Mazatzals wheeled into the sky, and dawn-flecked clouds fell to earth, or where the earth should have been. Carried along like a chip of wood on the Thames, he paddled madly, trying to avoid obstacles looming in his path; a giant boulder, a towering saguaro, a smoke tree. Traveling at express-train speed, he closed his eyes in horror as the desert Niagara raised him high on its crest to fling him at a patch of spiny cholla. At the last moment a freakish shift of the current deposited him with a splash into a shallow pool at one side of the main course of the Agua Fria.

Stunned, he lay in the mud and ooze until he realized he was drowning. Thrashing, he staggered to his feet, drawing gasps of air into his lungs. Someone was screaming, a shrill insistent female keening that hurt his ears. He ran toward the sound.

"Phoebe! Oh, Phoebe! Dear Lord, where is she?"

The roar of the water had grown fainter. Against its diminishing rumble he heard Mrs. Glore scream again, saw her white face, her open mouth, the pointing finger paralyzed with horror.

"There! There she is!"

The great wave had scoured out a pool in the once-tranquill bed of the river. On its foam-flecked surface Drumm saw something floating, a white flower unfolded on the surface. Desperately he threw himself into the water, now well over his head, and swam to the white blossom. It was Phoebe Larkin's petticoats; he grabbed a handful of silk and started to backstroke with one arm, holding the petticoats with the other. Faintly, above the frantic splashing of his efforts, he heard shouts, commotion, Mrs. Beulah Glore still screaming with fire-whistle intensity.

"She's drowned! She's drowned!"

Blackness engulfed him. His arm felt leaden and he gasped for breath, feeling his mouth fill again with the muddy water. But Eggleston had splashed into the pool to help him.

"You're almost there, Mr. Jack!"

Just as he could swim no more and was about to release his hold on the floating fabric, Drumm's feet touched bottom. He staggered from the water, hauling Miss Larkin by her petticoats. Depositing her on a grassy hummock, he collapsed. Dimly he realized that the roar of the waters was almost gone. As he listened, it dwindled downstream, the sound like that of a goods van passing into the distance.

Eggleston turned Miss Larkin over while Mrs. Glore vainly patted Phoebe's face, trying to rouse her. Drumm pointed. "Get that keg over there!"

Mrs. Glore did not understand, but Eggleston had lived in Brighton and knew how to handle drowning victims. Quickly the valet snatched up a small barrel that had held preserved herrings. Drumm picked up the recumbent figure like a rag doll and flopped it over the barrel. With Eggleston taking Phoebe's bare feet and himself the limp arms, they began to roll her back and forth.

"What are you doing?" Mrs. Glore cried.

"Reviving her," Drumm explained.

"I never seen anything like that!" Mrs. Glore sobbed. "Is that a proper way to handle a female?"

Drumm glanced at the camisole, the lacy petticoats, the exposed thighs.

"At this moment," he said, "I do not give a tinker's damn if she is male or female or something in between! What matters only is to save her life!"

Phoebe Larkin made a hiccuping sound; a gout of water drained from her bluish lips. The rescuers paused in their frantic see-sawing.

"She's alive!" Mrs. Glore cried. "She's alive!" Sinking to her knees, she raised her hands in a prayer of thanks.

The limp body stiffened, seemed now to oppose their flailing. Miss Larkin hiccuped again; her body twisted under their hands. A small object fell from her bodice onto the muddy ground. It was a derringer pistol, a two-barrel weapon with a pearl handle glinting in the growing sunlight.

Afterward, what with the emotion of the moment and the quickness with which Mrs. Beulah Glore snatched up the tiny gun and dropped it into the pocket of her wrapper, Drumm was not even certain he had seen it. A derringer was certainly a peculiar item for a lady to carry in her bosom. He was trying to assess this development when their subject curled herself into a ball, like an eel. Eggleston lost his grasp

54

on her ankles. Jack Drumm slipped on the muddy ground; he and Miss Larkin fell heavily together, her wet body plastered against his.

It was an awkward position. She lay across him, pinioning him to the ground. Exhausted from his own near-drowning and his efforts to rescue her, he could only lie there, panting and helpless, her face against his. He saw with great clarity the sprinkling of freckles across the bridge of her nose, the delicately shaped eyebrows — plucked, surely — the glorious red hair now hanging dankly about her face.

"Let me help her to her feet," Eggleston suggested. "I think she is coming round."

Drumm waved him off.

"She had better not be disturbed," he explained. "It is dangerous to awaken unconscious people too quickly. It can lead to disorders of the brain."

Phoebe opened her eyes, stared into his. Bemused by their cerulean depths, he could only stare back. She hiccuped. "Where am I? What — what —"

"You come back from the dead, dear!" Mrs. Glore told her. "Mr. Drumm here threw himself into the water to pull you out!"

Phoebe continued to look into Drumm's eyes. He was uncomfortably aware of his maimed mustache and the blood-caked scar. But she seemed bemused.

"You saved my life!" Her lip trembled.

They lay together in the bright sunlight, the valet and Phoebe's traveling companion hovering over them. Jack Drumm cleared his throat in embarrassment. "I — I suppose so." He turned to Mrs. Glore. "If you will help her up now, ma'am —"

Eggleston and Mrs. Glore hauled her to her feet and supported her between them. She continued to stare at Drumm with admiration.

"At the risk of your own life!"

In the dry air his drawers were clammy. Embarrassed at her show of emotion, he shivered and looked about for his blanket.

"Nothing," he muttered. "It was nothing! I am a good swimmer. And Eggie here helped me."

Phoebe pulled away from them and rushed to Drumm. Throwing her arms about his neck, she kissed him hard on the lips. Astounded, he could only stand mute, hands dangling at his sides, feeling the soft body pressed against him, the full red lips wetly on his. He tried to speak but found it difficult. Finally he managed to disengage her.

"Thank you!" she gasped, looking into his eyes.

Embarrassment spoke for him, put words into his mouth he did not intend.

"I — I — well, I guess I would have done the same thing for anyone that was drowning."

Her face changed; the blue eyes became wide and hurt. She drew back.

"But — but I'm not just *anyone!* I'm Phoebe Larkin! You risked your life for me, and I'm bound to be grateful!" When she seemed to step toward him again, he stepped awkwardly, warily, back.

"Well," he muttered, "I'm — I'm glad you're all right, anyway."

A flush came into her pale cheeks. One hand attempted to arrange the wet strands of hair. When she spoke her voice trembled slightly.

"I — I'm sorry! I didn't mean to — to bother you!"

Frustrated, trying to find the proper words, he shook his head. "You didn't bother me! You didn't bother me at all! That wasn't what I meant!"

"I know what you mean," Phoebe said icily. "It's my fault, Mr. Drumm. You see — I have a very loving nature. Sometimes it betrays me. I am grateful you saved me, but sorry you misunderstood my gratitude!"

Almost desperately he looked around at the camp, devastated once by an Indian raid and now by a perverse flood. Everything was coming out wrong. He had planned the Grand Tour well, but the Arizona Territory had a way of upsetting things.

"Eggie," he muttered, "we must get some order back into things."

For the first time Phoebe Larkin seemed conscious of her scanty attire. Mrs. Glore found a blanket that was not too wet and drew it about Phoebe's shoulders. Even in the warm sun the girl shivered.

"There, there!" Mrs. Glore soothed. "It's only the after-effects of your dreadful experience! Come sit with me on that box under the tree."

Phoebe accepted the blanket, and an opportunity for the last word.

"Mr. Drumm," she said bitterly, "whatever you think of me, I must say — you're a damned cold fish! I heard Englishmen were like that, but so far I never had the bad luck to meet up with one!" Tossing her head, she turned her back on him and went to sit with Mrs. Glore.

Discouragement only brought out the stubbornness in Jack Drumm's character. While Phoebe sullenly watched, and Mrs. Glore searched downstream for enough unspoiled food to nourish them, he and the valet worked to bring order out of chaos. Noon-tide came and went, and they were sweating and exhausted. In the late afternoon Mrs. Glore squinted into the distance and pointed.

"There! Do you see that? Something is coming — a stage, maybe — or wagons!"

In the distance they could see a plume of dust in the mouth of Centinela Canyon. Drumm snatched up his spyglass. Shaking water from it, he focused on the distant disturbance: wagons, several wagons, escorted by a patrol of cavalry.

"Thank God!" Mrs. Glore said. "Now maybe we can leave this Godforsaken place and travel to Prescott, like we planned!" She glanced at Jack Drumm. "No offense meant — you've been kind and helpful, Mr. Drumm. But there *is* Phoebe's Uncle Buell in Prescott! He'll be worried."

"That's right," Phoebe Larkin agreed, tossing her head. "I'm anxious to mingle with some kind and understanding people for a change!"

Safely out of the canyon, the train crawled forward while the cavalry escort galloped toward Drumm's camp. Moments later Lieutenant George Dunaway reined up his mount and dismounted, hat in hand as he spied Miss Phoebe Larkin.

"Well, Drumm!" He looked at the wreckage of the camp. "What in hell — pardon, ladies — what happened here?"

"Apaches!" Drumm said sourly. "After we left you, Agustín and his bullies attacked us and ran off all our animals, except that one mule over there. Then, early this morning, a flood came down the mountain and overran the camp." He stared at Dunaway. "What's so damned funny?"

The lieutenant preened his mustache. "Didn't you see the storm over the mountain last night? No one but a greenhorn would camp in the middle of the Agua Fria this time of year!" He bowed to the ladies. "Introduce me, will you?"

Jack Drumm was annoyed with Dunaway's flippancy but muttered an introduction. "The ladies," he explained, "were going to Prescott on the stage. But when it was forced to turn back because of Apaches, they chose to stay here and wait for other transportation."

"I know," Dunaway said. At his gesture the men dismounted and lay wearily on the ground, munching hardtack and cold bacon. "Passed old Coogan and the California and Arizona Stage Line coach yesterday, hightailing it back to Phoenix. Sam Valentine said to take care of the ladies." Hat in hand, he approached Miss Phoebe Larkin. "Ma'am, the accommodations are kind of rough, but there's room for you and your friend in one of the freight wagons yonder if you want to travel to Prescott."

Phoebe Larkin seemed to bat her blue eyes at Dunaway, which annoyed Jack Drumm further.

"What about us?" he demanded. "And our equipment?"

Dunaway fondled his mustache and grinned. "If there's room. Ladies first, you know!"

"Have you got the Apaches put down, Lieutenant?" Phoebe Larkin asked. "I shouldn't like to be scalped before I see Uncle Buell in Prescott!" She laughed, looking charmingly at Dunaway.

"Not exactly, ma'am. Eighth Infantry sent a company out from Camp McDowell, and other forces will be here in a few days. But my B Company has hazed Agustín pretty well into the mountains already. Things have eased enough for wagons and stages to come through the valley. Oh, the Apaches may swoop down in a few raids like at Weaver's Ranch, but we've got Agustín pretty well trapped up on the mountain." He gestured toward the Mazatzals and grinned. "See that smoke? Probably old Agustín barbecuing one of your mules, Drumm! Nothing an Apache likes better than a mule steak!"

"I should think," Drumm muttered, "that with their need of transportation they would be very foolish indeed to eat their animals!"

The brigandish-looking corporal whom Drumm remembered from the encounter with Dunaway in the canyon hooted with laughter. A trooper slapped his thigh and grinned a gap-tooth grin. Dunaway was also

60

amused. He swigged water from a canteen and put the cap back on, savoring the moment. "An Englishman couldn't be expected to know, I guess, but Apaches don't *ride* horses — they eat them!"

"Eat them?"

"That's right."

Drumm was bewildered. He gestured at the infinite space of the playa. "But how do they get around, then?"

"They *walk!*" Seeing Drumm's astonished stare, Dunaway chuckled. "You know Port Isabel, down on the Gulf?"

"Of course. We landed there, on the *Sierra Nevada*, from San Francisco."

"Then you know it's a hundred miles from Port Isabel up to Yuma?"

"About that. Yes, I should guess a hundred miles."

"Colorado Steam Navigation Company had some tame Apaches hired a while back to run mail from Port Isabel to Yuma. The red sons of —" He coughed, delicately. "An Apache runner delivered the mail on regular schedule; a hundred miles in twenty-four hours." He glanced toward the train of freight wagons, now drawing up at the river to water their teams of oxen. "Well —"

"If the rascals are walking," Jack Drumm said in a tight voice, "then it seems to me your mounted command should have captured them by now, and have them safely back on the Verde River reservation, where they cannot plague innocent travelers!"

Dunaway scowled. "We've been in the saddle for six days running! An Apache on foot is harder to catch than a flea in a sand-storm! I've seen 'em travel all day and all night with no food but a handful of mesquite beans, and gain on us! A man on a horse shows up a long way off, but an Indian on foot looks like another damned bush till he raises up and shoots your ass off!"

Drumm had found a sensitive spot, and probed deeper.

"Nevertheless, I should think a few men from our Middlesex Regiment could handle this situation rather better. They have fought Indians — real Indians, from India — for a long time. They probably know better how to handle the aborigines than you people from the Colonies!"

George Dunaway turned red. The scorching afternoon was suddenly quiet. The teamsters, scenting trouble, gathered around. Someone laughed, a jeering laugh probably intended for Jack Drumm.

"Miss Larkin," Drumm said coolly, "perhaps you and Mrs. Glore had better get your things together now. Lieutenant Dunaway will see you safely to Prescott and your uncle — that is, if Indians on foot do not overwhelm him on the way!"

He was being deliberately insufferable; he knew it, and he enjoyed it. Dunaway's insolence and contempt, added to the other indignities he had experienced since coming to the Territory, drove him to it. Besides, Miss Larkin was watching the exchange with interest. Jack Drumm was not used to being put down at all, even less before an attractive female. Satisfied, he turned on his heel in curt dismissal of the U. S. Army and its fumbling attempts to deal with the rebellious Agustín.

But Dunaway cleared his throat and said, "Just a minute!"

Surprised, Drumm turned.

"Corporal Bagley," Dunaway said to the brigand, "I ask you to witness that George Dunaway, Sixth Cavalry, U. S. Army, Fort Whipple, near Prescott, is now going off duty. Whatever happens next has got nothing to do with the Army." Carefully he unpinned the silver bars from his shoulders and removed the collar insignia from his sweat-stained shirt. "I've got plenty of leave coming. There's nothing in Army regulations says I can't take some right here and now, is there?"

"No, sir!" Bagley said joyously, accepting the insignia in a horny palm. "Being company clerk, I can swear to that, if there's any fuss about it later!"

The grinning men ringed Drumm and Dunaway. From the corner of his eye Drumm saw Miss Phoebe Larkin put a slender hand over her mouth; the blue eyes widened.

"Leave?" Drumm asked, puzzled. "Whatever for?"

Dunaway rolled up his sleeves. "I guess," he said, "old Agustín tried to rearrange that fancy waxed mustache of yours, Drumm, but he didn't do a proper job. Maybe I can finish it for him." One booted foot planted solidly forward, he raised clenched fists. "Put up your hands! I'm going to give you the thrashing you've been spoiling for!"

Drumm was startled. The lieutenant was a roughneck, an un-couth and uncurried frontier character; no credit at all to the finer traditions of the Army. But though he did not believe in brawling, Drumm would have to give the braggart a boxing lesson. He himself had once gone five rounds in Birmingham with the great Jem Mace, the fighter who had won the middleweight title in '61. Mace was old then, and slow, but had praised Jack Drumm's agility and quick hands.

"You don't mean it!" he said incredulously.

"Put up your hands," Dunaway insisted, "or I'll wear you out with a willow switch!"

Drumm struck the classic pose Jem Mace had taught him.

"All right, then — come at me!"

Cautiously they circled each other. Dunaway feinted with his left hand and Drumm stepped easily inside the wide-swinging right cross that followed. At the same time he jolted Dunaway's chin with a short uppercut. He could have hit harder, but did not want to hurt the lieutenant.

Stunned, Dunaway crouched and came forward like a turtle, chin tucked below his shoulder; he stabbed outward with a jab. Drumm waited till the jab was committed, then swung a quick left to the pit of the lieutenant's stomach. Again he moderated the punch, but it was enough to make Dunaway grunt and stagger back.

"Come again!" Drumm taunted. "Have another go at it, why don't you?" Jem Mace, he felt, would have been proud of him.

Abandoning caution, the lieutenant rushed forward, both fists swinging. Expertly Drumm stepped aside, elbows pulled close to his body and clenched fists

64

protecting his face, coolly waiting out the blind rush. But this time something went wrong, dreadfully wrong. As Drumm trod on a gopher tunnel (*Geomyidae Thomomys*, he remembered dismally) the earth gave way under him and he toppled backward.

According to the Queensberry rules, he was entitled to a count of ten to recover his footing. But Dunaway rushed forward and threw himself on Drumm, knees crushing the wind from his chest, hands groping for the throat. Locked together in what Drumm assumed was frontier style, the two rolled muddily on the ground while spectators cheered and made bets.

"Middlesex Regiment, is it?" Dunaway snarled. "Know how to handle Indians better, do they?" Fingers twined around Drumm's neck, he lifted Drumm's head high and banged it repeatedly on the damp earth, uttering cavalry obscenities all the while. "There, take that! And that! You Englishmen are so damned good at handling things — handle *that* now!"

He banged Drumm's head down so hard that planets, constellations, a complete zodiac, reeled through his skull. Eggleston, seeing his master abused, ran to help him. Corporal Bagley reached out a languid paw and caught him by the collar.

"Had enough?" Dunaway jeered.

With his wind cut off he could not respond. The world dimmed, turned black. "Guess *that'll* teach you!" Dunaway panted, relaxing his hold.

Drumm lay winded like a beached salmon while Dunaway casually retrieved his insignia to the cheers of the B Company rowdies. Eggleston tried to help his master rise but Drumm waved him away and staggered to his feet, aware that Miss Phoebe Larkin was regarding him pityingly. That hurt more than his defeat at the hands of George Dunaway.

"It wasn't fair!" he gasped, spitting out a foreign object that proved to be a tooth. "The rules say —"

"No rules out here, no rules at all!" Dunaway casually tucked in a shirttail. "As to what's fair, Drumm — depends on where you come from. Nothing out here is fair — the Apaches aren't fair, the weather isn't fair, the whole damned Arizona Territory is the un-fairest thing you ever saw, and it's no place for a weakling that comes along whimpering about fair! Arizona is for *men* — men that scratch and claw their way and stick it out no matter what the weather, or the Indians, or the Lord God Himself!" Dunaway turned toward Miss Phoebe Larkin and her companion. "Is that your baggage, ladies? Corporal, take the valises and put them in the lead wagon, will you?"

Drumm watched the corporal pick up the bags. He was afraid he would add to his humiliation by vomiting. "Now that we've settled our little score," Dunaway said conversationally, getting again into the saddle, "there was a Pinkerton man named Meech, Alonzo Meech, left Phoenix about the same time you did, Drumm. Hasn't been heard from, and the home office has been making inquiries. Seen him around?"

Jack Drumm's throat hurt; he spoke hoarsely.

"Meech was with us when Agustín hit our camp. Next morning he rode out toward Prescott; said he had business there."

"The Apaches probably got him," Dunaway remarked, brushing dust from his shirt where he had lately rolled on the ground with Jack Drumm.

"I doubt it." Drumm shook his head, wincing as his maltreated neck pained him. "Mr. Meech was an extremely determined man, and very resourceful."

Phoebe Larkin and Mrs. Glore were in whispered consultation, appearing concerned about something. The older woman kept insisting, but Phoebe continued to shake her head and say, "No, no, Beulah!"

"Well, ladies?" Dunaway asked.

The corporal was handing up the luggage into the wagon when Phoebe snatched at his sleeve. "I — just a minute, please!"

The brigand stared at her, then at his lieutenant.

"Ma'am," Dunaway asked, "what is the matter?"

Miss Larkin seemed distraught. "I — we've changed our mind, Lieutenant. We won't be going to Prescott after all."

"Not going to Prescott? But —"

"No." She was very firm. Taking the bags from the corporal, she set them down in the dust. "I think the journey will be too rough — in the wagon, I mean!" She looked nervously about, seeming at a loss for words, a condition that Jack Drumm had not before observed in her. Finally she said, almost desperately, "My friend here — Mrs. Beulah Glore — has a liver condition. A shaking-up, like she might get in a freight wagon, could aggravate her condition."

"That's the God's truth!" Mrs. Glore affirmed. "Oh, it's ever so troublesome! Keeps me awake nights, and I don't eat too good either! We better wait for the next stage."

Puzzled, Dunaway turned to Jack Drumm. "But they can't stay here alone!"

Drumm had long been thinking certain private thoughts. He first entertained these thoughts when he met the uncouth Dunaway in Centinela Canyon and the lieutenant was so contemptuous of him and his equipment; later, when Agustín and his pack of brutes wantonly attacked them; when a perverse flood gutted their camp and scattered their possessions all along the river. Everything in this hostile country — heat, thirst, wind — seemed especially designed to challenge, bully, drive Jack Drumm from the face of the Arizona Territory. The climactic incident, of course, was his present humiliation. George Dunaway had beaten him into submission, fairly or unfairly, cast doubt on Jack Drumm's qualifications as a man, and embarrassed him publicly in front of twenty snickering cavalrymen, several teamsters, and their Mexican swampers — and Miss Phoebe Larkin.

"They won't *be* alone!" he told Dunaway. "My man Eggleston and I intend to remain here also."

Dunaway frowned. "I don't think I heard you right. You're going to stay here, along the Agua Fria? For how long?"

Drumm looked steadily at his late antagonist. "For as long as it takes."

"What in hell does that mean?"

"I will stay here," Jack Drumm said, "until it is evident to me — and to others — that an Englishman

68

cannot be bullied, cannot be chivied, cannot be driven out of any legitimate place where he elects to remain."

Dunaway chewed at his ragged mustache. "I can't be responsible for your safety!"

"I didn't ask you to be."

"Agustín and his people are up somewhere on the ridge behind you, and it's just a whoop and a holler down the canyon to your camp. This is Agustín's old stamping grounds; that's why there's not been a stage station here, in spite of good grass and water." Dunaway turned to Miss Larkin. "Ma'am, I warn you — this place is dangerous! There may not be other transportation along for days."

"I'm not afraid," she said.

"Me neither," Mrs. Glore agreed. "We'll stay awhile, if it's all right with Mr. Drumm here."

The lieutenant shrugged. "Suit yourself, ladies!"

In spite of his brave front, Jack Drumm felt weary. He had a longing to lie in the green grass of Hampshire with his head on Cornelia Newton-Barrett's lap, free of great resolves and weighty responsibility. But he thrust the image from his mind; there was work to be done. As Dunaway rode off with his men toward the safe haven of Prescott, he turned on his heel and spoke briskly.

"Get a shovel, will you, Eggie? We must dig that rifle pit deeper, and face it with stones."

CHAPTER
FOUR

Before the last wagon left, Jack Drumm flagged down the driver and drove a few bargains. They were not bargains exactly; gamy mutton under a cheesecloth was forty cents a pound, and beans, unwashed and containing pebbles, went for a quarter. Though the goods were consigned to L. Bushford and Co., a Prescott grocer, the whiskered driver apparently saw a way to dispose of them at an even greater profit than the goods would fetch in the capital. What arrangements Jake would later make with L. Bushford and Co. were of no concern to Drumm; he suspected the arrangements would be as unsavory as the rest of the Arizona Territory and its inhabitants.

Fortunately, he had greenbacks, converted from English pounds at the Merchants' Exchange Bank in San Francisco. There he had hesitated at giving away sound English currency for the gaudy greenbacks; now he boggled even more at bolstering the economy of the Territory with his purchases. But there was no remedy for it. If he were to stay here he would have to have supplies. Perhaps his decision, born out of injured pride and humiliation, had been a rash one, but it was now made.

Jake stuffed the bills into a hip pocket. "It's a shame, Mr. Drumm," he said, "that I ain't got a few cans of salmon for you."

"How's that?"

"When I was teamster down at Camp Bowie, we had some tame Apaches on the post. They'd steal anything — stuff they couldn't even use, like the bandmaster's tuba. But Apaches is scared to death of fish; figger they're cousin to the snake. So all a man had to do was open a can of salmon and they wasn't no Apache'd come within a hundred yards of his belongings!"

"I'll have a few pounds of sugar too," Drumm decided, counting his money.

"Cost you six bits a pound!" Jake warned. "That's a bargain, though, considering it come all the way from Frisco!"

If he continued to stay along the Agua Fria, Drumm would soon have to have more money. Perhaps there was a way he could have Andrew arrange a letter of credit with a Phoenix bank. There was certainly no sustenance along the river for anything but jackrabbits; everything would have to be brought in.

"Tell you what I'll do," Jake decided, weighing out the sugar. "You bein' such a good customer —" He reached under the high seat and handed Drumm a wide-brimmed straw hat of the kind Mexicans wore, complete with a gaudy braided cord for the chin. "Compliments of the management!"

The Bombay topi was indeed in bad repair. A rent in the crown let in the sun and the brim had nearly been torn away during the Apache raid. "Thanks," Drumm said glumly, hooking the garish scarlet cord under his chin. He must look a fright; Cornelia would recoil in horror.

Jake unwrapped his long whip, looking calculatingly at the fourteen oxen. "Them critters is bushed," he complained. "Since Weaver's Ranch went under there's no place to pasture fresh stock." He looked around, scratched his chin. "The right man could make himself some money here running a stage stop. Plenty water, grass, lots of politicians traveling to the capital." He waved farewell; the whip cracked like a rifle shot. Wearily the oxen leaned into the yokes and the heavily laden wagon creaked away.

While Phoebe Larkin and Mrs. Glore watched, Eggleston helped Drumm carry the food back to the litter and confusion of the wrecked camp. The setting sun cast shadows long and black as they staggered under the burdens. The valet put down his load with a sigh.

"Mr. Jack," he asked, "do you really mean to stay here, along the banks of the river?"

"I do, indeed," Drumm said. "I am sorry if I compromised you, too, Eggie, but perhaps there is some way I can get you safely back to Clarendon Hall. As for myself, I intend to stick it out to show these people what an Englishman can do under adverse circumstances!"

"Then I will stay with you," the valet decided.

"It is not necessary! Already I have taken great advantage of your loyalty."

72

Eggleston shook his head. "My place is with you! My people served the Drumms for over a century, and I cannot abandon my duty now." He looked calculatingly at Jack Drumm. "You do need a shave, Mr. Jack! Shall I get out my basin and razor?"

Drumm shook his head. "This wound on my cheek does not yet permit it." Anyway, he thought, a beard could help to conceal the damage done to his mustache. A beard would also be more appropriate to the Mexican sombrero.

Mrs. Glore strolled over to inspect the supplies. "I've got some bacon," she volunteered. "I could boil up a mess of them beans. With a little meat they wouldn't taste bad for supper. And if Mr. Eggleston will gather some poke salat along the river there —"

The valet looked baffled.

"Along the bank, in the riffles," Mrs. Glore explained. "That stand of green shoots sticking up! My land — don't you have poke salat in England, Mr. Eggleston? Why, there's nothing better than a mess of them shoots with a little bacon grease poured onto 'em!"

Drumm picked up the shovel, watching the dwindling tracery of dust as the wagon train, under Lieutenant George Dunaway's protection, creaked toward Prescott. A breath of French scent made him turn sharply.

"Is there anything I can do?" Phoebe Larkin asked.

Put off by the shameless way she had flirted with Dunaway, afraid also that she would pity him after his trouncing, he planted the shovel in the trench and stamped viciously at it, driving the steel deep into the earth.

"No," he muttered. "Nothing you can do — not in those clothes, anyway!"

"But I want to help!"

Silent and tight-lipped, he went on shoveling.

"You're real grouchy!" Phoebe complained. "Whatever is the matter with you? Has the cat got your tongue?"

Drumm didn't know what that meant; he supposed it was an American witticism. "There's no need for you to do anything!" he snapped. "Just sit over there in the chair, and Mrs. Glore will have some supper ready directly!"

Phoebe Larkin set her lips; under the lace ruching her breasts rose and fell quickly. "Now you listen to me, Mr. Drumm!" she cried. "Maybe you're mad because I invited Beulah and me to stay here, but it really was not convenient for us to go to Prescott right now! Soon we hope to — to travel on, but right now we have no choice!"

Doggedly he kept on shoveling.

"I'm strong as a horse, and willing! Show me what needs doing! All my life I worked hard for my board, and I intend to keep on doing so!"

While he was trying to pry loose a rock, the handle snapped off in Drumm's hand. Disgustedly he threw the broken shovel from him. Phoebe Larkin pushed him aside. Snatching up his mattock, she swung it high over her head. Fearing feminine awkwardness, Drumm stepped back. But the blade, accurately aimed, buried itself next to the offending rock. Phoebe Larkin, tugging the weight of her body against the handle, neatly popped up the obstinate boulder.

"There!" she cried triumphantly.

Jack Drumm glowered at her. *All my life I worked hard for my board, and I intend to keep on doing so!* What had happened to the previous story — her father, Judge Larkin, and the crowd of wealthy suitors always "hanging around the place"?

"You see?" Phoebe cried. "A determined woman can do a *lot* of things!"

There was also the matter of the derringer she carried in her bosom. And why, after being in such a hurry to reach Prescott, did she refuse George Dunaway's offer of transportation there? But Miss Larkin stared at him so challengingly Jack Drumm decided not to press the matter — at least, not for the moment.

They needed a small dam to impound the scanty waters of the Agua Fria. In addition, the work would keep him and Eggleston gainfully employed; if they did nothing but sit in the rifle pit all day they would surely go mad. It was now early October. The nights turned cold and crisp, and the heat in the valley moderated. In a perverse way Jack Drumm enjoyed the hard labor — the swing of the repaired shovel, the chunking noise as gouts of dirt flew through the air and landed in line with the cord he had strung between two stakes. Mrs. Glore and Phoebe insisted on working, also, cleaning up the litter of the camp, repairing the wrecked reed hut, leading Drumm's solitary mule down to the river to drink. Phoebe named the mule Bonyparts, from the jutting hip bones and impoverished ribs.

Gradually the camp began to take on a neater appearance. With an ax Phoebe broke up old boxes for firewood, repaired camp chairs with wire she found in the wreckage, cut stalks of bamboo and made a brush awning to shelter the makeshift kitchen where Mrs. Glore worked. Phoebe was still angry with him, Drumm suspected. He watched covertly as she busied herself about the camp. In soiled traveling dress, red hair done up in a bun, and her face dirty, Miss Larkin did not in the least resemble the attractive female who had stepped off the Prescott stage. Unfavorably Drumm compared her to Cornelia Newton-Barrett. He could not imagine Cornelia chopping firewood. It was unladylike, to say the least, though he was bound to admit he appreciated Miss Larkin's efforts.

Watching her, he saw also what seemed a movement in the tall reeds along the river, a rustling not accounted for by the breeze. Seizing the Sharp's rifle, which lay always nearby, he rushed into the greenery, calling out, "Who's there?"

Eggleston, carrying his pick, ran after him. Together they stood among the reeds, sun filtering down on them in a lacy pattern like a Japanese print.

"What is it, Mr. Jack?" Eggleston finally whispered. "Did you see something?"

"I don't know." Drumm parted the reeds, rifle cocked. "It seemed to me something moved! Well —" He shouldered the gun. "Perhaps it was only an animal of some sort. At any rate, there appears to be no danger now."

That night they ate more of Mrs. Glore's boiled beans, along with mutton she fried up to prevent it from spoiling. The meat was strong but they all had good appetites. Drumm thought of dinner at Clarendon Hall; how unlike this! But the rains would soon be coming to Hampshire. The weather would turn cold and dank, the great house uncomfortable except for an island of warmth before the fireplace and in the kitchen around the cookstove. Here, on the other hand, the evening turned soft and mellow. Swallows flitted about in search of insects, and the western sky was streaked rose and saffron and the soft lavender of lilacs.

"Surprise!" Mrs. Glore cried. Beaming, she placed on the table a tin plate. "I found a can of peaches and some flour, and made a kind of — well, *pie*, I guess you could call it, though I could have done better with lard and a proper rolling pin!"

After the scanty rations, Mrs. Glore's pie was a treat. Drumm lolled in a camp chair, lighting a tattered but generally serviceable Trichinopoly cigar that Eggleston had discovered in a broken chest. In the glow of the moment, he felt almost charitable toward his unwelcome guests. He spoke briefly to Phoebe Larkin.

"You mentioned an uncle awaiting you in Prescott. Won't he be worried when you don't arrive there?"

She scraped the bottom of the tin plate with a spoon, dredging up the last juice. "My, that was good! It's been a long time since I et — ate pie!" She turned to Drumm, sucking a sticky finger. "Uncle Buell? Oh, he won't worry! He's lived out here long enough to know how uncertain schedules are on the frontier."

Drumm puffed on his cigar, watching the blue-gray smoke mingle with the sunset colors. "I do hope," he murmured, watching Beulah busy herself with soap and a pan of dirty dishes, "that Mrs. Glore's liver condition has improved."

"Her what?"

"The liver condition! You said her liver was bothering her — that jolting in a wagon to Prescott was medically inadvisable."

Phoebe looked puzzled but Beulah Glore drew quickly near, waving a damp dishcloth in the air to dry it "That's right!" she confirmed. "That's the God's truth, Mr. Drumm! That's why we couldn't go to Prescott!"

Phoebe looked relieved. "Yes," she said quickly, "that *was* the reason, all right. Her liver still pains her, too, though it's some better." Changing the subject, she looked up at the stars beginning to wink on against the velvet mantle of the night. "I've read a lot of astrology, Mr. Drumm. Do you know — the stars tell everything?"

He drew on the cigar. "So it is said."

"I cast up my horoscope last night, by candlelight. Right now is really *not* a good time to travel anyway. Jupiter is in Aries, I think — maybe it's the other way around — but traveling is not advisable for a Pisces person like me — or Beulah, either."

There was something almost beseeching in the way she spoke. Casting aside the stub of cigar, he rose to join her in the gloaming. Eggleston was busy helping Mrs. Glore put supper things away on improvised shelves. "I believe," he said, "it is somehow unwise for you to travel to Prescott, though I must admit I am not sure of the real reason."

For a moment she tensed; he feared that she was going to be angry again. But finally she sighed, looking at him with mournful eyes. "Life," she murmured, "is very difficult for a spirited woman. A woman alone, I mean, who has to fight for what she wants. Mr. Drumm, I shouldn't want you to think Beulah and me ungrateful, kind as you've been to us, taking us in and all."

He was looking beyond her, staring into the darkness along the river.

"What is it?" she asked.

An owl hooted, the sound eerie against the faint splashing of waters. "Did you hear that?" he asked.

"I heard the owl."

Shaking his head, he moved slowly toward the awning where his needle-gun was propped against the table. Washing beans for the morrow, Eggleston watched him.

"Don't anybody move!" Drumm warned. He picked up the rifle. The sound of the hammer was loud as he cocked it. Holding the camphene lamp, he walked again toward the reeds. "Who's there?"

Nothing moved; the slight breeze had died at dusk. The stalks of bamboo stood stiffly erect, unmoving.

"Who's there?" he called, waving the muzzle of the rifle menacingly. "Hallo, there! Throw down your weapons! We have you surrounded!"

The sound of his bravado died away in the silence; the reeds still did not move. There was only the faint gurgling of water in the pools of the Agua Fria.

Feeling foolish, he started to go back to the camp, when the reeds wavered, trembled.

"Come out!" Drumm ordered. "Come out with your hands in the air, or I'll shoot!"

The reeds parted. A wizened face, small and brown like that of a monkey, peered through.

"Careful!" Drumm warned. "No sudden moves!"

The intruder was an Indian, but not an Apache; at least, he did not resemble Agustín and his raiders. He was below even the height of the stocky Apaches, and dressed in a ragged pair of once-white pantaloons and leather jerkin. The feet were bare and horny; a tangle of glass beads hung around his neck. He wore a tattered felt hat that once must have belonged to a white man.

"Keep your hands over your head!" Drumm ordered.

In response to his gesture the wrinkled little man shuffled from the thicket. He was trembling; in the light of the camphene lamp the seamed and leathery face worked convulsively.

"Why, the poor thing!" Mrs. Glore murmured. "He's *scared!*"

Drumm gestured. "Search him for concealed weapons, Eggie! This man could be dangerous! He is certainly not one of our good simple English countrymen!"

The valet patted the intruder's clothing, rummaged through the leather bag the man carried, tossed a hatchetlike knife with a cord-wrapped handle to his master.

"No firearms, certainly," he reported. "and in his knapsack are only some of those flat pancakes —"

"Tortillas, they are called."

"And little sacks filled with seeds — beans, peas, Indian corn, things like that."

Mrs. Glore pushed between Drumm and the visitor. "My goodness!" she protested. "You're scaring the tripes out of him with that gun! He's hungry — look how his ribs stick out!" Ladling beans into a tin plate, she offered it to the man.

Warily he eyed it; then the monkey's paw of a hand shot out and he snatched the plate. Squatting, the newcomer dredged food into his mouth with his fingers, finally wiping the plate clean with a tortilla from his knapsack.

"There — I told you!" Mrs. Glore said. "There's no harm in the poor creature!"

Drumm lowered his gun, but continued to observe the Indian. "He is probably a Pima, or a Papago. They are peaceful farmers, and the seeds he carries very likely represent his only wealth."

The little man got to his feet and made a gesture that indicated fealty and respect anywhere in the world. He spoke rapidly, hands fluttering like small birds in a kind of sign language. Drawing a finger across his throat, he pointed toward the Mazatzals. Putting his hands over his face, he cowered and held out two fingers, working them back and forth in a manner reminiscent of a man running.

"He is fleeing from the Apaches!" Drumm decided. "That is certainly his meaning!" Striding to the dying fire, he kicked the embers. "Eggie, put out the lamp! His presence here may mean that Agustín and his cutthroats are not far behind!" He opened the case, loaded his Tatham pistols, and handed them to Phoebe Larkin.

"If we are attacked and there is no hope, do me the favor of shooting Mrs. Glore directly. Save the other pistol for yourself. There are horrible tales of what the red brutes do to captured white women!"

"I'm not afraid," Phoebe said. Her voice trembled only slightly. "If one of them comes near me, he will get what for!"

"That's right," Mrs. Glore said. "We are from far up the holler, and was weaned on a bullet!"

"Eggie," Drumm instructed, "you and I will defend the camp from the earthworks we have dug. Bring all our weapons and cartridges. A flask of water, too, and a dish of Mrs. Glore's beans to stay us during the night's watch."

Phoebe touched Drumm's arm. "You — you be careful, now!"

She was looking directly at him, eyes luminous in the starlight. He expected to find fear there, perhaps panic. Instead there was a queer look he did not have time to analyze.

"I will be careful," he assured her. "Now you and Mrs. Glore go into the hut and get some sleep. If anything untoward happens, you will certainly be aware of it."

The camp settled into stillness. A rind of moon hung low in the western sky and finally disappeared. An infinity of stars sprinkled the sky, so densely distributed that it was difficult to separate one from the other. Only the Pole Star seemed a separate entity, hanging high over distant Prescott.

"That Mrs. Glore," Eggleston said softly in the darkness, "is an unusual woman, Mr. Jack!"

Warmth fled the earth, evaporating quickly into the dry air. Along the river the coyotes started their nightly chorus. The sound was almost welcome to Jack Drumm, a familiar thing against the menacing uncertainty of an Apache attack.

"She is, indeed," he agreed. "A good cook, also." He squatted in the trench, peering over the parapet of stones, watching, listening. Orion's belt crawled slowly overhead.

"A hard worker, Mrs. Glore," Eggleston continued. "Very clean and neat, also!"

"That, too," Drumm agreed.

The wound on his cheek itched. Though it had partially healed and the ugly scab had fallen away, he was conscious of its disfiguring nature. The beard, now a good half inch long, covered most of it; he was grateful for that.

Through the night they lay behind the parapet, tense and expectant. Eggleston slept — Jack Drumm was sure he once heard a muffled snore, quickly cut off — but Drumm himself could not think of sleep. Cramped and sore, he stared into the starlit darkness with eyes aching from the intensity of his gaze. He had two females to protect; it was a heavy responsibility.

He felt, rather than saw, the pallid dawn. Well, it had all been a false alarm, he supposed. Eggleston truly slept, now; his mouth was open, a lock of thinning hair fallen over his face so that the valet looked almost like a child — a lost middle-aged child. Drumm smiled paternally.

"Eggie," he whispered. "Wake up! The night is almost over!"

Yawning and stretching, the valet sat up. "For a moment there," he admitted, "I think I dozed a little."

Drumm started to laugh but bit it off hard. From the river, where they must have lurked unseen, the Apaches burst out on the camp, a dozen or more of them. Silently and viciously they spread about the camp, intent on murder and rapine. Clubbing the butt of his carbine into a looming painted face, Jack Drumm had the satisfaction of seeing the man stumble backward, dropping a ribboned hatchet. Pulling the trigger, he saw another attacker drop his lance and fall. At his feet Eggleston knelt, aiming carefully, to drop an Apache who was running toward the reed hut.

"Good shot, Eggie!" Drumm shouted.

Perhaps low on ammunition in their mountain fastness, the raiders hoped to slaughter them with knife and club and hatchet. But this time Drumm and his valet were prepared. Together they laid down a blistering fire, forcing the Apaches to retort in kind. Though the big Sharp's rifle was a single-shot weapon, Eggleston had his pistol, and Drumm covered him with carbine fire while the valet reloaded. The survivors quickly took cover and for a moment the din ceased. Drumm peered over the parapet but withdrew when a bullet ricocheted from a flat boulder and caromed off, singing wickedly. In the first rays of the rising sun he saw a puff of smoke from the reed hut, a flash of orange; an attacker running toward the reed hut suddenly bent over, as if struck by an immense wind, and crumpled. Phoebe Larkin and Mrs. Glore were defending themselves. He hoped they would save the last cartridges for each other.

In the brief lull he swung to scan the perimeter of the trench, fearing that a new attack was planned from another quarter. He was just in time to see the Union Jack, his own Union Jack, fluttering high over the far side of the parapet. Now they were attacking from that side.

"They are coming, Eggie!" he shouted. "Be ready!"

The flag was carried by the man in the ornamented leather hat — surely Agustín himself — whom Jack remembered from the first raid. Bone whistle between his teeth, keening like the call of a wild animal, Agustín leaped into the trench. Behind him swarmed the rest of the attackers.

The chieftain swung a gleaming machete, as it was called. Drumm blocked it with the barrel of his carbine. Iron clanged against iron. Agustín dropped the swordlike weapon, cursing an Apache curse. As he danced in pain, Drumm caught Agustín's brown hand in his and twisted hard, bending the wrist backward in a jujitsu maneuver he remembered from Kurushiki, in

Japan. Agustín dropped the flag. They both scrabbled on the ground for it.

Wrenching at the staff, Jack tore the flag from Agustín's grasp but the wily Apache kicked him in the groin. Giddy with pain, he doubled over, hearing at the same time a woman's scream. It seemed very far away, distant, almost like a voice from beyond the Styx.

Aware of a sudden shadow, he rolled away in panic. But it was Eggleston standing over him, swinging the big Sharp's like a club. The weapon spun in a deadly arc, the steel buttplate crashing into a rag-bound skull.

"Get back there!" the valet snarled, and broke a man's bones with another vicious swipe of the butt. "Ho, sirrah, stand back! Mr. Jack, are you all right?"

Someone leaped on the valet, bearing him down. The trench filled with smoke, confusion, wolfish snarls, the report of firearms. Drumm tried to get to his feet but could only writhe in agony, clutching his groin. He was dimly aware of Agustín snatching up the maltreated banner, holding it triumphantly aloft where it caught the rays of the rising sun.

Almost resignedly Drumm closed his eyes, waiting for the end. This was his last sunrise. Lieutenant George Dunaway had been right. He should have — how was it the lieutenant had put it? *Shuck off all this junk and ride as fast as you can to Prescott before you get bushwhacked.* Interesting word, bushwhacked! Now he had been bushwhacked. Never again would he look on green grass and blooming roses, never again see Clarendon Hall, never again see Andrew and Cornelia Newton-Barrett and —

Impatient at death's delaying, he finally opened his eyes. That was when he saw Phoebe Larkin. Like an avenging fury, she stood on the parapet, pistol in each hand, squinting along the barrels with such professionalism that he knew instantly the derringer in her bosom was a well-known tool, her familiarity with weapons a matter of custom. Probably she was a professional murderess, though this category of employment was not one he had previously come on. But murderess or not, he did not want her to die.

"Run!" he yelled. "Run away, Phoebe! Save yourself!"

Propping his body on outstretched arms, he tried to rise. But a last bullet from the fleeing Apaches struck him heavily in the shoulder. The force of the impact spun him sideways so that he fell with face pressed against the dew-wet earth. He became very tired. Curious, he tried to touch his wounded shoulder. The effort was painful, and his fingers came away warm and wet. *Blood — his blood, Drumm blood.*

He continued to lie in that strange position, cheek pressed against the ground and buttocks in the air, hearing the sounds of battle grow fainter and ever fainter.

CHAPTER
FIVE

When he awoke Jack Drumm did not know where he was, even less where he had been. He seemed swimming in some nameless void, a fathomless pool where there was no up or down, no now or then — only the cloying blackness. From time to time he caught a glimpse of light, perhaps a lamp burning in a window a long way across the moors. At times there was a face lit by the lamp glow, but so faint and blurred that he could not recognize it. Too, at times he heard sounds: voices, small rustlings, footfalls. When he cried out, tried to reach these evidences of humanity, the dark enveloped him again and he sank again into the void.

Finally, with the tenacity of the Drumms, he decided that this business of the darkness was very silly. If he was alive, then a black void was no place to waste time. If he was dead, there must be something beyond the void; pearly gates, perhaps, and a waiting harp — or fiery furnaces. In either case it seemed best to find out immediately.

Opening his eyes, he stared dazedly about. It took a long time to identify the splash of color on the back of a folding canvas chair near the bed. Finally he identified it as a China silk kerchief — a woman's kerchief, such as females used to bind their hair or secure in place a bonnet. Exhausted by the concentration, he lay back; the familiar void once again engulfed him.

He did not know how long it was before he opened his eyes again. With a start he realized that he lay in Eggleston's reed hut. The movement lanced his shoulder with spasms of pain. He lay quietly again, feeling the awkward bulk of bandage. Recollection flooded back — the Apache attack, Agustín in his leather hat waving the Union Jack, the numbing impact of the bullet, the final sight of Phoebe Larkin standing on the parapet like an avenging angel, firing down into the trench with his Tatham pistols, one in each hand.

Run! Run away, Phoebe! Save yourself! Dimly he remembered the words, remembered shouting to Phoebe Larkin. Then he had collapsed on his face, knew no more.

But he was here. He was alive. From outside the hut came reassuring sounds: the bray of a mule, a woman's voice, someone laughing, the rippling of wind in the reeds along the river. He was alive!

Gritting his teeth, he rolled to the edge of the crude bed and swung his naked legs over. The whole world reeled, tipped upside down. Desperately he grasped at the chair. Finally his equilibrium returned, though he seemed out of breath and very tired.

Dressed scantily in his shirt, he staggered upright, the earth floor cool and damp under his feet. Still holding on to the chair, he stared unbelievingly at the scarecrow regarding him from the fragment of mirror

89

fastened to the wall. The apparition was surely a fugitive from Dartmoor prison, a gaunt hollow-eyed ruffian with scruffy red beard. Even the slatted light from the sun, filtering through the reeds, painted the sorry figure in stripes appropriate to a convict. His mouth opened in wonder; he saw a gap where a tooth should be. Remembering the fight with George Dunaway, he was now certain that the apparition was he, John Peter Christian Drumm, of the Clarendon Hall Drumms. In spite of himself, he came close to grinning. The bearded ragamuffin leered back at him. What changes the Arizona Territory had wrought!

Shuffling painfully across the floor, blanket wrapped around his bare legs and dragging the chair as a prop, he stood in the doorway, accustoming his eyes to the sunlight. Eggleston had Bonyparts, the mule, hitched to a bizarre assembly of slats from a broken keg laced together with wire to form a crude drag; he was scraping dirt to finish the dam across the Agua Fria that Drumm had planned. The little Papago man who had visited the camp the evening before the attack was making bricks with a wooden form and mud from the river. Under a brush shelter Mrs. Beulah Glore stirred something — probably more beans — in a pot over a mesquite fire.

Puzzled, Drumm stared at a fresh mound of earth. At the head of the raw new mound a stake was driven into the ground; a scarlet cloth headband fluttered from it. With elation he realized that their little party had indeed given the Apaches "what for," as Phoebe Larkin had promised.

He saw her, then, standing in the shade of a spread canvas, drinking from the water butt with a tin dipper. As he did, she appeared also to hear the faint sound of gunfire from the mountains, and turned to stare into the purple distance where George Dunaway was still harassing the Apaches.

"Phoebe!" he called. "Miss — Miss Larkin!"

At first she did not see him, only tightened her grasp on the heavy Sharp's rifle and continued to look at the slopes of the Mazatzals, dipper poised halfway to her lips. He tried to speak louder, but all that emerged was a strangled croak. Phoebe heard him, however; she dropped the rifle, crying out. Eggleston let fall the makeshift rope reins, Mrs. Glore abandoned her beans, and Papago left off his brickmaking. They all ran to Jack Drumm.

"I only left for a minute!" Phoebe complained. "Oh, whatever are you doing out of bed?"

Mrs. Glore and the valet took him by the arms and tried to steer him back into the hut but Drumm would have none of it.

"I am all right!" he protested. For the first time he noticed the copper-brown youth sitting under the brush ramada, tied firmly to a wooden bench.

"Who is that?"

Eggleston had a blood-stained bandage around his head, but he spoke with great pride. "A prisoner of war, I guess you might say, Mr. Jack! We captured him day before last —"

"Day before last?"

"You've been out of your mind," Phoebe explained, "for well over forty-eight hours! It was probably due to all the blood you lost from where you were shot in the shoulder."

"Lucky for you," Mrs. Glore beamed, "the ball passed right through and didn't bust anything! Mr. Eggleston here stood over you like a lion and fought them off! Oh, I tell you, he was a real ring-tailed roarer! How he did ramsquaddle them red brutes!"

Basking in her approval, the valet smiled modestly. "And Miss Phoebe here, in addition to playing the perfect Amazon with your pistols, put you to bed and managed to stop the bleeding with cold compresses."

Jack Drumm remembered a hand on his brow, a light and gossamer touch that was for a while his only link with this world of sunlight and triumph.

"I am — I am grateful," he stammered. "I mean — to you all, but especially to you, Miss Phoebe. And we fought them, the Apaches, to a standstill! We showed them we are here to stay, residents of the Territory!" He caught sight of the grinning leathery face of the Papago. Where had he been during the battle?

"He skedaddled," Beulah Glore explained. "Don't know as I blame him, either! He wouldn't go ninety pounds with sashweights in his pockets. But he's been real useful around here."

"Now, Jack," Phoebe urged, taking his arm, "you must get back to bed! You are as white as a bedsheet, and have got to rest."

She had never before called him Jack, and the familiarity made him uncomfortable. Too, how had she described him? *A cold fish?* That had been unfair, and inaccurate. Cornelia Newton-Barrett could have informed her differently. He wondered what Cornelia would have done during an Apache attack.

"First," he said, "we must decide what to do with this scoundrel here — this Apache youth you have captured."

"Beulah here," Eggleston said, "hit him over the head with a shovel! When the rest finally broke and ran, they left him for dead. We tied him up, but let him walk about each day for a little while under guard. He eats a great deal, though, and will soon pauperize us."

The little Papago sidled up to Jack Drumm and looked fearfully at the Apache youth in his bonds. He jabbered something, then retreated.

"I know," Drumm said. "They are very fierce."

He looked into the black eyes of their captive. It was like staring into the eyes of a snake — a flat impassive opacity that showed nothing of humanity behind the glittering pupils.

"Look here," he said. "Do you speak any English? I mean —" Frustrated, he broke off. "*Englisch? Anglais? Ingles?*"

The youth only stared coolly, muscular bronze arms folded over a hairless chest.

"Flag!" Drumm made a waving motion. "Do you understand 'flag'?" He took a stick and drew a Union Jack in the dust, complete with staff and waving folds of cloth. "*My* flag!" He pointed to the flanks of the Mazatzals. "It belonged to my brother Andrew, damn it all, when he was in India, and I want it back! Flag —

do you understand? I want my flag back, or Agustín will have to answer to me!"

At mention of Agustín the obsidian eyes seemed for a moment to clear, to show depth, to indicate interest. The youth was tall for an Apache, with a kind of indolent grace even in his bonds. He lifted his chin proudly, and the black eyes became large and luminous. Then, suddenly, it was if a curtain descended. Once more, Jack Drumm might have been addressing a stone.

"I don't think the creature understands a word you say," Mrs. Glore observed.

Jack Drumm felt his knees weakening; he swayed a little. Phoebe caught him under the arm, looking anxiously into his face.

"Hadn't you better —"

"I — want — my — flag," Jack said between clenched teeth. "Flag — *bandera!* You understand that?"

The Apache watched him, immobile, without emotion, but Jack felt somehow that the youth understood. He turned to the valet.

"Cut him loose, will you, Eggie?"

Eggleston was surprised. "Are you sure, sir, that —"

"Cut him loose," Drumm repeated, surprised to find his voice suddenly husky and reedlike, almost inaudible. "Let him go, and tell his master Agustín we are here to stay, along the Agua Fria! Let him tell Agustín he can not dislodge us! Let him tell Agustín I will have my flag back, and before I leave this miserable

94

land I will see Agustín himself hanged on a gallows in Prescott!"

He toppled, then, and would have fallen. Eggleston and Mrs. Glore managed to catch him under the arms and drag him protesting into the reed hut. He had a fever and his mind wandered again. But Phoebe Larkin was always nearby; it gave him a grudging complacency.

By the middle of November the combined forces from Camp McDowell and Fort Whipple had confined Agustín and his raiders to the Mazatzals. Escorted by small detachments of troops, stages and wagons and even an occasional straggling train of hopeful settlers began to filter along the Prescott Road, although there was still danger of scattered raids. Sam Valentine and the newly elected Territorial representatives rode north to the capital in an armed band. Valentine was amazed at the growing activity along the river. Eating a slice of Mrs. Glore's peach pie, he strolled along the earthen dam, where the water now backed up to a depth of almost a foot.

"So you just decided to stay, eh?"

Drumm did not mention his fight with Lieutenant George Dunaway but he suspected that Valentine had heard of it. News traveled fast in this arid land.

"Yes," he said, "we Drumms are a stubborn lot."

Valentine ate the last of the pie and looked toward Mrs. Glore's new kitchen, built with odds and ends from a Phoenix-bound shipment of lumber by the sawmill in the new capital of Prescott.

"The ladies too, I see."

"Eh?"

"Those two indomitable ladies stayed also — the ones who refused to go back to Phoenix when the stage was attacked in Centinela Canyon."

"Yes," Drumm said, "they are stubborn too, I think. At any rate, they decided to stay over awhile and help me get things in shape here. I think, though, they will be leaving soon for Prescott. Miss Larkin has an uncle there, I understand."

Valentine's eyes narrowed. He stroked his beard. "I see two more pies cooling on the table over there. They are covered with cheesecloth against the flies, but I can smell pie a hundred yards off. Do you suppose Mrs. Glore would sell me one?"

"She baked a few extra," Drumm admitted. "They cost a dollar apiece."

"Done." The legislator finished the last of his coffee, and added, "I appreciate the coffee, too, but you ought to charge for it. If you're going to stay here, you can make yourself a mint of money with a good cook." He mounted his big bay and looked thoughtfully at Drumm. "You know, this Territory needs people like you — hard-working savvy folks that'll settle down and make the desert bloom. But Arizona needs people like George Dunaway too. George cusses a lot, never been curried below the knees, but he's actually a prince of a fellow when you get to know him. And if it wasn't for tough nuts like George Dunaway, the rest of us might just as well go home to Indianapolis or Nashville or Atlanta — wherever we came from."

Ike Coogan stopped off, too, driving a Tully and Ochoa freight wagon bound for Prescott with a load of melons, pumpkins, sweet potatoes, and peaches. Sitting in the shade of the ramada with Jack Drumm, he sliced open a ripe melon with his jackknife. Handing a dripping half to Drumm, he noted his host's wincing as he reached for the succulent fruit. "Got you through the shoulder, eh?"

Drumm nodded. "It's not healing right. There's pus around the wound, and a suppuration."

Juice dripping from his whiskers, the old man shook his head, grinning. "*Rancho Terco*, that's what I'd call it. *Rancho Terco!*"

Drumm knew some Spanish. "*Rancho Terco?* Let's see — *terco* means —"

"It means stupid!" Ike cackled. "Idiot — blockhead! Hee hee! That's it, all right! Blockhead Ranch! No one but a blockhead would camp in the middle of an alkali desert and wait for old Agustín to swoop down and cut out his giblets!"

Drumm was annoyed. "I don't think it's so foolish! Anyway, Sam Valentine tells me Agustín probably won't bother us any more. And this is good soil along here — all it needs is water!" He pointed to the river bottom where the gentle Papago, whom they had named Charlie after an ancient London dustman, was hoeing newly sprouted shoots of corn. "With plenty of winter sun, and water, a man could get several crops a year along the Agua Fria!" *Not*, he thought, *as in Hampshire*. There it was already cold and dark, blustery and raining.

"You serious?" Coogan demanded.

"I am in dead earnest. I mean to stay here until I am ready to leave — and I do not know when that will be."

Coogan scratched his tobacco-stained beard. "By God, you sure cut a different figger from that silly-ass Englishman that first come here!" He stared at Drumm's ginger beard, the straw sombrero, the jagged scar on the cheek. "You're beginning to look like a real Arizony hardcase!" He got creakingly to his feet, leaning on the old rifle. "If you're actual intending to stay here for a while, I got a proposition for you from Tully and Ochoa in Phoenix."

"What kind of a proposition?"

"Run this spread as a regular stop. They'll leave extra animals here to graze and water, busted wagons that need fixing, whatever. Old man Tully thinks he might even put in a little warehouse. Fifty dollars a month to run the place. Stage line needs a stop, and they'll pay you something too. You can make a few dollars on the side selling grub to people, maybe putting someone up for the night in that shanty over there."

Eggleston's uncle had indeed been a wheelwright, and the valet had once worked at the trade. So long as they stayed, Mrs. Glore could cook meals and Phoebe could help her. Charlie, the Papago, could be the porter when he was not tending his vegetables.

"I'll do it!" Drumm decided.

George Dunaway rode by with B Company. Dusty and sweating, he slid wearily from his mount to stare at the bearded figure in the tall conical hat. "Drumm?"

Jack nodded. "Hello, Dunaway."

Phoebe had been helping Charlie dig weeds from the garden. Flushed and glowing, cheeks pink from effort and the sun, she came to greet the lieutenant. Her feet were bare, the balmoral dress torn and stained. Beulah Glore came too, face sweating from the heat of the kitchen fire, and Eggleston.

"Well, I'll be God damned!" Dunaway stared from one to the other, too astonished even to apologize for his language, while the troops watered their mounts in the small lake beginning to form behind the earthen dam. "I'll be simply God damned!"

"We're still here," Drumm said with some pride.

Dunaway shook his head in disbelief.

"And we intend to stay here — at least, Eggleston and I."

Phoebe Larkin moved a bare toe thoughtfully in the dust. "Mrs. Glore and I are staying, too — for a while. We'll leave for Prescott soon, I guess, but Mr. Drumm has been so good to us we're bound to help out."

The lieutenant eyed her admiringly. Even with her disheveled appearance she was beautiful. The China kerchief attempted to restrain the red hair but much of it escaped in a rich cascade of curls; smudges of dirt on her cheek only accentuated the gentian blue of her eyes; the feet were narrow and well shaped in the Arizona dust. Leaning on the hoe, she looked to Drumm like a goddess of the harvest — Ceres, perhaps. He was annoyed at Dunaway's pleasureful gaze, especially when Phoebe Larkin smiled winningly back.

"Well?" he said, rather sharply.

Dunaway took the crockery cup Mrs. Glore handed him. Still looking at Phoebe Larkin over the rim, he spoke to Drumm. "Heard you captured one of Agustín's Apaches during your last dust-up."

"That's right."

"And let him go!"

Drumm nodded.

"That was a damned fool thing to do!" Dunaway snapped. He wiped his mouth, turned hard eyes on Jack Drumm. "We've been trying to get one of 'em alive for weeks." He pointed toward the slopes of the Mazatzals. "There's no way to flush old Agustín out of there unless we know where he is, how to get in through all those *barrancas* and rocks and passes. Mr. Drumm, you just set back our campaign about a month — maybe more!"

Drumm's shoulder pained him, and he winced. "I don't see how —"

"Let me tell you how, Englishman! If you'd held on to him till we got here, like any proper citizen of the Territory would do, we'd have sweated it out of him — where the old man was holed up, how to get there, the story we need to know to settle Agustín's hash for once and for all!"

Drumm became indignant. "Torture him, you mean?"

The lieutenant scowled, slapped his dusty hat against a thigh. "We'd have gotten it out of him, one way or another! But you let the bastard go! It was a damned irresponsible act!" Dunaway jammed the shapeless hat on his head and climbed again into the saddle. "I hold you responsible for the wounding of Private Murray, do you know that? Murray was hurt down at Mud Springs. Some of Agustín's rascals slipped down the mountain and bush-whacked my pickets at daybreak yesterday!"

"I'm sorry," Drumm said. "Truly sorry — but —"

Dunaway gave him a withering look, tipped his hat to the ladies, and rode away in a cloud of dust. On their last encounter the lieutenant had bested Jack Drumm conclusively; this time Drumm felt he had again come off second best. But he was learning.

The shoulder did not improve. Instead, Jack developed a fever again. Suppuration from the wound turned yellow and foul-smelling. He felt it sapping his strength but he continued to work alongside the others. They were concerned for him, uneasy at his dogged persistence, and finally almost angry when he refused to rest.

"But there is much to be done!" he insisted. Leaning on the shovel he was using to dig irrigation channels to newly leafed beans, he looked about. "Where is Charlie? He should be here to show me where to run these damned ditches!"

"I don't know, Mr. Jack," Eggleston said, mopping his bald head. "He went out early this morning with a sack on his back. Perhaps he is looking for edible plants of some sort."

Mrs. Glore trundled by a load of mesquite wood cut for the kitchen fire. "He don't like *my* cooking, that's a fact!" Laying down the load, she struggled for breath.

"You know what Charlie favors? Yesterday I seen him with a snare, trapping them little mice that runs around the bushes. He throws 'em in the fire to singe 'em, and gobbles 'em down like they was patty foo graw!"

Phoebe shuddered; her face grew pale. "I'm glad *I* didn't see him! I'd have lost all my suppers for a week back!"

That night Drumm sat by candlelight and wrote a long letter to his brother Andrew:

It is so very strange — I was on the final leg of my Grand Tour, yet here I find myself suddenly the major-domo of a flourishing settlement along the banks of the Agua Fria River in this backwater of civilization! You spoke of the doggedness, the determination, which I think most of the Drumms possess. Well, perhaps mine has betrayed me into a foolish adventure! Yet there are compensations. The winter air is like wine; the sun shines beneficently, the birds sing in the *saguaro* and *pitahaya* — they are cactuses, you know — and a very pretty young lady, Miss Phoebe Larkin, has stopped here along with her companion until they find suitable transportation to Prescott. I think our Eggie is rather fond of Mrs. Glore. However, I do not find Miss Larkin to my taste. She is a very forward female, inclined to be rough and strident, though she did participate magnificently in the latest attack on us by the renegade Agustín and his bloodthirsty Apaches.

He concluded with a request for Andrew to cable him the sum of five hundred pounds, payable at the Merchant's and Drover's Bank of Phoenix, A.T. (that meant "Arizona Territory," he explained), and sealed the letter, meaning to send it by stage to Prescott and thus eastward on the cars. Hearing rustling outside the lean-to, muted voices, he started in alarm and reached for his pistol. "Who is it?" he called. "Eggie, is that you?"

The valet was supposed to be on watch atop the tower they had built from precious lumber.

"Phoebe?" he asked. "Mrs. Glore?"

The intruder was Charlie, the Papago. Grinning from ear to ear, he entered the lean-to. "*Ostin*," he said to Jack Drumm, holding up a hand in salute. Jack did not know what the word meant, but it seemed a term of respect, like "sir," perhaps, or "your honor." Phoebe Larkin was behind Charlie, carrying a bucket, and Eggleston brought up the rear of the procession.

"What is this?" Jack demanded. "What is this all about?"

Phoebe set down the bucket, filled with black mud from the river.

"Charlie and I," she explained, "are going to cure your shoulder. You've gone long enough with that festering wound. Now it's time for back-country remedies to take over."

Over his protests, Phoebe unbuttoned the ragged shirt. "You remember — you asked this morning where Charlie was? Well, I don't speak Papago but with signs I made him understand what I wanted. He went out and

103

got certain plants and together we ground them up and mixed them into this mud. Now we are going to manufacture a poultice and put it on your shoulder."

He tried to resist but Eggleston and Charlie easily bore him to the pallet. Phoebe mixed the evil-smelling concoction with a stick.

"Mr. Jack!" Eggleston said severely. "This is for your own good, sir! I am only a valet, but I am getting very tired of your stubbornness!"

Jack Drumm stared unbelievingly. Eggleston appeared frightened by his own temerity but kept a firm hold on his master while Phoebe Larkin smeared the black stuff on the wound. She covered it with fragrant-smelling leaves, the whole bound in place by a strip from a ruined blanket.

"There!" she said. "Now you just lay back there and let those yarbs work! In Pocahontas County my Uncle Buell knew every yarb — herb — there was. Were? Anyway —"

The poultice did not smell as bad as he had feared. There was a resiny fragrance to it, and the coolness of the mud was balm to the inflamed shoulder. Eggleston and Mrs. Glore tiptoed out to let the two of them alone. Phoebe sat beside him, candle flickering on her hair and lighting responsive flames. When for a long time he did not speak, she asked, "Isn't that better?"

He nodded, bemused by the candlelight and her presence.

"We never really got a chance to talk," she said. "Maybe it's my fault. I know I come on pretty strong at times, like a mule with his ears laid back. But I *like* to

104

hear you talk, you're so educated and all." She paused for a moment. "Tell me about England," she said softly. "What's it like? When I was a little girl I had a book about England — all about the old kings and such."

He told her about the Plantagenets; about the Wars of the Roses, Henry and his innumerable wives, Queen Elizabeth, the Stuarts, the Restoration, all about Pitt and Castlereagh, to whom he was distantly related; and about the Whigs, and Queen Victoria.

"Did you ever see her — Queen Victoria, I mean?"

"Once. My father took me to Buckingham Palace. I was very small — don't remember much about it."

"And — about you!"

He was getting drowsy. "What about me?"

"Tell me about you!"

He felt peaceful; his shoulder no longer hurt. Sleepily he murmured, "I'll make a bargain with you, Phoebe."

"What bargain?"

"If you tell me," he said, "the truth — the *truth*, mind you — about how you came to be here, and why you are staying here, I'll tell you all about John Peter Christian Drumm."

She looked at him, eyes somber, almost black, in the glow of the candle. "I *told* you! My father —"

He shook his head. "All that business about your father being a judge in New York City, a crowd of suitors begging for your hand, the judge packing you off to travel, your wealthy uncle in Prescott —"

"Don't you believe me?"

Perhaps, being drowsy, he was insensitive to her agitation.

105

"It is cut from the whole cloth," he told her. "You do not talk or act in the least like a refined young lady from a great metropolitan center. You know about 'yarbs' that certainly do not grow on Manhattan Island, and are very familiar with guns. Mrs. Glore speaks of being 'from far up the holler and weaned on a bullet.' You refuse to return to Phoenix, speaking of some dreadful experience there. Yet when you have a perfectly good chance to travel to Prescott, you beg off with some cock-and-bull story about Mrs. Glore's liver. I am not a complete idiot, you know, in spite of Lieutenant Dunaway's opinion." He shaded his eyes from the candle with a hand and looked at her. "Tell me — what is your secret, Miss Phoebe Larkin, or whatever your name is?"

He had meant it jokingly, in the best of good humor, but she grew distraught. "You — you —" She broke off, twisting the handkerchief in her fingers. "I have told you everything — at least, what I was lief to tell." She gave him a long and tragic look. Never had he seen her so lacking in composure. Gone was the clever and confident young woman; Phoebe Larkin suddenly became a fearful child, eyes misting with tears and pain.

"I am sorry," he blurted, trying to rise on an elbow. "Phoebe, excuse me! I did not mean to —"

Suddenly she fled; he heard footsteps diminish into the night. Along the river the coyotes howled; the frogs stopped for a moment at the sound, then resumed their drumming.

What was the mystery?

106

The next day he found out. After lying late abed, he wandered out into the sunlight. Raising an arm over his head, he found his shoulder almost free of pain. The fever had abated, also. Standing thus, flexing his arm, he watched a traveler approach from the direction of the capital. Alonzo Meech, the Pinkerton detective, got creakingly down from the decrepit mare and shook hands.

"Bon joor," Meech said. "That's French for 'it's a hell of a nice day.' "

Jack looked around for Mrs. Glore, hoping she had coffee on and boiling, but Beulah was not in the kitchen. He did not see Phoebe Larkin, either. Eggleston was feeding the chickens that a teamster had traded Mrs. Glore for peach pies, and Charlie stalked mice under the spreading ironwood tree.

"So the Apaches didn't get you," Drumm remarked.

The detective shook his head. He looked dusty and funereal as ever, and weary also. But there was something enduring in his manner.

"No," he said. "Oh, they stepped on my corns a little in a gulch near Prescott, but I give them as good as I got." He accepted a dipper of water; drinking part of it, he splashed the rest in his face and rubbed at his eyes. "My butt feels like a dime's worth of stew meat from all the saddle time I been putting in." Throwing the reins over the mare's head, he watched the animal shamble toward the greenery along the river. "Been on the road all night. Best time to travel, with old Agustín and his cutthroats loose."

Drumm remembered the detective's mission. "You were pursuing someone."

Meech nodded. "A pretty young lady named Phoebe Buckner. Her companion is a middle-aged lady goes by the name of Beulah Glore. They was seen around here. A freighter said he'd heard —"

"Two — two females?" Drumm tried to keep his voice casual.

"That's right." Meech walked slowly toward the bright patch of color thrown over the back of a chair under the ramada. It was Phoebe Larkin's China silk scarf, the garish print to keep her hair in place against the wind. The detective picked it up, spread it, examined it. "I'd know that anywhere," he muttered.

"I guess she forgot it," Drumm said. "But — what crime did they commit?"

The detective folded the kerchief and slipped it into his pocket. He stared around, taking in the reed hut, the half-finished adobe, the lean-tos, the earthen dam, freshly sown crops, the graves of the two Apaches.

"The young one," he said, "plugged Mr. Phineas Buckner, her husband, with a little derringer. Didn't kill him, but that wasn't *her* fault! Rifled the old man's strongbox, run off with Buckner's cook, an old friend of hers from Pocahontas County, West Virginia. Where are they, Mr. Drumm?"

108

CHAPTER
SIX

Suddenly Drumm realized that the two females must have observed the approach of Alonzo Meech from a distance. Eggleston was laying up adobe bricks in a mortar made by burning rocks, and the Papago shoveled dirt atop the dam to accommodate the steadily rising waters. But there was no sign of Phoebe Larkin or Mrs. Glore; they had fled.

"Why — ah — I —"

"They stopped here, didn't they?" Meech demanded. "Heard the two of 'em come through on the Phoenix stage, then stayed when Apaches turned the stage back."

Drumm's words came so glibly, so naturally, that he himself was astounded. He had up until now been a truthful man.

"That's right," he lied. "They *were* here. But one of Tully and Ochoa's wagons took them into Prescott the other day. They packed up and left, both of them. It seems Miss Larkin has an uncle in Prescott, and —"

"That was her maiden name — Larkin," Meech observed. "Her married name is Buckner."

"Well, anyway, they are not here now. They have gone on to Prescott. Quite suddenly, as a matter of

109

fact." He wanted desperately to look around, to see whether Phoebe and Mrs. Glore might even now be rolling out pie dough or chopping wood for the kitchen fire to give the lie to his statement, but did not dare.

Meech strolled to the water butt and drank another dipperful. "They ain't in Prescott," he grumbled. "By now I know everyone in Prescott, except for the greasers. Them two ain't there — ain't *been* there!" Shaking water from his grizzled beard, he stared at Jack Drumm. "Seems like you favor that shoulder."

"Apaches again, a few days ago. They shot up the place, but we — Eggie and I — drove them off."

"Heard in Prescott you was planning to stay here along the Agua Fria. Seems to me like a damned fool idea, but —" Casually the detective wandered toward the kitchen, but Drumm steered him to a chair under the ramada.

"You must be tired after riding all the way from Prescott. Sit there and rest — I'll bring something to eat. I was about to have a bit of lunch myself."

While Alonzo Meech slumped in the chair, fanning himself with his broad-brimmed hat, Jack spoke in low tones to Eggleston.

"That is Detective Meech — do you remember? The people he was searching for are Miss Phoebe and Mrs. Glore."

The valet's eyes opened wide. "But what —"

Jack quickly put a finger to his lips. "Where are they?"

"Mr. Jack, I don't know! A moment ago they were working in the kitchen, but I heard Mrs. Glore make a

110

funny noise and they hurried into the reeds along the river!"

Drumm nodded. "I thought so." He looked again toward Meech, lolling in the chair. "If you will, bring us something to eat. Remember — say nothing whatever about the ladies! I told him they left here several days ago for Prescott."

"But —"

"Shhhh! I will explain everything later. In the meantime, let us act perfectly natural. Perhaps Meech will be satisfied and go on about his business."

Together Drumm and the detective ate pie and drank coffee under the ramada. The sun climbed high in the sky; the Mazatzals turned blue and hazy. A wren dipped brazenly through the shelter and then perched atop a cactus, singing a cheerful song. Meech spooned up the last of his pie.

"Ain't had a treat like that since I come out here! Crust just like my wife makes." He looked thoughtfully at Jack Drumm and belched. "Mrs. Glore was said to be a good cook."

"Eggie is almost of chef level," Jack said carelessly. "You remember his cooking the night we had dinner here, just before Agustín and his Apaches attacked. Eggie is a real coper — he can bring off almost anything you care to mention. Really, a marvelous servant!"

Meech wiped his mouth, staring at laundry spread over the bushes. Jack suspected they were Phoebe Larkin's underthings. From where he sat he could not quite make out the laces and bows undoubtedly there.

"Eggie is quite clean, also," he added. "He insists on laundering our linen daily. Since we settled down here, we have become very regular in our habits."

"Well —" Meech sighed and put on his broad-brimmed hat. He filled his canteen from the water butt and buckled the big Colt's revolver about his waist. "Got to get on about my business."

Jack's inquiry was casual. "Where are you bound for now?"

Meech stared with reddened eyes down the road; his gaze followed the winding track into Centinela Canyon. "Just around, I guess, to pick up their trail and start all over again. I had 'em dead to rights in Phoenix but they gave me the slip." He mounted the buckskin and waved. "Churchy la femme. That's French for 'don't never trust a woman.'"

Jack sat for a long while under the ramada, watching the detective and his mount dwindle in the southern distance. Finally they were gone, but perhaps the detective had field glasses in his saddle-bags. He walked slowly, casually, to the dam. Eggleston looked up, brow shiny with sweat, face smeared clownlike with dirt.

"He has gone, then?" he asked.

"How far, I don't know! But I think he is suspicious. Even now he may be watching the camp."

The valet leaned for a moment on his shovel. "I do not think the women are very far away, Mr. Jack. A moment ago I was sure I heard voices."

Jack parted the reeds. Damned females — what had they gotten him into? Now he was an accomplice after the fact, when all he had to do, really, was admit their

112

presence and let Meech take them away to a well-deserved fate! Murder was a serious business.

"Phoebe?" he called. "Miss Larkin?"

The sun beat down in a lacy green pattern. Something plopped into a scum-edged pool. His boots gurgled and sucked in the rich ooze.

"Phoebe!" he called again. "Where are you?"

A bee lumbered near his ear. The buzz was loud in the silence.

"Phoebe?"

He stepped into a hole and fell headlong, grasping the tough stalks in an effort to regain his balance. As he toppled, his eye registered the scene as a photographic plate is struck by light to fix a permanent image. Phoebe Larkin stood in a clearing, aiming carefully with her derringer. Mrs. Glore screamed; Jack saw her also with utmost clarity, terror-struck, hand over her mouth. Fortunately the shot went wide, cutting through the grasses over his head. Indignantly he clambered from the muck to snatch the weapon.

"One murder," he protested, "is enough for any female, I should think! You almost killed me!"

Phoebe sank down on a grassy mound, face in her hands.

"I thought it was Detective Meech," she quavered.

"That's right!" Mrs. Glore cried. "That's the God's truth! May I be set afire without no hose company if that ain't the truth! We was hiding here, and when someone come blundering through the reeds, we figured the jig was up!"

Eggleston came running, Sharp's rifle at the ready. "What is it? What's happened?"

"Nothing," Jack said. "Nothing at all, Eggie. Just a little misunderstanding. Go back to your work."

Now he understood their strange behavior: the initial refusal to return to Phoenix, their later refusal to go on to Prescott with the wagons under the escort of Lieutenant Dunaway. The Pinkerton had lost their trail in Phoenix. Thinking they had finally eluded Meech, the two women took the stage to Prescott and Phoebe's uncle Buell, only to have the stage turned back by the Apaches. They could not, of course, return to Phoenix, where Meech was, and so insisted on staying at the Agua Fria with Jack Drumm. Then, when safe transportation to Prescott was assured, Drumm told Dunaway that Meech was in Prescott, still on the trail of his quarry. It must have been an agonizing moment for Phoebe and Beulah Glore, trapped between Phoenix and Prescott. But Drumm hardened his soul. Phoebe Larkin was a murderess.

"Come with me!" he ordered, slipping the derringer into his pocket.

"Where?" Phoebe asked.

He nodded toward the reed hut.

"But —" A hand crept toward her throat. "Where is that devil Meech?"

"He has gone, but may be watching us from a distance." Taking her hand, he guided Phoebe and Mrs. Glore to a thicket that bordered the reed hut; they were able to slip in unseen, so far as he knew.

114

"I don't understand this," Phoebe murmured. She sat in their shelter, cluttered about with fripperies. A lacy nightgown hung from a nail, bottles of cologne and containers of face powder littered an upturned box, the place smelled feminine and foreign to Jack Drumm. Face pale but head proudly erect, Phoebe clasped hands in her lap. "Mr. Meech must have told you the whole story! Why didn't you just turn us in?"

He had no ready answer. "I don't know, exactly. Maybe it was only that I wanted to hear your side."

That was not it — not the whole thing, anyway. He found himself in the grip of a powerful emotion he did not quite understand. He distrusted emotion, especially his own; better always to be cool and practical. To cover his discomfiture, he added, "Anyway, that's neither here nor there."

"But it is!" Phoebe insisted. "It makes you an accomplice, or some such legal foolishness! I know *that* much! Since I was caught up in this nasty business I studied the law to find out where I stood!"

"And where," he asked, "*do* you stand, Miss Larkin?"

Phoebe swallowed hard, looked down at her clenched fingers.

"I want you to know the truth! Since you helped us so — me and Beulah — I'll tell you everything, just as it happened." In a monotone, not looking at him, she went on. "I was a poor girl from Clover Lick, in Pocahontas County. That's in West Virginia, the coal-mining country. I worked hard, and hunted and fished with my uncle Buell. Mr. Phineas Buckner owned most of the mines. He was a rich man, a real rich man, that lived in Philadephia. He used to come to Pocahontas County to visit his mines and see how much money they was — were making. One time he came to our house — my pa was a foreman in the Black Diamond Mine — and saw me. I was only eighteen then, and I guess something of a looker —"

"That's right!" Mrs. Glore interrupted. "Peaches-and-cream complexion, and that red hair falling all over her shoulders —"

"Be quiet, Beulah," Phoebe said. "Anyway, Mr. Buckner courted me. He was nigh on to fifty then, and old enough to be my father. But I was a loving girl — still am. I am full of love, and sometimes regret it. I — I —" She broke off; tears misted her eyes. "I gave him my hand, and we were married in a big church in Philadelphia. That was ten years ago, come spring."

Jack Drumm cleared his throat, uncomfortable. "If these details pain you so, you need not —"

"No!" She shook her head; the red tresses swirled about. The close air filled with feminine fragrance. "I've got to tell somebody, maybe just to get it all straight in my own mind!"

Brushing a vagrant strand back from her forehead, she went on. "Philadelphia was a big town, and I didn't fit in with his society friends. And Mr. Buckner was so much older than me that there was no one to talk to. I did get him to bring Beulah to his big house when he needed a cook, but she was the only friend I had. For a while he kind of showed me off, like I was a prize he won. But then he began to fuss at me. He got real

116

mean." She closed her eyes. "He — he began to beat me. Said I was obstinate, when all the matter was that I just — I just was a country girl. I didn't know how to act in society and there wasn't anyone to teach me."

Mrs. Glore shuddered. "He was a brute, that old man!"

"I had a little derringer Uncle Buell gave me when I was fifteen, before he went off to seek gold in Arizona. Uncle Buell said I was so pretty — *he* said it, you see, I didn't — that sometime I might have to defend my body against wicked men. I thought it was a joke, but it wasn't." She bit her lip. "One night Mr. Buckner came to my room — we slept in separate rooms — and had —" She swallowed again, and her voice trailed off. "Well, he had his way with me. He abused me, beat me with his belt. I couldn't stand it anymore. I got my derringer from where I kept it in my — my underwear. I always have and always will kill my own snakes, so I shot him. I don't know where I shot him, but he fell down covered with blood."

Reliving the scene, Phoebe was overcome. She began to weep. Mrs. Glore sat with an arm around her, trying to comfort her.

"There ain't much more to tell," Beulah finished. "Phoebe come and told me what she'd done. While the rest of the servants was milling around upstairs, we took a crowbar and busted the lock off the old man's strongbox. I had my savings, but the old alligator hadn't paid me for weeks because I stuck up for Phoebe. I took what he owed me and we lit out of there. And that's the God's truth, the only kind of truth there is!"

117

Drumm scratched his chin. The beard itched. "Detective Meech gave me only the barest details. But your version puts a different light on things."

"What can we do? The Buckners are big bugs in Philadelphia, and Beulah and I are just little people. No one will believe us!"

"I have a plan," Drumm said.

They listened.

"With Meech about, as he may well be, we have to be very careful. I told him you two had gone on to Prescott, to visit your uncle Buell, but I do not think he believed me."

"You never!" Mrs. Glore cried.

Phoebe was surprised, also. "But why did you do that? That puts you in as much trouble as us!"

"Never mind that! At any rate, here is what you must do. I want you and Mrs. Glore to remain here, in the hut, night and day. Do not venture out. There will be people passing by, more and more now that Agustín is barricaded in the Mazatzals — stages, freight wagons, travelers and settlers, miners. Even Alonzo Meech may unexpectedly return, hoping to catch you unawares. But you are not to show yourselves. In a few days, I expect a friend of mine — a Mr. Ike Coogan — to come by in the Tully and Ochoa wagons with a contract for me to sign. Coogan is a good sort. I think I can arrange to smuggle you and Mrs. Glore to Prescott in one of his wagons. There your uncle can take over your protection; perhaps help you to get to the Sandwich Islands or Australia, where you will be safe."

A tinge of color returned to Phoebe Larkin's cheeks. The freckles paled. She touched her lips with a wispy handkerchief. Phoebe looked dainty and very feminine; Jack marveled that this was the female who swung a mattock like a man, drove off Agustín's braves with a pistol in each hand — and shot a brutal husband.

"Why, I must ask you again," she said, "are you doing all this for us?"

"Because you have been badly used. We Britons believe in fair play."

She rose, looking him in the eye with that strange gaze he had once before observed. "Mr. Drumm," she said, "I thought you were cold as Mose's toe. But I'm bound to admit I'm a poor judge of men! All anyone has to do is remember I married Mr. Buckner. So I apologize for what I said. Maybe there *is* a little milk of human kindness in you."

"Me too," Mrs. Glore agreed. "That's the God's truth! We both got a little different slant on you now."

Jack Drumm had a different slant, as she put it, on himself, also; it bothered him. Belatedly he realized he must soon find time to write a few lines to Cornelia Newton-Barrett. For some time he had neglected her.

Behind the new dam the water level grew. Now there was a pond containing small fish, deep enough to bathe in. Charlie and Eggleston finished the adobe building and roofed it with thatch. Jack Drumm blistered his hands cutting brush to build a corral. The beans and corn that the Papago had planted began to

119

burgeon, show miniature fruits. Too, a semblance of peace came to the valley of the Agua Fria. Traffic increased along the road to the new capital. Now there were frequent freight wagons and a twice-weekly coach service. A man named Sloat from Emporia, Kansas, tied up his mules two miles down the road from Rancho Terco and settled there with his wife and six children. The winter sun was good for Mrs. Sloat's rheumatism, and Sloat was impressed by the rampant growth of Charlie's corn and beans. "In Kansas, in November," Sloat enthused, "everything's snowed over, but out here a farmer can work the soil right through the winter! That's for me!"

George Dunaway rode by, also. Jack was currying old Bonyparts, the mule, when the lieutenant and two men tied their horses to the new hitching post before the adobe and dismounted. Dunaway looked spruce. The ragged black beard was neatly trimmed, his blue shirt ironed till the creases stood out like knife blades, and his boots gleamed in the noonday sun. Jack looked at the flowers clutched in the lieutenant's fist.

"You're welcome," he said, "but surely you're not bringing me a bouquet."

One of the troopers snickered but Dunaway fixed him with a malevolent eye.

"They're for Phoebe," Dunaway explained. "I picked 'em from Mrs. Major Trimble's front yard. Where is she?"

Jack was startled. "Miss Larkin?"

"Of course. Where is she?"

He brushed Bonyparts carefully, not looking at Dunaway. "Oh, I thought you knew! She and Mrs. Glore left. They — they went into Prescott several days ago on the stage."

Dunaway watched his men lead the mounts to the pool.

"I'm sorry," Jack said. Though he and Dunaway were hardly friends, there was something almost touching in the way the lieutenant stood disappointed, bouquet still clutched in his hand. Too, Jack Drumm was now the *patron*, as the Mexicans would say, of Rancho Terco, a host to desert travelers. "Sit down, here, in the shade," he invited, and handed Dunaway a gourd of water from the butt.

"Thanks." With a sigh Dunaway slumped on an upturned box. "Got quite a spread here."

"We manage," Jack admitted, not without pride.

"I'm sorry I missed the ladies. They went to Prescott, you say?"

"That's where they were bound for."

"Funny! I've been in and out of Prescott lately, but I didn't run across 'em. Of course, it's the capital now, and growing. There are a lot of people there."

"I suppose so."

Dunaway put down the gourd and patted water from his black whiskers with the back of his hand. "It's a hard life, a soldier's," he said. "I never married, maybe on account of that. Wouldn't be fair to ask a woman to follow you to a place like this." He stared into the purple distances.

"I suppose not."

"She was real pretty," Dunaway said. "Miss Larkin, I mean. There was a — well, a kind of a *substance* to her. I mean — she seemed like a real *person*."

Phoebe Larkin was real enough; that was true, Jack thought. He glanced toward the reed hut, hoping the reality of Phoebe's person could not be seen. The two women, quickly bored with forced inactivity, were probably watching him and Dunaway, straining ears to hear the conversation.

"I'm not young anymore," Dunaway admitted. "God, I'm thirty-six already, and I don't know how it happened I got old so quick! But it gets you to thinking, Drumm, thinking how a good woman might make a difference in your life. Well —" He got up, sighed again, put on what was obviously a new hat of the Stetson variety Jack Drumm had often seen in the Territory. Dropping the flowers into the dust, he looked at them for a moment, then ground them with his heel. "Got pickets out all along the wagon road. Just riding out to check on them."

Jack followed him to where his trooper escort waited. "How's the campaign against Agustín going?"

Dunaway shook his head. "We keep him penned up pretty well in the Mazatzals, but till we find some way to get infantry up there and flush him out, he's going to be a problem. He can always swoop down and bloody a few noses. Keep an eye out, Mr. Drumm, and don't be fooled. Just when you least expect it that bastard is going to strike!"

"I know," Jack said. "I surely know."

122

The women *had* been watching, listening. After the soldiers left, Phoebe called from the hut. "Who was that, Mr. Drumm? Was it Lieutenant Dunaway?"

He stood near the doorway, pretending to sharpen his knife on a chunk of granite. "I am sure you know it was."

Phoebe peered around the edge of the doorframe. The slatted light filtered through the reeds onto her hair, lighting it in random glints.

"He — he brought you flowers," Jack added, not wanting to tell her but feeling obligated to be fair to George Dunaway.

"Me? Flowers? But why?"

"Dunaway is a lonely man. He said a soldier's life was hard out here, and I suppose it is. Anyway, I gather he — well, he thought you beautiful, and wanted to bring about a — a closer acquaintance."

Someone giggled.

"Anyway," Jack said, "I told Dunaway you were not here, that you and Mrs. Glore had gone on into Prescott. He was very disappointed."

Again someone giggled. This time he thought it was Phoebe Larkin. What was the term for it he had heard — cabin fever? Was the long and boring confinement beginning to addle the two females?

"So he thinks me beautiful," Phoebe mused.

"That is his opinion."

Bearing down so hard on the knife, he cut his finger and swore.

"And what is your opinion?" Phoebe asked.

He sucked at the wounded finger. "What is my opinion of what?"

"Do you think me beautiful?"

"I have not got time," he said coldly, "to stand here engaging in idle talk! Of course you are beautiful, Miss Larkin! I think you are only trying to make me say something ridiculous."

Stalking away, he still heard female laughter from the hut.

Next day a Tully and Ochoa wagon came by. Ike Coogan got stiffly down, calling a greeting, but before Jack could speak the old man was supervising the removal from his wagon of what appeared to be a corpse. Jack watched the Mexican swampers carry the frail body to the shade of the ramada. The man was old, looking to be seventy years of age or more. The white beard stuck stiffly into the air, and his lean body was as rigid as a board.

"Who is that?"

Coogan wadded a gunnysack under the old man's head. "Uncle Roscoe."

"Uncle Roscoe what?"

Coogan shook his head and spat. "No one ever heered his last name, but everyone in the Territory knows him. Been prospecting these mountains for forty years, I reckon. Uncle Roscoe was here before I was, and I been here nine years longer 'n God, so that should give you an idee."

Jack knelt, put an ear to the ragged shirt. "The pulse seems regular, though slow. What's wrong with him?"

124

Coogan pointed toward the loaded burro the Mexicans were un-tying from the rear of his wagon. "Old Pansy was loose in Centinela Canyon. I knew then something must be wrong. I climbed up the hill, and shore enough there was poor Roscoe laid out under a bush with an empty canteen. Maybe it was apoplexy — I dunno — and he got that far hopin' to flag down help. Anyway, I drug him onto the wagon and brought him here. Ain't nothin' much we can do fer him, is there?"

Jack Drumm had spent two years in Glasgow at medical school before deciding he was not cut out for a physician, but he did remember some of his lectures. He rolled back a wrinkled lid and stared at the dilated pupil. Uncle Roscoe groaned, tried to raise a hand. It fell back; he subsided.

"There's a bed in that new adobe," Jack said. "If you'll have your swampers carry him there, I'll bleed him of a quart or so. That should help."

Coogan grinned. "Why, that'd be salubrious! Pore old coot! The landscape wouldn't be the same without old Roscoe! By God, that's nice of you, Mr. Drumm!"

When they had settled Uncle Roscoe comfortably, and Jack Drumm had signed the contract with Tully and Ochoa to manage the Agua Fria station, Coogan suddenly asked, "Where are them two ladies that was here — Miss Larkin, I think, and the old lady that was traveling with her?"

Though Coogan's Mexicans appeared to have no English, Jack drew him confidentially aside. "That's what I wanted to talk to you about."

Briefly Jack told the story — how the two women had fled prosecution, how Detective Meech dogged their tracks, how they were trapped along the Agua Fria and were now awaiting salvation, how Meech might even now be watching.

"What do you say?" he asked. "Will you help them?"

Coogan bit off a chunk of Wedding Cake plug.

"Do *you* believe their story?" he asked.

"I believe them. They are being unjustly persecuted."

Coogan chewed, leaning on the long rifle, staring at the dust. "I could get in trouble."

"That's right," Jack admitted. "I myself am already in deeper trouble. But there is a time when a man must be ready to accept trouble in a good cause."

Coogan grinned a tobacco-stained grin. "Ain't no cause better 'n a pretty gal!"

"Then you'll help?"

"Shore enough!"

Between them they arranged for Coogan to drive the wagon down the road and into a stand of bamboo along the river. The two women could then leave the reed hut with their valises, walk under cover of the river greenery to the wagon, and board the vehicle without being seen by a lurking Detective Meech. Coogan would cover them with wagon canvas and take them to Prescott.

"No hurry," Coogan called. "I got to grease them wheels, and wrap a felloe with wire where it got busted."

Across the river the brittlebush with its dusty gray leaves was blooming; butter-yellow flowers laid a carpet

126

on the rocky slopes. Quickly Jack picked a bouquet and hurried to the reed hut. They did not hear his scratching at the door. When he did enter they were startled and nervous. The long confinement was telling on them. Phoebe's face was pale, and Mrs. Glore had developed a tic.

Hurriedly Jack explained the plan. The two women started immediately to pack. Phoebe noticed the brittlebush flowers; she stared silently at the bouquet.

"Ah — this is for you," Jack muttered, feeling awkward and uncomfortable. It was a foolish idea, of course; emotion had betrayed him. The blooms were only common, and Phoebe Larkin must have seen them all along the river.

For a moment he thought she was going to fling her arms around him, as she had that day when he pulled her from the flooded Agua Fria. But she seemed to have learned a lesson.

"That was very nice of you," she murmured, looking down at the yellow flowers. "It — it was thoughtful."

"You're a real gentleman," Mrs. Glore confirmed. "And that's the God's truth! There ain't many of 'em left around anymore!"

He shifted from one foot to the other. "A — well, perhaps a kind of going-away present. The Spanish called them *incienso*. They used the dried sap for incense in their early churches in Arizona."

"Jimmie brought me flowers, once, in Clover Lick," Phoebe said.

"Who?"

She seemed in a reverie. "A boy I knew, a long time ago. He — he was killed in the mines." She looked at him unseeingly. "Jimmie Frakes. He was blond, blond like you, Mr. Drumm."

Uncomfortably he rubbed his hands together. "Well," he said, "are we ready?"

Mrs. Glore fastened her bonnet in place with a swordlike pin and picked up the bags. "Ready or not, Prescott, here we come at last!"

"Good-bye, Mr. Drumm." Phoebe held out her hand. It was warm in his calloused fingers. "You've done so much for us — no one could ever thank you enough. I won't even try."

He wanted to say something memorable, something cool and composed yet significant, but there was a strange lump in his throat, an emptiness in his breast. He could only stand in the doorway and watch them walk away through the reeds, the sun dappling them as it shone down through the high grasses. Watching them go, he strained his eyes, seeing at last only a patch of color here and a minuscule movement there. Finally they were gone.

He went back to the Tully and Ochoa wagon. Coogan had completed his repairs.

"They will be waiting for you," Jack said. "I'm everlastingly grateful to you, Mr. Coogan."

"Ike," Coogan corrected. "Hell, I ain't been called Mr. Coogan since I was brought up before the judge in Phoenix for drunk and disorderly!"

For a long while Jack Drumm stood in the dusty road, watching Coogan's wagon until it went out of sight around the bend. He scanned the low hills, the brush, the rocky slopes, fearing to see a wink of sun, a flash of reflected light from the lens of field glasses. But he saw nothing. Alonzo Meech had probably abandoned the search. Eggleston came to stand beside him.

"The two ladies are gone, then?"

Silently Jack nodded.

"I will miss Beulah Glore," the valet said. "She was a fine woman, no matter what sticky business she may have gotten into back in Baltimore."

"Philadelphia," Jack said.

"Look at the chickens, Mr. Jack! They miss her too. She used to feed them about now."

Suddenly he missed Phoebe Larkin more than he cared to admit. He went quickly into the adobe to attend to Uncle Roscoe while Eggleston coaxed the reluctant burro into the corral. For a moment, just before entering the sickroom, he thought he saw a man's figure atop a ridge to the south of the ranch. But as he narrowed his eyes against the glint of the November sun, the figure disappeared — or perhaps it had never been there. He was getting jumpy.

The old prospector was able to talk, though only weakly and briefly. The heart was sound, though, pumping determinedly. Some color had come into the pallid cheeks. Jack bled him, and made a broth of sage leaves, which the *Traveler's Guide* said were a specific for stroke. Boiling the infusion, he tried to remember the Latin name of the shrub, but could not. Sage was no longer an exotic plant to be identified and entered in his field notebook; it was becoming the common furniture of the desert, this Arizona desert that was for the time being his home.

The next morning Uncle Roscoe was markedly better and wanted to sit up, though Jack forbade it.

"God damn it!" the old man protested. "I ain't no weakling! It was just a little dizzy spell come on me in the canyon there!"

Leaving Eggleston to feed Uncle Roscoe a dish of chicken soup, Jack wandered listlessly to the road and stared in the direction of Prescott. They should be in the capital by now — Phoebe and Mrs. Glore — and perhaps safe in the hands of the redoubtable Uncle Buell. Looking around at Rancho Terco, it seemed somehow deserted, incomplete, unfriendly.

Looking, he saw something else. Pinned to the new hitching post with a bone-handled knife a note fluttered in the wind. He tugged at the knife, driven deep into the post, and read the note. It was lettered in block characters with what appeared to be a stub of charcoal, and was obviously the work of an untutored hand. The choice of terms was strange, also, and the phrasing queer, though the words had a certain dignity:

This is my place. This river my place all right. I do not want white men heer where I born & my *parientes* bury.

The writer's scanty English had failed. *Parientes*, Jack recalled, meant "kin" in Spanish.

130

You fight good but spirits ask you go from this place. You send back *sobrino* —

Jack wrinkled his brow. More Spanish; what was *sobrino?* Uncle? No, that was *tio. Sobrino* — yes, that meant "nephew."

You send back *sobrino* but I cannot friend you no more. I finish saying.

He stared at the wrinkled paper. It was signed with a straggling A; an inexpertly made A that lay almost sidewise at the bottom of the warning, but still — an A; A for Agustín.

CHAPTER
SEVEN

Uncle Roscoe might be seventy, or eighty, or ninety. He was short and wiry, bandy-legged, tough as an old boot and smelling almost as bad. Fretting at the refusal of his left arm and leg to accommodate him, he sat in the shade and unwillingly drank the sage tea that Eggleston brewed.

"But you're getting better," Jack pointed out. "Look — you can move your fingers now!"

"Can't hold a pick! Can't hold a shovel!"

"You're coming along nicely," Jack comforted. "I daresay if I had had such a stroke, I wouldn't be as far along now as you are!"

"Well, mebbe so," Uncle Roscoe sighed, "but I wish things'd move along more pronto! I'm an old man. I don't think the Lord's got me down for any more time." He told Jack Drumm about the Gypsy Dancer Mine he had spent twenty-odd years searching for. "Hungarian feller — name of Laszlo something — stumbled on it." He took a tattered scrap of paper from a pocket. "Met him in a saloon in San Diego and he showed me this map and some nuggets big as goose eggs. He was in town to buy supplies but a gang of Mexicans laid for him and hit him over the head. They stole the nuggets, but when Laszlo was laid out for the coroner I slipped the map out of his shirt and took off for the Agua Fria. That was in — let me see — fifty-six, fifty-seven — something like that."

"And you've been looking for the Gypsy Dancer ever since?"

"Oh, I'll find it!" the old man assured him. "I got the location pretty well narrowed down by now!"

Roscoe was a rich source of information about the Apaches, the Mazatzals, the whole Territory. He knew Charlie the Papago and Ike Coogan, claiming also to have been a ceremonial brother of Kayatinah, the father of Agustín himself, and once adopted into the tribe.

"What you want to know all this stuff for?" he demanded.

"Because the Apaches insist on trying to drive me away from the Agua Fria. We are enemies. To do a proper job of resisting, I must understand them."

"Ain't nothin' much to understand," Uncle Roscoe grumbled. He waved his hand toward the hazy distances. "Once they owned all this — now the politicians and the merchants and the Army is trying to take it away and make 'em live on the Verde River reservation. I don't mean no offense, Mr. Drumm — you been good to me. But you can understand how *you'd* feel if bandits run you out of your big castle in England!"

"It isn't exactly a castle," Jack said, "but I know what you mean."

"They're proud," Uncle Roscoe went on, "and resourceful. They lived off this dry land for thousands

133

of years. They make bread from mesquite beans, and beer called 'tiswin' from the mescal plant. They bake mescal roots in a pit in the ground, too. It tastes like molasses candy; they got a sweet tooth, like anybody. They eat the fruit of the *nopal* cactus — some folks calls it 'Indian fig.' Their lingo is all gobbles and gargles, but there's a pleasant sound to it."

Jack looked to the greening fields where Charlie hoed weeds. "Do the Papagos speak the same language as the Apaches?"

"Purty close," Uncle Roscoe said. "At least, they can make each other out."

"Charlie calls me 'Ostin.' What does that mean?"

Uncle Roscoe grinned a toothless grin. "'Ostin' is Apache talk for 'Lord.' Anything they respect or fear they call 'Ostin' — the bear, snakes, lightning. 'Lord Bear,' 'Lord Snake,' 'Lord Lightning.'"

Jack helped him light his pipe. The old prospector lay back in the chair, staring at the great bulk of the Mazatzals, remembering a long time ago when he lived with the Indians.

"They don't never call *themselves* 'Apache.' That's just a Mexican word that means 'enemy.' Their name for theirselves is *Tinneh*. It means 'The Men' — and that's what they are: men, real men." He watched a circle of blue-gray smoke drift in the wind. "Missionaries never had any effect on 'em. The Apaches got their own religion, and stick by it — all kinds of gewgaws and ceremonies. Sacred cords, sacred shirts, medicine arrows and lances, pieces of quartz and petrified wood. What means most is *hoddentin*. That's cornmeal, usual dyed red or blue, they hang in a bag around their necks. Kind of a charm, to protect 'em in battle."

Now Jack understood the little sack filled with blue grains he had taken from the neck of the Apache killed in the first fight at the Agua Fria, the sack he later hung on the broken lance of the dead man.

"The men folk," Uncle Roscoe went on, "are good sewers, do all the sewing for the family. But an Apache is scared to death of his mother-in-law." He chuckled. "He won't talk to her or face her if he can help it. I've seen 'em walk a mile out of their way just to sashay around a mother-in-law!"

Cornelia Newton-Barrett's mother, Jack remembered, was also somewhat of an ogress.

"They love to play cards, gamble, run footraces. Mostly they're happy. But when someone dies they set the whole village afire — they live mostly in brush huts — and move away. They don't want to be reminded."

Jack looked toward the graves, amulets swinging in the wind. He had thought of the Apaches as murderous beasts; certainly they had tried to kill him. It was unsettling to view them as human beings; family men, people who doted on mescal candy and feared a mother-in-law and were in their own way religious.

"They eat horses, too," Jack was reminded, and looked where old Bonyparts grazed, along with a lame ox and some horses left at the Rancho Terco station under the terms of his recent agreement with Tully and Ochoa. There was a spring wagon, also, that was being towed to Prescott when an axle broke. Eggleston, at a crude forge, was making repairs.

"Horses and mules is a special treat," Uncle Roscoe agreed. "They eat sunflower seeds, too, and wild potatoes and berries and rabbits and whatever else comes to hand. They grow a little corn, when folks leaves 'em alone. But now most of 'em has been herded onto the reservations. The rest is being chased from pillar to post. No, times are a-changing for them, I guess —" For a moment the old man seemed to doze, then opened his rheumy eyes. "And for the rest of us old geezers, too, like me and Ike Coogan."

Times were changing the fastest along the Agua Fria. Rancho Terco was a natural site for a stage stop; midway between Phoenix and the new capital, it began to grow like the tent towns in the gold country of California twenty-five years earlier. Prescott furnished fresh vegetables, lumber, beef cattle, and excellent beer from a new brewery. Phoenix supplied wheat, barley, pumpkins, sweet potatoes, mutton, and wool. It was also an important distribution point where goods and supplies unloaded from the steamers of the Colorado Steam Navigation Company at Yuma could be shipped by wagon to Florence, Tucson, Prescott, and the many mining camps and Army posts.

The merchants of the Territory — Fish and Collingwood, Lord and Williams, Leopoldo Carrillo, Zeckendorf, Tully and Ochoa — maintained fleets of freight wagons that weekly plied the rutted roads with bolts of gingham, lard and sides of bacon, saddles from

St. Louis, kegs of bourbon, rum, and brandy, cartridges for the Army, patent medicines. Sometimes the cargo even included barrels of oysters and clams shipped all the way from San Francisco in ice renewed at the new ice-making factory in Yuma. Temporarily balked by the Apache rebellion, the economy now boomed again. But still Agustín sat stubbornly atop the Mazatzals, a brooding threat the Army could not eradicate. From time to time he reminded the Territory of his presence by quick, stinging raids along the river, Jack Drumm's Union Jack carried aloft as a totem.

Though Jack had not yet heard from his brother Andrew, enough money was coming in to keep Rancho Terco viable. Corn, beans, and winter melons flourished under Charlie's care; Eggleston discovered pan-size fish in the river; Uncle Roscoe, recovering from his stroke, found a bed of wild potatoes. "Dee-lishus!" he cackled. "All you got to do is fry 'em, peel and all, with a little wild onion!" Roscoe found the wild onions, also, and they feasted on fresh new potatoes. But the mealy taste made Jack think of Clarendon Hall. He and Andrew used to filch potatoes from the kitchen to roast at their secret hiding place in the depths of the forest behind the house. Unwillingly, he found himself thinking also of Cornelia Newton-Barrett. What must she think of him? When last he wrote Andrew he had neglected even to mention Cornelia in his letter, to speak of his intention toward her, his anticipation of seeing her soon. Guilty, he found a stub of candle and started to write:

I think of you so often and of the times we were together.

He struck that out; it was not true. Really, he had not thought of Cornelia for a long time. Starting again, he wrote:

Do you remember the time we were alone together in the great hall, sitting by the fire? The hour was well after mid-night, and the house very still. You —

The pen, corroded from disuse, scratched into the paper and blotted. He tore up the letter and started another, but found himself staring moodily into the flame of the candle. Cornelia had been in nightclothes; a filmy gown that shimmered in the firelight lay lightly on her thigh yet molded itself silkily to the rounding curve of flesh. Cornelia's hair was long and blond, falling around her shoulders in cascading ringlets that — that —

Eyes half closed, he frowned. Cornelia's hair was blond, certainly, but in his vision something had changed. He narrowed his eyes further, insistent on retaining the misty image. This woman's hair was red, a titian red that caught the flames, made a halo around her pale face with its blue eyes. Blue eyes? Cornelia's eyes were brown, a melting brown like those of a good setter, but the eyes in his dream were blue — remarkable cerulean blue, soft lashes overarched by delicate brows.

138

"Phoebe!" he blurted. "Phoebe Larkin!"

Wadding up the half-finished letter, he threw it angrily from him. How dare she? Phoebe, he meant — not Cornelia. Reaching for the pen, he tried another start. That did not work out either.

Ashamed and repentant, he stalked out and sat for a long time in the moonlight, smoking one of Fish and Collingwood's "stogies," as they were called — five cents apiece, and hardly of Cuban quality. His thoughts were confused. Relieved of the glow from the treacherous candle, his eyes finally became accustomed to the dark. In the gloaming he could just make out the great purple bulk of the Mazatzals. The wound on his cheek itched, and he scratched it gently. Agustín was up there, in the Mazatzals. From the corner of his eye he saw a spark of light on the mountain; it glimmered briefly, then disappeared. Agustín? An Apache campfire? He did not know. But somewhere, sometime, he and Agustín would meet again; he knew it in his bones, in his being, in the wound on his cheek and the newer one in his shoulder.

Early one morning, leaving the defense of the ranch to Eggleston, Uncle Roscoe, and the Papago, Jack Drumm hitched Bonyparts to the repaired spring wagon and drove to Prescott for supplies. Not only for supplies was the trip necessary, but he remembered Jake the teamster's comment about the land along the river as potentially valuable property. He did not know the procedures involved but intended to visit the Land Office and make inquiry.

It was a December day, breezy, the desert wind soft and warm. Wrens trilled in the cactus, a few of the ocotillo retained red-tipped branches from bloom of the previous summer, and the sky teemed with snowy caravels of cloud. Jack had a good baritone voice. He began to sing an old ballad he remembered from his father. It was called "The Girdle"; a hymn to a lady's belt. Lord Fifield, in his early days, had been somewhat of a rover. Basking in the sunshine while Bonyparts plodded ahead toward distant Prescott, Jack recalled the final words:

A narrow compass, and yet there dwelt
All that's good and all that's fair.
Give me but what this ribbon bound,
Take all the rest the sun goes round!

Feeling content, he lolled on the seat. For the first time in a long while he had a feeling of satisfaction, of accomplishment. In that assurance he allowed his thoughts to wander. Phoebe Larkin's waist had a narrow compass, indeed. Her hips were full and rich, nipped at the waist by a circumference that must be no more than twenty-odd inches. *Give me what this ribbon bound, take all the rest the sun goes round!* A bit racy, that! Well, he thought loyally, Cornelia Newton-Barrett had a small waist also. He could not imagine Cornelia swinging a mattock, or for that matter shooting anyone, even greatly provoked. Cornelia was a lady of quality and breeding, which Phoebe Larkin — or Buckner — was not.

Lost in thought, suddenly he blinked. On a ridge paralleling the road a light flashed. An Apache mirror?

140

Were they watching him, signaling his presence, a raiding party out for guns and ammunition, which they must desperately need? Reins in one hand, he picked up the needle-gun in the other and made sure it was loaded. The contentment fled.

"Get along, mule!" he barked, slapping the reins over the animal's broad sweating back, festooned with gnats and flies. Bonyparts swiveled his ears and broke into a shambling trot while Jack scanned the ridge. Prescott must be at least another twenty miles distant; he would be lucky to arrive by noon. Beginning to feel vulnerable, he wished traffic on the road were more frequent. There was something macabre in thoughts of death on a fine day. But Weaver's Ranch had probably dozed in the sun when the Apaches attacked.

Prescott was over six thousand feet in altitude, much above the playa. The road climbed steadily, passing through *barrancas* and canyons. His mouth felt dry and cottony. Sweat filmed his brow and dampened his grasp on the reins. An Apache might lurk beneath each saguaro, a painted warrior behind every boulder, a bandy-legged assassin in every wash. He felt cold, which might have been expected with the increase in altitude, but he suspected that part of it was due to fear. When he saw the rambling out-buildings of Fort Whipple and heard the sound of a distant bugle playing mess call he was relieved.

As a child Jack had visited his father in the state of New York, near Albany, where Lord Fifield held a consular post. Prescott was not only picturesque in location and dainty in appearance, but after the

141

sprawling Latin character of Phoenix and Yuma it seemed a village transplanted bodily from the Mohawk Valley of New York State. Houses were built in American style, with little of the adobe and brush common to Phoenix. The doors were American doors, fastened with American bolts and locks, opened by American knobs instead of being closed by a heavy cottonwood log falling against them. The houses of sawn lumber were neatly painted and surrounded with paling fences. A light snow lay on the ground; fat milk cows watched him as he drove into town, wheels of the spring wagon crunching in the icy ruts.

Tying up the wagon, he balanced the needle-gun under his arm and went to look for Sam Valentine. In one respect, walking through the bustle and confusion of the midday throngs, Prescott was similar to Phoenix. The gambling saloons were in full swing; the game "went" and the voice of the dealer was heard in the land. Tobacco smoke ascended from cigarillos, pipes, and cigars, filling the rooms with the foulest of odors. Even in midday the lamps were lit. High above the hum of conversation and the click of chips sounded the cry: "Make yer little bets, gents, make yer little bets! All's set, the game's made, the ball's a-rolling!"

After inquiry, Jack found Sam Valentine sitting in the lobby of the Imperial Hotel, reading the latest copy of the Daily Miner.

"Sit down!" Valentine invited. "What brings you to the capital?" He gestured toward the bar for two whiskeys.

Jack told him.

142

"Rancho Terco still thriving?"

"We make do," Jack said modestly, laying aside his sombrero. He told the legislator his needs, and Valentine recommended stores where quality goods might be purchased.

"And cornmeal," Jack added. Eggleston had developed a passion for tortillas; Jack liked them too, with morning eggs.

"Mexican's got a mill out on the Bear Spring Road," Valentine said. "Best damned meal you can buy! Name's Manuel Peralta. Tell him I sent you and he may knock a few pennies off the bill. We don't have too many Mexicans up here — they prefer the heat in the valley — but they're good citizens." He lit a long stogie, offered one to Jack Drumm. "To tell the truth, I never thought I'd see you again! Figured by now you'd have cashed in your chips."

Drumm looked puzzled; Sam Valentine laughed.

"Just an expression! Means I thought you'd have lit a shuck — left the game — gone back to England." He drew deep on the slender cigar.

"No," Jack said, "I'm staying — at least until I'm ready to leave."

"How long will that be?"

Jack shrugged a Mexican shrug.

"Listen," Valentine said. He leaned forward, tapping Jack on the knee. "Have you ever thought of becoming an American citizen?"

"No."

"Why not?"

Jack shrugged. "I'm an Englishman, Mr. Valentine. All that is left of my family is in Hampshire. My brother is managing the estate, and is not doing too well — he needs help. Anyway, my roots are deep in Hampshire. I must admit your Arizona is a fascinating place, especially in the winter when Hampshire is like a great meat locker. But I am only a visitor here."

"Shame!" Valentine said. "A great shame! We need people like you in the Territory, especially in the Legislature. There are problems, problems that take brains like yours, education like yours, stick-to-itiveness like yours, Drumm."

The stogie was vile. Jack tried hard to hide his distaste with a sip of the whiskey. It, too, was raw and harsh.

"I appreciate your compliment, Mr. Valentine," he said.

"Well, think about it!" Valentine urged. "This is a land of great opportunity! We're not stuck in the mud like your old England — no offense meant, of course! But the Territory's growing! Do you know what I heard only yesterday?"

"No, sir."

"Already the Atlantic and Pacific Railroad is planning a branch line into Prescott from the main route at Bear Spring! Once that happens, the sky's the limit! Land values will shoot up — a smart man can make a stake in a few months!"

"I'll certainly think about it," Jack promised, and did not intend to. "Ah — by the way," he went on, "do you

144

know a man named Larkin? A Mr. Buell Larkin, here in Prescott?"

The legislator furrowed his brow, stroked his beard. "Larkin? Don't know as I do." He called to the bartender, busy polishing glasses behind a mahogany bar. "Pete, you know a man hereabouts named Larkin?"

Pete pursed his lips, stared long and hard at the glass he was shining. "Larkin? Sure — old Buell Larkin! He was from somewhere back in the States — Kentucky, I think."

"West Virginia," Jack suggested.

"Pocahontas County, he told me," Pete remembered. "Wherever that is!"

"Where is Larkin now?"

"Under six feet of sand and gravel! Someone jumped his claim up in Hardscrabble Canyon — shot the old man in a disagreement."

"How long ago was that?" Jack asked.

Pete shrugged. "Two years ago. Mebbe three. Time passes — I don't strictly remember."

So Phoebe Larkin and Mrs. Glore had not found refuge with her uncle Buell! Getting to his feet and thanking Sam Valentine, Jack went out into the street. A light snow was falling. He pulled the poncho tighter about him. Though it was only teatime, lamps were turned on against the early dark; each cast a ring of golden light in the misty downfall.

He stepped aside to avoid a dray wagon hauling kegs of beer. What had happened to them — Phoebe and

145

Mrs. Glore? Had they managed to elude Meech? Were they still fleeing? Or —

After he had completed his other purchases and filled out the necessary papers with the clerk of the Legislature, he drove out on the Bear Spring Road to look for Manuel Peralta's mill. Here was atmosphere reminiscent of Phoenix, picturesque and exotic in the gentle rain of snow: a few adobe buildings, log lean-tos, the gentle chords of a guitar muffled by the downfall. Tall conical hats like his own, women wrapped in rebozos, the liquid lilt of Spanish. He sniffed appreciatively; the winter air was laced with the smell of chiles, the slap-slap of female hands making tortillas, the cries of children playing games like *el charro* and *escondate* — hide and seek.

Manuel Peralta was a talkative man with a fierce brushy mustache. "I hear of you," he said, shaking hands with Jack. "I hear a lot about you, *Señnor* Drumm! You fight the Apaches on the Agua Fria, eh?"

"Yes," Jack admitted. "We try to prevail against them."

Peralta spat through a gap between his teeth. A mouse scurried away from a torn sack of meal.

"I have my own place, once, down on the Santa Cruz, near Cojeta — raise melons and grapes and vegetables to sell in Tucson. But the damned Apaches drive me out!" The miller wiped his dusty face with a sleeve. "Kill my wife and two *niños!* That's why I come to here, to get away from the Apaches." He gestured toward the kitchen, a lean-to huddling against the mill. "I got me a new wife now, a young one, and more *niños*. But I miss Concepción and the two babies."

146

Jack remembered the string of beads around an Apache raider's neck that first night on the Agua Fria. Maybe the rosary had belonged to Concepción Peralta. The miller was helping him load the bags of meal when a woman passed, trudging down the lane with a sack over one shoulder. In the falling snow Jack caught only a brief glimpse, but recollection stirred; the stout figure, the measured stride, the purposeful manner.

"Mrs. Glore!" he called.

For a moment the figure broke stride.

"Wait!" Dropping the meal, he ran after her. "Wait a minute!"

The cloaked figure started to run, suddenly disappeared. Jack paused, staring into the rabbit warren of *jacales*, lean-tos, tumble-down adobes where the figure had vanished. Somewhere a concertina played, a woman laughed. Light from a lamp in a window shone into the snow-dusted alleyway. "*Dispénseme, señor*," a small boy carrying a basket of fresh tortillas murmured, and squeezed by him.

Beulah Glore? Or was it only a trick of his imagination? Maybe it was just that he longed to see Phoebe Larkin once more. But the two ladies were probably long gone from the town of Prescott.

"Ladies?" Peralta tugged at his mustache. "Two ladies? *Gringo* ladies?" He pondered the question. "Seem to me —"

"A Mrs. Beulah Glore," Jack said, "and a younger lady — Miss Phoebe Larkin." He waited. "With red hair," he added.

147

Peralta seemed undecided. Finally he said, "You don't mean them no harm?"

"Good Lord, no!" Jack said. "I'm a friend!"

"Because," Peralta said, "there is a man looking for them, too, I hear. A detective."

"Meech!" Jack blurted.

"I don't know his name. I don't know their name, either. It is none of my business." The miller shrugged. "You understand, *señor*, people come to Mex Town to hide, sometimes, when the law is after them. But it is not good for a Mexican to stick his nose into things. We give them a bed, maybe *frijoles* and a cup of coffee — you understand, it is not any of our business. They pay us, then they go away. That is all there is to it!"

"Yes, yes!" Jack said, impatient. "That's all very true, I'm sure! But where can I find these two ladies?"

The snow was falling more heavily now; a church bell rang. It was six o'clock. A dog shambled up to Peralta, and he kicked at it. Whimpering, it loped away on three legs.

"Go down to the church," the miller said. "Turn left and walk to the end of the lane. Under the hill there is a little house with a stone chimney, and a cow and a burro behind a fence. The padre lives there — Father Garcés. Maybe he can tell you something."

Leaving the wagon and old Bonyparts, Jack hurried toward the corner. In his haste he hardly saw the figure standing in the deep embrasure of the church doorway.

"Well!" The man caught him by the arm. His flat-brimmed hat was crowned with a peak of snow; the

148

stuff lay heavy on the dark cloth of his coat. His breath merged in frosty puffs. "It's a small world!"

Jack swallowed hard, and could only stare.

Alonzo Meech nodded. "Bonus snowshoes! That's Spanish for 'ain't it a hell of a night out?' What are you doing in Prescott, Mr. Drumm?"

CHAPTER
EIGHT

Seeing no other way out of the predicament, Jack Drumm paid for beans, tortillas, and a bottle of fiery *aguardiente* brandy at a tiny *cantina*.

"It's mighty nice of you," Meech acknowledged. "I'm about out of cash, and the home office is getting real fussy about sending me expense money. I been out here a long time now without nothing to show for it. And the Buckner family is getting mad, I guess, because I ain't clapped the cuffs on those two she-devils yet!" Draining a tin cup of brandy, he tapped Jack on the arm. "You know what? People are *helping* them two! Everyone seems in cahoots with 'em! Take now, for instance. I was sure I'd run 'em down to Mex Town here, but I lost the danged trail again! When a feller don't speak the Spanish lingo, and these miserable little shacks all piled together the way they are, it don't make my job no easier!"

"Yes," Jack agreed, "a detective's job is difficult, I should imagine." A thought began to form in his mind. "Well, I think I'll take a room at the Imperial tonight and drive back to the ranch in the morning. I'm not anxious to go down that grade in a snowstorm."

150

Seeming not to hear, Alonzo Meech reached for another hot chile and sucked reflectively on it. Jack had tried one, spitting it out when it seemed to be incinerating his tongue, but the detective seemed to relish them.

"I ain't especially *smart*," Meech admitted. "Oh, I read about all these great detectives — the Bow Street Runners in London — that fellow — what was his name? Oh, yes — Javert, in Mr. Hugo's book, which I can't pronounce —"

"*Les Miserables.*"

"Yes, that's it! Anyway, I'm not smart and deducting all the time, the way those fellers did. But what I got on my side is patience. Even the smartest crinim — crinim —"

"Criminal?"

"I don't usual drink on the job, but it's a cold night." Meech poured himself another brandy. "Anyway, even the smartest of 'em will slip up sooner or later, and that's when old Meech is on hand with the cuffs!"

Remembering the detective's weakness, Jack crooked a finger at the Mexican woman who ran the *cantina* and asked for another bottle of *aguardiente*. He poured Meech and himself a cupful, only sipping at his.

"Well," he said again, "I've got to be going. The Legislature is in session. I'll probably have a hard time getting a room."

Meech drank half the brandy and set the cup down so hard it sloshed on the table. "It don't make no difference," he said loudly, "whether Pinkerton's pays me or not! It's a matter of pride, see? Professional pride! I'm getting up in years — fifty-six next July — and I'll not have my record spoiled now!"

When Jack slipped away Meech was pouring himself another drink, seeming not to hear the Latin laughter, the quarreling from a corner where a *monte* game was going on. Jack was not even sure Meech noticed his own departure.

The snow was falling faster. There was no wind, only the steady downfall that muffled sound, cast iridescent rings around the lamp-light from an occasional window. Peralta had locked the mill and gone to supper. Bonyparts stood in the traces, broad back mounded with snow; he snuffled impatiently and tossed his head.

"Good mule," Jack muttered, and gave him a nosebag of oats. *Go down to the church*, the miller said. *Under the hill is a little house with a cow and a burro behind a fence. The padre — Father Garcés —*

Hesitantly he knocked at the door. It was more substantial than the rest of the house — heavy oak planks, an iron ring set in the middle.

There was no answer. The burro looked at him with disinterest. Shaking its coat to throw off the snow, it ambled into the brush-topped ramada to join the cow.

He knocked again, watching over his shoulder for Meech. A man with that kind of persistence had to be taken into account, even when he was tipsy with aguardiente. There was no answer. Putting his lips close to the door, he called softly.

"Miss Larkin! Mrs. Glore? Are you there?"

Pressing his ear against the door, he heard nothing. But suddenly the door opened. He fell headlong into the room.

"Don't move!" a voice commanded. "Just lay there, spread out like that!"

He obeyed. The yellow rays of a lamp spread over his prostrate form, something hard and metallic pressed into the hollow behind his ear. The door closed, a bar fell heavily into place.

"Turn over!"

Gingerly he rolled over, blinking in the light.

"Why, it's Mr. Drumm!" Beulah Glore cried. She moved closer with the lamp. Phoebe Larkin, kneeling next him, slipped the derringer into the cleavage of her bosom.

"Jack!" she cried. "Jack Drumm! It's you!"

Somewhat miffed, he got to his feet. Readjusting his poncho, he picked up the sombrero and said, "You gave me a very strange welcome!"

Phoebe beckoned him to a table and poured a cup of coffee. "We thought it was Meech," she explained. "Our friend — Father Garcés — has seen him here, in Prescott. And tonight, when Beulah went out to buy a few potatoes and a piece of meat for the father's supper, someone in the street called her by name and began to chase her!"

"That was I," Jack said. "But Alonzo Meech is indeed here! I found him standing near the church, watching people pass by, probably hoping to catch sight of one of you." He waved aside the coffee. "We must hurry and get out of here! Where is the padre?"

153

"At the church," Phoebe said, "hearing confessions or whatever they do in the Catholic church. But what —"

"I have a wagon," Jack explained, "and old Bonyparts. I came to town for supplies and they are in the wagon, covered with canvas. Get your things ready and come with me! I will put you under the canvas, and we will drive out of town and back to Rancho Terco!"

In the lamplight Phoebe Larkin's face was pale and distraught. Her freckles stood out. Nervously she put a hand to her brow, pushing back the vagrant hair. The lamplight behind her shone through the red-gold hair with a shimmering halo.

"What good will that do?" Phoebe asked quietly. "No, Jack — it's no good! That man will never give up! He chased us three thousand miles, and now he's as near as the church! It's time to give up, to let him take us back to stand trial, no matter how unfair the whole thing is bound to be."

"Never!" Jack cried. "If I have anything to do with it, he will not catch you! I can tell you — we Drumms from Clarendon Hall are stubborn people! We do not give up, and you and Beulah would be well advised to follow our example!"

Mrs. Glore shook her head. "If we get back to the ranch safe — the Lord knows how I miss that place, and Mr. Eggleston — then Meech'd just find us there, sooner or later!"

"We will cross that bridge when we come to it," Jack said curtly. "Right now you are in *immediate* danger, and we must deal with that directly! Hurry and pack what things you need!"

154

Phoebe wrote a note to Father Garcés. They turned out the lamp, slipped furtively into the snowy night, and locked the door after them.

"The padre, as they call him, is a good man," Beulah sighed. "Myself, I'm a Baptist. But I guess Catholics has got a stake in the true faith too!"

The dirt lanes were deserted. A dog shambled over to sniff them. "Good boy!" Phoebe said, and the dog slunk away. Over their heads the bells of the church rang, and they all started nervously. "Just around the corner here," Jack whispered, "at Peralta's mill!"

At the sight of Phoebe, Bonyparts whickered in recognition.

"Quiet!" she cautioned, rubbing the velvety muzzle. "I'm glad to see you too, old fellow!"

Jack stowed the valises in the wagon, then held up the canvas for them to climb in.

"There are blankets in there," he advised. "If you huddle together among the meal sacks and cover yourselves it will not be too cold, I think."

Phoebe helped Mrs. Glore into the bed of the wagon. While Jack continued to hold the canvas high, she paused before him. Her face was pale in the gloom, her eyes only deep shadows.

"I asked you once before! Why are you doing this for us? You're risking your own safety, your reputation, maybe even your own freedom!"

"I told you," he said, "the Drumms always fight injustice. If you go far enough back, they resisted King John himself and made him sign the Magna Charta."

For a long time her eyes looked into his. Snow fell on her hair. A ray of moonlight filtered perversely through the misty down-pour.

"There isn't — there isn't any other reason?"

He was uncomfortable, not knowing what she was trying to get at.

"If we stand here," he blurted, "discussing ethics, we are all apt to be collared by Detective Meech! Will you hurry and get into the damned wagon?"

It must have been well after ten at night when he clucked to Bonyparts and slapped the reins over his broad back. There was only one way out of Mex Town, one rutted lane leading back to Prescott, the long grade, the valley of the Agua Fria — and that way had to pass the church. The wagon moved away, iron-shod wheels crunching in the mud. Alonzo Meech had probably gone to bed somewhere. Perhaps he only had his head on a table at the *cantina*, empty *aguardiente* bottle before him, while a *mozo* swept out.

In any case, no one stopped them. The neatly fenced houses of Prescott slept in the snowy night; the brewery and blacksmith shops and mercantile stores were closed. Only from the Ten Strike, the Jack of Diamonds, and the other saloons came the sound of activity. Lights showed through frosted windows, a fiddle squealed, haze of blue tobacco smoke drifted from an open door. Singing and roistering, a few late revelers staggered from the gaming houses.

"Drumm? Is that you, Drumm?"

A soldier in a cavalry greatcoat lurched alongside the wagon, tugging at Jack's sleeve.

156

"Stop, damn it! Stop your mule! Is that you, Jack Drumm?"

The soldier was Lieutenant George Dunaway, in his cups. Dunaway motioned to another shambling figure; Corporal Bagley, the mustached brigand who seemed always near. "Jim, c'mere!" Dunaway gestured, almost losing his balance, preserving himself only by clutching at the wagon seat. "Here's Drumm, good ol' Drumm! Shake hands with Drumm, Jim! *You* remember old Englishman Drumm! I licked him once, but he's a better man than I first give him credit for!"

Corporal Bagley was also in his cups. Putting out a hand, he swayed and fell in the snow. Dunaway disregarded him.

"What you doin' in Prescott?" he demanded.

Even from the high seat Jack could smell the bouquet of bourbon whiskey.

"Just came into town to buy a few supplies." Nervously he looked over his shoulder. Meech might be following them.

"Goin' back to your ranch *this* time of night?" Dunaway demanded. "In a damned snowstorm?"

"I — I thought it might be a little safer," Jack stammered. "I mean — the Apaches aren't likely to bother a wagon in this weather, are they?"

Dunaway hiccuped. "Never know. Old Agustín is unpre — unpre —" He hitched up his breeches, spat into the snow. "He's un — pree — dickable!"

"Well," Jack said, "I'd better be moving along."

Dunaway, however, was in a conversational mood. He looked down at Corporal Bagley, prone in the snow and apparently sleeping.

"Officers aren't supposh — supposed to fraternize with enlisted men. But Jim Bagley's an old friend. Shaved — saved my life at Shiloh in April of '62. Course, the damned West Pointers look down their noses at me, but I don't give a damn!" He looked up at Jack Drumm. "Do I, now?"

Jack was uncomfortable. He wondered what the two females in the wagon were thinking about the delay. They were probably terrified.

"I suppose not," he murmured.

"My time's about up," Dunaway went on. "The hell with this tin-soldier Army! It's gone to hell since the war! You know what I'm going to do?"

Jack shook his head.

"In two more weeks I'm going to Australia! Down there I hear there's lot of cheap land, good wages, pretty girls looking for a husband! *That's* where I'm bound for! No more chasing raggedyass Apaches for me!" In a reedy tenor Dunaway began to sing:

"We went to Arizony
For to fight the Injuns there.
We came near to being made bald-headed
But they never got our hair!"

Corporal Bagley wandered unsteadily to his feet, wiping mud and snow from his breeches. Together they bawled out the chorus:

158

"Forty miles a day on beans and hay
In the Regular Army, O!
We bless the day we skipped away
From the Regular Army, O!"

"I must go!" Jack insisted. "I've got a long way to travel!"

The lieutenant slapped him on the knee. "When a man gets to know you, you're not a bad sort, Drumm!" Hiccuping, he draped an arm about Jim Bagley's shoulder and the two staggered into the night, singing off key.

Descending the rocky grade, well clear of Prescott, Jack halted the mule under a windswept grove of trees. Shaking snow from the canvas cover, he called, "Come out and stretch your limbs if you want to! I think we're out of danger — immediate danger, anyway!"

Stiff and cramped, the two females clambered down. The snow had stopped and the moon shone, scudding high in a rack of clouds.

"I was so afraid, back there in town, when you stopped the wagon," Phoebe said, shivering.

"That was Dunaway — George Dunaway."

"After a while," Phoebe said, "I realized it was him. I'd know his voice anywhere. It would have been nice if I could have said hello. George Dunaway is such a good man. Oh, he's kind of rough, I give you that, but he's all wool and a yard wide!"

Jack remembered the lieutenant bringing Phoebe flowers. He said, with some asperity, "There was hardly any time for visiting!"

159

"I know," Phoebe cried. "Oh, yes, I know!"

He helped them back into the wagon. This time they could safely lie together and look up at the stars, free from the smothering canvas. As he drove, he heard their drowsy chatter, the female talk; it was somehow domestic and comforting. An excellent idea came to him — one that might solve a lot of problems. Why not? he asked himself. Why not? The idea seemed eminently practicable, and he resolved to try it at the first opportunity.

During his short absence Rancho Terco had grown — perhaps only a little, but one more gun to defend against Agustín and his Apaches was worthwhile. The newcomer, Eggleston reported, was a man from Columbus, Ohio, with weak lungs, a wife, and three towheaded children. Ben Sprankle had come to Arizona for his health. He had a small stock of chewing tobacco, coal oil, nails, tinware, and bolts of gingham.

"He wants to start a little store here," the valet explained. "He never had a real home himself, he said, but he thought along the Agua Fria was a good place to raise children, with all the sunshine and fresh air. He says in Columbus, Ohio — where is that, Mr. Jack? — this time of year it's all snow and slush and sniffles."

Phoebe, glad to be "home," as she said, breathed deep of the warm dry air. Uncle Roscoe, now completely recovered, shook her hand like a pump handle. "Ain't nothin' like a pretty woman to dress up a spread like this!" he said, and Phoebe blushed becomingly. Eggleston and Mrs. Glore had disappeared

160

into the now-completed adobe to greet each other in a more private way.

"That's right," Jack agreed. "Women are a proper and fitting part of the landscape, even on the frontier, Uncle Roscoe. I am glad we have attractive females on Rancho Terco."

Phoebe looked at him with a peculiar look, and said, "Well, if I must settle for being part of the landscape, I suppose that will have to do."

"Like the yucca plant," Jack amended. "That is part of the landscape, too. When it blooms, all the birds are attracted to the beautiful waxy flowers. The — the yucca is useful, too. The Indians make all sorts of things out of it."

"And I suppose we females are useful too, Mr. Drumm?"

He was not sure whether she was ragging him. Somewhat stiffly he said, "You and Mrs. Glore have been a great help to us here."

"And you've helped me and Beulah too," Phoebe murmured. "So we must be grateful." She turned away to wander among the outbuildings, inspecting everything new, leaving Jack Drumm with the remembrance that the yucca plant had sharp spiky leaves resembling small daggers. He was pondering this botanical resemblance when Eggleston emerged from the adobe. Mrs. Glore was already preparing a fresh kettle of beans and had a batch of biscuits going.

"I was so glad to see Beulah again," the valet said earnestly. "Really, Mr. Jack, I missed her dreadfully."

"I, also."

"But —" Eggleston broke off and looked down at his fingers, scarred and toughened by the hard life. "What I mean to say is — I missed her in an entirely different way from you, Mr. Jack."

"How is that?"

Eggleston coughed, clasped his hands nervously behind his back. "Well, I have never married. But there comes a time in a man's life when he thinks about growing old alone, and lonely. I do not care if Beulah has committed some offense against the American law. I am sure she meant well, and was probably even justified in what she did. That would be no bar to my marrying her."

"Marrying her?" Jack was astonished.

"Marry her!" Eggleston spoke firmly. "Yes, Indeed, I would be happy spending my declining years with such a female as Beulah Glore! I would, of course, someday want to take her home with me to Clarendon Hall, but — well, she is such a different kind that I wonder how she would fit in in Hampshire."

Jack put his hand on the valet's sleeve. "Eggie, if you love her and she loves you —"

"Oh, Mr. Jack, she does, and I do!"

"Then she is the mate for you in Hampshire, or in Halifax! Perhaps the old families in Hampshire — like yours and mine — would benefit from new blood, some of the new American blood, teeming as it does with life and energy and determination."

Feeling awkward at having spoken so emotionally, he clapped Eggleston on the back and hurried away to make his plans. Time was of the essence. He called them together to advise them.

"We had a narrow escape from Mr. Meech in Prescott. No one knows when he may reappear. In the meantime, we must all be cautious. The adobe is finished, and is commodious and comfortable. You, Phoebe, and Mrs. Glore will spend your time inside, emerging only at night, so as not to be seen."

"But how will I cook?" Beulah demanded. "I'll bet none of you has had a decent meal since I left!"

"Eggie will attend to the cooking," Jack said.

"I know we're in danger," Phoebe protested, "but we can't spend the rest of our lives caged like animals in a zoo!"

"It will not be long," he promised. "I have a plan. If everything works out, you will be confined only for a few days."

"What kind of plan?"

He shook his head. "Only trust me for a little while."

"But —"

"I have every reason to think it will come off successfully. But first — we must plan a little gathering. A Christmas party, that's it!"

"Christmas?" Phoebe asked doubtfully.

"Yes, indeed! It is almost that time, is it not? At home, in Hampshire, good neighbors are gathering for syllabub and innocent games. The goose is fat; English countrymen are roaming the forest for a proper Yule log. The cellars are filled with apples and pears, preserves, fat gammon, braces of fowl. Snow is deep, and children are singing of good King Wenceslas. Here,

163

in this Arizona desert, we should also be mindful of the Christmas season, should we not?"

"But your plan —" Phoebe insisted.

"The celebration is all part of the plan," he said, and would tell them no more. But they liked the idea of a celebration and fell to with a will, planning a menu, cutting down a sapling cottonwood and draping it with strings of paper flowers and bits of tin and glass, deciding which chickens would grace the festive board.

"And there will be a guest," Jack added. "If we are to give each other small gifts as Phoebe suggests, there must of course be one for the guest."

Phoebe, caught up in the excitement, was cutting a large star from a tin can. "A guest? Oh, Jack — who?"

"You will see," he promised. "You will see come Sunday."

He wasted no time in getting in touch with the guest. Yes, word came from Prescott, the guest would be honored to attend. He would ride out before dawn and arrive at noon. The Sloats, and the Sprankles down the road, were reminded also of the holiday season and planned their own celebrations. Charlie the Papago disappeared; in a few days he came back with a wife and several brown children in ragged shifts and bare feet. Though not understanding exactly what Christmas was all about, Charlie dug up a clump of saltbush with its clusters of papery fruit and planted it near his hut for his children to decorate as Ostin Drumm's tree was adorned.

"We've got to make presents for Charlie's family too," Phoebe decided.

In the hubbub and bonhomie of the season their precautions against Alonzo Meech were neglected. Stages came and went, passengers climbed down to eat beans and pie and drink coffee, freight wagons rolled ponderously to and from Prescott. They were so busy, not only with the routine business of the ranch but with the happy preparations for Christmas, that Jack was sure someone knew the females were once again at Rancho Terco. Meech would undoubtedly hear the rumors and take up the scent again. But tomorrow was Sunday — by nightfall everything should be happily resolved.

George Dunaway arrived shortly before noon, sweaty and dusty in dress blues. "I'm grateful to you, Drumm," he said. "Fort Whipple can be a lonesome place for a bachelor officer during the holidays. Oh, someone takes pity on me now and then and invites me for dinner, but I don't take kindly to pity!"

The lieutenant was astonished at finding Phoebe and Mrs. Glore at the ranch. Phoebe, excited, threw her arms about him in what Drumm thought was an excess of emotion, kissing Dunaway hard on his hairy cheek. Mrs. Glore, too, bussed him.

"It's George!" Phoebe cried. "Isn't that nice! He's come all the way from Prescott for our party!" She turned to Jack Drumm. "Well, isn't this the nicest surprise! You sly fox! So George was the guest, all along!"

Eggleston too shook hands with the lieutenant, and Uncle Roscoe had known Dunaway for a long time.

"Saved my gizzard one time, over at Mule Canyon!" he crowed. "Some renegade Navahos had me boxed in, but George and his roughnecks drove 'em off and took an arrer out of my behind!"

"But I don't understand!" Dunaway said, turning to Jack Drumm. "You said the ladies had gone on to Prescott, and now —"

"I'll explain later," Jack promised.

Dunaway sniffed at the aroma of roasting chickens, hot pie crust, and cinnamon and other spices. "Don't smell like Army fare!"

"Dinner's at twelve sharp!" Mrs. Glore beamed, her face red from the stove, arms floured to the elbow. "Now you menfolk just set and talk while I look to the pies!"

"And after dinner we'll open the presents!" Phoebe cried. "Oh, it will be such fun! There's something for you, George — I made it myself!"

When the rest had gone back to their work, Jack drew Dunaway aside to present him with one of the American stogies he had learned to tolerate. Sitting together in the shade of the ramada, they drank cold tea from an olla, laced with bourbon.

"Oh, by the way —" Dunaway fished in a shirt pocket. "Here's a telegraph message come for you to Fort Whipple. Must be important! Civilians usually don't get to use the military wire unless they're pretty high mucketymucks."

Jack had long been expecting word from Andrew about the money he had requested. He slipped the folded paper into his pocket. "We're glad to have you here, George," he said. "It was a long way for you to come, and I appreciate it."

Dunaway lay back in his chair and stared at the distant Mazatzals, already dusted with the first snows of winter. "A man never knows how things will work out," he mused. "A few months ago you and I were pummeling each other. I hated your guts, I guess. Now we're friends, having a sociable drink together. This Territory is a strange place — nothing goes according to plan, the way it does elsewhere." He blew a contemplative smoke ring. "So the two females were in the back of your wagon when I came up on you in front of the Lucky Lady in Prescott!"

"That's right."

"I'm glad you explained it to me. I heard Detective Meech was chasing them, but I knew two fine ladies like them couldn't have done anything wrong."

Jack spoke carefully. "They are fine ladies, indeed. And Miss Larkin is handsome, into the bargain, with that copper-colored hair and fine complexion."

"I know," Dunaway murmured, his eyes far away. "Yes, I know."

Encouraged, Jack puffed hard at his stogie. "You know, of course, we're pleased to have you here, George. But there's a little more to it than that." He cleared his throat, examined the ash of the cigar. "Maybe you've noticed — Miss Larkin is attracted to you."

Dunaway turned sharply from his contemplation of the distant mountains. "She is?"

167

"Surely you noticed how she threw her arms about you! Also, she kissed you on the cheek. In addition to being a fine figure of a woman, Phoebe is also affectionate."

Dunaway was silent, apparently at a loss for words.

"Look here!" Jack pressed on. "I won't shilly-shally any longer! The other night in Prescott you said you were going to leave the Army, go to Australia to make a new life."

"That's right."

"Take Phoebe with you! Make a new life for the both of you!" Dunaway stared at Jack Drumm. The stogie drooped. "Take — her? Take Phoebe with me?"

"Of course! Can't you see, man, it solves all sorts of problems! You get a pretty wife for your old age, Phoebe is at last safe from Detective Meech —"

"I'll be God damned!" Dunaway paled, chewed vigorously at his cigar. He rose, paced the dirt floor, furiously puffing. "I never dreamed —"

"She is certainly too much of a lady to throw herself at you! But I believe there is a real affection there."

"Are you sure? I wouldn't want to be made a fool of!"

Jack swallowed another mouthful of the bourbon and tea mixture. The earthenware olla, swinging on a cord in the shade, kept the drink delightfully cool and refreshing.

"These things always have an element of risk, I suppose. But I would say your chances were very good."

168

Dunaway took the tattered cigar from his mouth. "How do I go about it? I'm not exactly a lady's man, you know! Never had much to do with females, excepting whores."

"After dinner," Jack explained, "I'll arrange to get you and Phoebe alone for a little talk. Go at it slow, George; don't hurry. By and by you'll get the feel of it, and I know it'll come out right for everyone."

Dunaway spat out a shred of tobacco. "Speaking of everyone, what about Beulah — Mrs. Glore?"

"What about her?"

"What are you planning for her? After all, from what you tell me, she's in the soup too."

Impatient, Jack said, "Don't worry about Beulah! I'll arrange something for her too, though I don't know at the moment exactly what. In any case, Beulah is not your problem. Phoebe is! What do you say?"

Dunaway walked nervously about. A spider dropped from the thatch onto his shirt but he did not notice it. "By God!" he muttered, as if confronted by some blinding apparition. Chewing on the wet remnants of the cigar, he suddenly lifted his head. "What was that?"

Beluah Glore was ringing the piece of wagon tire that served as dinner pile. "Hash pile's ready!" she bawled. "All come a-runnin'!"

Dunaway turned to Jack Drumm.

"I'll do it!" he cried. "I'll have a go at it!"

After they ate and ate and ate, and drank and drank and drank, Drumm arranged for George Dunaway and Phoebe to take one of Beulah's pies to the ailing Mrs.

Ben Sprankle. "On the way back," he whispered to George, "just stroll along the river and make your case."

The lieutenant was as excited as a small boy. "I have you to thank for this!" he said, and wrung Jack Drumm's hand.

"Here I am with the pie!" Phoebe announced. "Are you ready, George?"

She wore a lacy shirtwaist; the long red curls fell fetchingly about her cheeks. Her eyes danced. "If George and I don't come back soon," she teased Jack, "don't bother to look for us! We'll be back in our own good time!"

Satisfied, he watched them go hand in hand down the road, Dunaway carefully balancing the pie, the muffler Phoebe had knitted for him around his neck. It was not a bad feeling at all, Jack mused, to play Cupid. Sometimes deserving people had to be put in each other's way. Phoebe would have a man to satisfy her loving nature, George Dunaway would gain a wife for Australia, Alonzo Meech would be finally balked. Of course, Phoebe Larkin would move beyond Jack Drumm's ken. He would no longer be distracted by her, no longer have to feel guilty of disloyalty to Cornelia Newton-Barrett.

Vaguely distraught, he watched for their return. They were a long time coming. Worried, he picked up the Sharp's rifle and started for the river. Perhaps wandering Apache scouts had seen them, silently ambushed them with knife and hatchet. But soon he saw Phoebe's blouse in the greenery, then George

170

Dunaway's dress blues. Phoebe quickly left George and ran into the adobe. Dunaway himself seemed perplexed and angry. He walked slowly toward the ramada where Jack Drumm was lounging and sat down.

"I've been a damned fool!" he muttered.

Jack was puzzled. "How did it work out?"

Dunaway contemplated his knuckles. "She got mad, real mad."

"Mad?"

"She don't love me! Oh, she was real nice about it! She thanked me and all that, said how it was a compliment she'd never forget. But she said she didn't love me."

Jack was as disappointed as Dunaway. The plan, so carefully nurtured and executed, had failed.

"I'm sorry," he said. "George, I'm truly sorry. I thought —"

"*You're* sorry!" Suddenly Dunaway bristled. "I guess you better be! God damn it, you got me into this situation! I must have sounded like a lovesick fool, my head all filled up with church music and wedding bells! I thought this was it! I thought that after all these years of paying for rides, I'd finally caught the brass ring on the carousel! Now I'm back where I started, only this time it's worse!"

Jack was startled at the emotion, and uncomfortable.

"I told you I am sorry! I meant well! And I'll talk to Phoebe and try to straighten it out with her."

"If she'll talk to *you!*" Dunaway said savagely.

"What do you mean?"

"Phoebe said she doesn't want to talk to you ever again! She said you can rot in hell before she ever utters another word to you, that's what she said. I tell you — she's madder about the whole thing than I am!"

"But —"

Swearing, Dunaway jammed the battered hat on his head and stalked away toward his horse.

"Now wait a minute —"

Rising, the yellow folded paper fell from Jack Drumm's pocket. Still swearing, Dunaway was searching the reeds for his mount. Baffled and unhappy, Jack slumped back in the chair and unfolded the crumpled form. After the usual military hieroglyphics, the message was terse. It had been sent by the Drumms' solicitors through Headquarters of the Department of the Missouri, U. S. Army:

ANDREW DRUMM DIED THIS DATE OF INDIA FEVER. CAN YOU RETURN CLARENDON HALL IMMEDIATELY TO ATTEND TO ESTATE BUSINESS AND ASSUME TITLE LORD FIFIELD?

CHAPTER
NINE

In the brush hut Jack Drumm sat silent and morose. Phoebe and Mrs. Glore had taken over the more luxurious structure of adobe. They all knew his bereavement, and left him alone to his thoughts. Andrew had been several years senior to Jack, always the protective elder brother. While Jack went to Cambridge and kept his head in books, Andrew was fighting rebel tribesmen in the Khyber. When Jack wanted to make the Grand Tour, Andrew, invalided home with the fever, took over the management of Clarendon Hall and its lands. Andrew had always protected him, accommodated him, cherished him. Now Andrew was gone.

He took his sextant from his case and examined it: 112° 13′ W., 34° 17′ N. — that was where he had been, far away from Hampshire and home, when Andrew, dear Andrew, died. His brother had probably died alone, except for Cousin Lionel, who lived nearby in Godalming and was the only other living heir. Trying to divert his grief, he picked up the dogeared *Traveler's Guide to the Far West* and thumbed through it. The plants, the animals, the mountains and deserts, all had once seemed foreign and exotic. Now, while Andrew sickened and died at Clarendon Hall, these things had become common and familiar, but at what a price! Angry, he flung the book from him. It fell to the earthen floor in a flutter of white pages.

Someone scratched at the door.

"Who is it?"

"Me — Phoebe."

She came in and sat on the edge of the sagging pallet, looking distraught. This morning she had done her hair very badly; it lay in listless coils and tangles. The freckles stood out, and the blue eyes were dark, with unattractive circles around them.

"I thought," he muttered, "you were not ever again going to speak to me."

She stared at the slender hands in her lap. "I — I wasn't. I'd made up my mind, that's right. But —" She shrugged, her face pale and wan. "I lost Uncle Buell, and I wasn't there either when he passed on. So I know how you feel, losing your only brother and being so far away when he died. So — I'm sorry. I came to tell you that."

He had been cruel, and regretted it, but could not let her off so easily. She *had* been headstrong about George Dunaway's courtship and his own plan for the two of them. But before he could speak she went on.

"Mr. Eggleston proposed marriage to Beulah. I suppose you know that."

"Yes," he said. "Eggie told me. He is very happy."

"She did not want to leave me, did not want to go to England without me, but I insisted. After all, I am the one who got her into this horrible mess, and I want her

174

to be happy. If I am at my wit's ends, there is no need for her to be desolate also."

He picked up the *Traveler's Guide* and smoothed the rumpled pages. "What will you do, then?"

When Phoebe Larkin first stepped off the Prescott stage she had looked like a Paris mannequin, the utmost in *haute couture*. Now she resembled poor sickly Mrs. Ben Sprankle down the road — dress torn and stained, feet bare, nails rimmed with grime. She had not been taking care of herself.

"I'll just go to Prescott and give myself up. What else is there to do? Mr. Meech, at least, should be glad to see me, if no one else is."

He looked sharply up from the *Guide*. "What do you mean by that?"

She took a deep breath. "Please — I don't want to be unpleasant about anything. I haven't the stomach for it anymore. I — I just came to tell you I was sorry for your loss."

"Go to Prescott!" he flared. "Give yourself up!" He paced the dirt floor. "What foolish talk!"

"But what else is there for me? You are going back to England, and I —"

"I tried to help you!" he cried. "Damn it, Phoebe, your happiness means much to me! I had all the arrangements made! George Dunaway was in love with you! George is a good man, an honest man, and a good provider, too, I daresay. But no! You had to knock everything into a cocked hat with your stubbornness, your willfulness, your headstrong ways!"

"Stubborn? Headstrong?" She rose quickly; her eyes flashed blue sparks, and under the shabby ruching her breasts heaved. "Mr. Jack Drumm, if ever there was a person stubborn and headstrong — pigheaded and obstinate and unseeing — it's *you!*" Her eyes dimmed with sudden tears. "Call *me* stubborn! Why, you take the blue ribbon for pure mulishness!"

He shook a schoolmasterly finger. "I devoted a great deal of trouble and thought to relieving your condition —"

"My condition!" Her voice was incredulous. "You sound like I was a mare with the glanders!"

"To relieving your condition," he insisted. "And when I had everything satisfactorily laid out —"

Angry, she raised clenched fists high in a hopeless gesture. "Stop it, I tell you! Stop it! Don't go on talking about me in that damned cold way!"

Women's tears unnerved him. Cornelia had used them artfully and effectively. Disconcerted, he paused.

"Listen!" Phoebe begged. "Listen to me!" She paid no attention to the great tears rolling down her cheeks, stitching their way into her bosom. "Maybe you're just stupid, or maybe it's your English ways that make you unable to show any affection, any love, and regard for others. You're like a damned icicle! So you *force* me to say something — something I would rather my tongue would rot out than say! Listen to me! Mr. John Peter Christian Drumm, I do not love George Dunaway! Do you understand that? I do not love him. I love someone else!"

Feeling faint and feverish, he goggled at her.

"I love *you!*" Phoebe cried. "There, I said it! And I am ashamed to have thrown away my love on a heartless and unfeeling Englishman!" Wiping her eyes with the soiled hem of her skirt, she fled.

He stared at the open doorway. Love *him?* Phoebe Larkin love him? It was impossible. He shook his head. He was much older than she. Besides — he was already engaged to Cornelia Newton-Barrett, and she knew that. In addition, Phoebe was an aggressive kind of female — strange and unpredictable. His own methodical and logical Drumm ways would never accommodate her spirit, her impulsiveness, her rashness. Cornelia Newton-Barrett was much more suited to his phlegmatic temperament. He could never imagine Cornelia acting as Phoebe Larkin had just done.

Someone seemed to be covertly watching him. Suspicious, he wheeled, and found himself staring into the cracked mirror on the wall. A bearded and shaken countenance stared back wildly at him. The beard, the woolen poncho, the coarse manta shirt-these things had by now become homely and familiar. But his face was somehow different. It betrayed powerful and unfamiliar emotion.

Stepping forward, he looked questioningly into the mirror. Love *him?* Impossible! How could anyone love a figure like that? Yet — what was this experience he had just undergone? Love? Did he love *her* — Phoebe Larkin? He shook his head. It could hardly be love. When he came to marry Cornelia, he supposed love would then come. They would be comfortable together,

177

they would have children to carry on the Drumm name, they would like each other very much, know each other's thoughts, they would grow old and gray together and finally lie side by side in the Drumm plot at Salisbury. That was love, real English love — the genuine article.

"Sir?"

He started, stepped away from the mirror. "Come in, Eggie."

The valet brought basin and razor, along with a woolen suit and fresh linens, long packed away.

"Are you ready for me, Mr. Jack? You seem a little —"

Jack waved a hand in a dismissing gesture.

"Miss Larkin and I were just — just talking."

Still shaken by the experience, he sat down and stroked the beard in a final gesture that was almost affectionate.

"You may proceed," he said, "when you are ready."

They were all sorry to see Jack Drumm leave. Sprankle wrung his hand, Mrs. Sloat baked him oatmeal cookies from her own family receipt, Ike Coogan brought a stone jug of homemade corn whiskey.

"You've changed a lot," Ike observed.

Under the thicket of beard the scar on Jack's lip had healed surprisingly well. Now that he was clean-shaven, it showed only a little. Though the stiff collar and bowler hat felt strange, he was already becoming used to them.

178

"Well," he smiled, "I guess it's a long time since you saw me in clothes like this."

The old man shook his head. "It ain't that. It's something inside."

"What do you mean?"

Ike shrugged. "It'll come out."

Uncle Roscoe was getting ready to go prospecting again in the Mazatzals. "Apaches don't skeer me none! After all, a feller can turn up his toes just onct!" He nodded toward the rugged ridges. "It might as well be up there as here." Extending a horny fist, he shook hands. "You been good to me, Mr. Drumm, and I won't never forget it. When I find the Gypsy Dancer, I'll send you a hatful of nuggets!"

Charlie and his wife and children came too, solemn-faced and dressed in their best white *calzones*, with a garland to hang around Ostin Drumm's neck. By now, Charlie had a little English.

"You come back — sometime?"

Jack shook his head. "I'm afraid not, Charlie. But I'll miss you and your woman and the children."

He could not stand to speak intimately to Phoebe Larkin. She avoided him also, until the final leavetaking. When he called them all together to say his farewells, she came in a freshly laundered white dress with a red sash Charlie's wife had given her. The titian hair was combed high in the Grecian style, tied with a ribbon. She wore a pair of the rawhide Mexican huaraches and her face was pale, the eyes betraying recent weeping. She stood silently with the others — the Sloats, the Sprankles, Charlie's family, Uncle

Roscoe — around the spring wagon. Charlie would drive the party into Prescott, thence to Bear Spring, where Jack and Eggleston and Mrs. Glore would take the eastbound Atlantic and Pacific cars.

"Speech!" someone shouted. Others took up the call.

Embarrassed, Jack allowed himself to be pushed up on the wagon. Clearing his throat, he pulled at the unaccustomed cravat.

"I'm really not much of a speechmaker. But I want you all to know I'm sorry to leave this place. The Arizona Territory is a rough and cruel place sometimes — sand, wind, cactus, Apaches. But the roughness is tempered for the man who looks beyond those surface things. And to make up for the hard times, too, there are the people of Arizona. They — you — are the salt of the earth, and I'll miss —"

Phoebe Larkin was staring at him with those great round blue eyes; for a moment he faltered.

"I'll miss each and every one of you. And after I've left, I hope you'll think of me as often as I think of you. The North Atlantic is stormy this time of year, and in Hampshire, in England, where I come from, it's cold and rainy and miserable. But there'll always be a warm place in my heart for the A.T., and for you old friends."

At the end his voice became a little hoarse, and cracked. Perhaps he had contracted an inflammation of the throat from the chill winter nights of Rancho Terco. But Ben Sprankle led a chorus of hip-hip-hoorays, Charlie's children lit Mexican firecrackers, and Uncle Roscoe tootled on a mouth-harp, while Sloat danced a jig. Beulah Glore, the moment of departure near, fell into Phoebe's arms and wept. Phoebe held her tight, patting her ample shoulder, saying, "Beulah, don't cry! You know it's all for the best. Someday, maybe, I'll come to Hampshire and visit you and Mr. Eggleston."

Jack climbed down from the wagon, held out his hand. Phoebe took it, silently. It felt cold and lifeless in his own.

"I — I will be thinking of you more than anybody, Phoebe," he stammered. His throat constricted in a spasm, and he popped a lozenge into his mouth. "I sincerely tried to do what I thought best for you — with George Dunaway, I mean — but it did not work out. Now I must leave you, and I want you to know I have paid Mr. Sloat to keep an eye out for you, run the ranch. In Prescott I will make some further arrangements which may better your state. I — I cannot be too specific at the moment but you will hear the details in the next few days, I think." He cleared his throat, stared into the bowler hat. "It is little enough I am doing, God knows, but perhaps it will help."

"I thank you," she said coolly, "but I always killed my own snakes, Mr. Drumm, and I always will. I do not mean to sound ungrateful — it is just the way I was made, I guess."

"Well," he said, "if sometime chance should put you in the way of a visit to England, I hope you will come to Clarendon Hall. Cornelia and I will be very happy to receive you." Things were getting awkward. Unnerved by her composure, her calm gaze, he bumbled on. "You would like Cornelia! She is a smashing girl — good at lawn tennis and things like that." He put his hat on backward and had to reverse it. "Rides well, too, Cornelia does." Hastily he climbed into the wagon, loaded high with Mrs. Glore, Eggleston, and their extensive luggage.

Swiftly the spring wagon rolled away in the dusty road. Beulah continued to weep on the valet's shoulder. Proud in the new coat and pants Jack had given him, Charlie chanted a Papago song, bare feet propped on the dashboard. Jack looked stiffly ahead, arms folded.

After a while, he could not resist the temptation to look back. There was the playa, shimmering in the winter sunlight. There too was the brooding bulk of the Mazatzals, dim and purple in haze, summits outlined in a rime of new snow. Along the greenery marking the Agua Fria he saw a brief sparkle of white — perhaps a dress, with a red sash. Maybe Phoebe Larkin was watching, waiting. He waved, knowing that at such a distance she probably could not see the gesture.

In Prescott, Sam Valentine was obliging. He riffled through the papers Jack Drumm gave him. "They all appear in order. No problem at all! I'll have the Clerk of the Legislature take care of it first thing in the morning. But why —"

"I *want* Phoebe Larkin to have Rancho Terco," Jack explained. "It's the least I can do for her, after the way I — I —" He broke off. "It's a personal matter, Sam. I'd rather not explain. But Miss Larkin loves the country, and I want the property to go to someone — sympathetic."

"And the money?" the legislator asked. "You've got a contract with the stage company, and with Tully and Ochoa, I hear. Then there's the income from other sources —"

"All of it." Jack was impatient to be done with the business. He suspected Valentine knew all about Alonzo Meech and his dogged pursuit of Phoebe Larkin and Beulah Glore, but did not want to mention it. And if Phoebe was caught, as seemed likely, the proceeds from the sale of the ranch would pay for a good lawyer to defend her. "I owe it to her, Sam," he said.

Valentine shrugged. "Whatever you say, though you're giving up a gold mine! And it goes without saying — the Territory is the loser when you go, Mr. Drumm. I had hopes you'd stay, maybe take out citizenship papers. I'm sorry our paths divide this way."

"You'll send her the necessary papers, then, when it's all arranged?"

"By the first stage," Valentine promised.

As they drove from the capital the next morning they passed the church, the sprawling huts of Mex Town. Bells chimed; the sound made him think, however unwillingly, of Phoebe, of Father Garcés's place with the burro and the cow within a pole fence, of Alonzo Meech standing in the shadow of the church. Meech had said the Buckner family was impatient with his failure to catch Phoebe Larkin. Well, perhaps the detective had given up the hunt and gone back to Philadelphia.

"A penny for your thoughts," Beulah Glore teased.

183

Jack shook his head. "Nothing. Nothing at all. My mind was completely vacant."

Beulah pursed her lips. "I doubt it, somehow. You was thinking of *something* — I could tell from the look on your face." Affectionately she pressed against the valet. "Mr. Eggleston here tells me Hampshire is just beautiful — all green and fresh and roses and country churchyards and things."

"In the summer that is true," he said. "And there is nothing like an English spring. The autumn is very pleasant, too, until the rains come. But I am afraid we are in for some rough times when we cross the ocean. The Prescott *Enterprise* reports gales on the Atlantic, with several vessels lost."

Beulah smiled. "With Mr. Eggleston by my side I'm not afraid of the wildest wind that blows! That's the Lord's own brassbound double-strength triple-distilled truth!"

Oddly, the first face Jack Drumm saw at Bear Spring was a familiar one. The burly Corporal Bagley, Dunaway's bosom friend, lounged on the platform at the Atlantic and Pacific station, oiling the action of a long-barreled Starr revolver. When Jack called to him, he was surprised.

"Mr. Drumm!" Dropping the weapon into the holster at his belt, he strolled to the spring wagon and shook hands, tipping his upswept cavalry hat to Mrs. Glore. "What in blazes are you doing here?"

Jack explained. Bagley listened, fondling his brushy mustache.

"But why are *you* here?" Jack asked. "The last time I saw you, George Dunaway and you were hanging on each other in front of the Lucky Lady saloon in Prescott."

Bagley looked abashed. "That's right. We were really spifflicated that night. George got a reprimand out of it. Major Trimble burned him good! They sent *me* to watch this Godforsook railroad station with a detachment of guardhouse lawyers! Watch against what?" He waved his hand about. "Sagebrush, jackrabbits, wind, and sand! God, what a thirst a man can raise out here! I'd give my —" He coughed, delicately, looking at Mrs. Glore. "I'd give a purty for a mug of ice-cold lager!"

He invited them to sit on the platform, helped unload their baggage, and told them the eastbound train was delayed. "Last week she was to steam through here on a Wednesday. It was Friday night before she showed."

"My goodness," Beulah said, paling. "Whatever are we to do, Mr. Drumm, if there's no train?"

"We'll make out all right," Jack reassured her. "Now just don't worry, Beulah!"

Sitting in the shade on boxes Corporal Bagley provided, they listened to the clatter of the telegraph instrument inside, scanned the cactus-studded distance for the train. The wind blew, sand filled the air. Wheeling low over the station, a hawk pumped skyward again with a snake in his talons.

"This Presbyterian church," Beulah mused, while Eggleston snored against her shoulder. "Mr. Drumm,

185

I'm a River Baptist — always have been. When Mr. Eggleston and I get married, I ain't going to be committing a sin, am I? I mean — is it all right for Baptists and Presbyterians to marry each other in England?"

"Perfectly all right. Eggie's church will welcome you, and you will become quite a respectable member of the organization — known for your good works and all that kind of thing."

Beulah was comforted, and after a while also dozed off. Jack itched; the heavy wool suit was scratchy, and though it was January in the Territory, he sweltered. Where was the train? He strained his eyes looking into the distance. After a while he dozed too, or thought he did. He dreamed the A. and P. cars were arriving at the station. The diamond stack chuffed smoke; the conductor swung a flag — they were at last ready to go. But the smoke pursued Jack Drumm. Through the open window it boiled; thick, almost viscous. The smoke was red, red as a vampire's lips, red as blood, red as Phoebe Larkin's flowing tresses. The stuff curled around him, clinging tentacles of scarlet, wrapping him with their coils, pinioning him, sapping the strength from his body. He was helpless, bound tightly with the scarlet strands. Crying out, all he could manage was a despairing croak. "Phoebe!" he cried. "Please, why are you doing this to me? Phoebe!"

Someone gripped his shoulder. "Whatever is the matter, Mr. Drumm?" Anxiously Beulah Glore peered into his face, mopped his fevered brow with a

186

handkerchief. Eggleston watched over her shoulder, his face concerned. "Were you dreaming?" Beulah asked.

Shamefacedly he sat erect. The wind was still blowing sand and tumbleweed, the sun beat down, the tracks shimmered in the heat. The eastbound train had not yet arrived.

"I — I suppose so," he stammered. "I dozed a little, then —"

Embarrassed, he got up to stroll the station platform. Inside the board shack the telegraph sounder clattered its metallic language. Corporal Bagley and the operator bent over a penciled message.

"Christ!" Bagley muttered. He chewed at his mustache. The operator, a wispy man in shirtsleeves and eyeshade, looked at Corporal Bagley uncertainly. "Last night," he said in a hushed voice. "Not twenty-four hours ago!"

They became aware of Jack Drumm's presence.

"What is it?" he asked. "What has happened?"

Bagley swallowed; his Adam's apple bobbed, twitched, came to an uneasy rest. He picked up the paper and scanned it again, lips moving silently.

"Mr. Drumm," he said finally, "this is railroad business, and they told me I wasn't to stick my nose in it. It's Army business, too, and on that account, beggin' your pardon, it ain't any of *your* business. But I'm bound to admit you got a kind of a stake in it." He spread the paper flat on the desk. "This here is from Major Trimble at Fort Whipple. He says to be on the lookout for some action. Agustín has busted out of the Mazatzals and is raising a hell of a lot of sand."

187

"Causing trouble, you mean?"

Bagley nodded. "I guess you could say that. Last night he raided along the Agua Fria."

Jack Drumm felt suddenly cold. The desert sun lost its warmth. Something in Jim Bagley's voice made him tremble. There was more coming, he knew. The scar on his lip began to smart, to burn.

"Last night," the corporal said, "Agustín come down hard on your place. Rancho Terco — ain't that what you called it?"

Jack nodded dumbly. After a moment he asked, "Was anyone — was anyone — hurt?"

Bagley took a deep breath. "Luther," he said to the telegraph operator, "you got any gin put away? Or whiskey? I want to give Mr. Drumm a little snort."

"I don't need anything!" Jack insisted. "Tell me — what happened?"

"Feller named Sloat was killed," Bagley said grimly. "Some of the others was cut up, but they'll live. And that girl — the one with the pretty hair —"

"Damn it!" Jack shouted, taking him by the butternut sleeve. "Tell me! What happened?"

Bagley's face was somber. "Miss Larkin — that her name? Agustín carried her off to the Mazatzals, Major Trimble thinks."

CHAPTER
TEN

He loved her. He loved Phoebe Larkin. He must have known it all the time, from the moment she stepped off the stage at Rancho Terco, hair done up in that China silk scarf. There had been the sprinkle of freckles across her nose, the proud and independent way of her, the coltish eagerness so strange and unsettling to his staid British soul. Yes, he must have known all the time that he loved her, but had been too Drumm-stubborn, too Anglo-Saxon reserved, to admit it. Now the realization stunned him. This was — this must have been — love all along! He tugged at his tight collar, stared wild-eyed from Bagley to the telegraph operator.

"I'm going back! Right now!"

"Take it easy, Mr. Drumm," Corporal Bagley cautioned. "There's no need to —"

"I'm going back! Can you let me have a horse from your corral out there?" He pointed through the dusty window. "Look, if it's money —"

Bagley pushed the wallet away. "There's nothing you can do, believe me. Major Trimble and George Dunaway and B Company are there by now."

A steam whistle blew. The musical note, rich and complex, sounded like the chimes of Salisbury

Cathedral. "Mr. Drumm!" Beulah Glore called. "Hurry! The cars is coming!"

He ran out on the platform. Around the distant bend came the Atlantic and Pacific Railroad's Western Express, stack puffing smoke as the train toiled up the grade to Bear Spring station. Eggleston and Charlie the Papago carried baggage to the edge of the platform.

"I'm not going," Jack blurted.

They stared in astonishment.

"Listen," he said, fumbling in his pocket. "Listen to me! Something has happened at the ranch. The Apaches attacked again. They killed Mr. Sloat and carried off Miss Phoebe." He handed the envelope to the valet. "Here are your railroad tickets, and money."

Beulah Glore, listening, nearly swooned. Eggleston caught her under the arms. "My God, Mr. Jack! Can it be so?"

The Western Express reached the plateau of Bear Spring. The chuffing quieted, the whistle blew again, this time louder and nearer.

"There is no time to talk!" Jack insisted. "I must somehow get back to the ranch and see what I can do in this terrible situation!"

"But what are we to do when we reach New York City?"

"Go directly to the offices of the White Star Lines at Pier B and book passage for yourself and Mrs. Glore. I will try to catch up with you, but there can be no assurance. There is no reason for you and your —" He tried to smile reassuringly at Beulah Glore, but the gesture was strained. "For you and Beulah to delay your return to Clarendon Hall."

The Western Express slowed, ground to a halt. Brakes squealed, there was a release of steam, a shower of ashes, clouds of pungent woodsmoke.

"Now go!" Jack commanded. "Look — the conductor is already signaling the engine driver!"

In spite of Beulah's protestations, he rushed her and Eggleston into the car. When Charlie attempted to put his own bag in the vestibule, Jack snatched it away, saying, "No, no, Charlie! I am not going!"

Weeping, Beulah leaned from the open window. "I can't go! What will happen to poor Phoebe?" She turned within. "Mr. Eggleston, let go my skirts!"

Gently Jack pushed her back into the car.

"There is nothing you can do," he comforted. "I myself can probably accomplish little. But Corporal Bagley says Lieutenant Dunaway and B Company are already on the trail of the kidnappers, so please put your mind at ease."

"All abo — o — oard!" called the conductor.

As the cars gathered speed Jack ran along the platform, shaking Eggleston's hand. "Mrs. Glore is your concern now, Eggie! When you arrive, tell everyone at home I will be along as soon as possible!"

Shaken and out of breath, he watched the departing Western Express, bound for places with strange-sounding names like Albuquerque, Trinidad, Wichita, and Topeka. Suddenly he realized Charlie was tugging at his sleeve. The Papago's face was clouded with fear.

191

"Ostin, what happen? Something — something bad?"

"Charlie, Agustín and his Apaches attacked our ranch last night." He spoke slowly and carefully; the Papago's English was poor. "You are not to worry, though. Corporal Bagley says that only poor Mr. Sloat was killed."

Charlie's leathery face contorted. "*Esposa* — my wife — my *niños* —"

"I am sure they are all safe, else Corporal Bagley would have told me."

He had not been aware that Corporal Jim Bagley was standing near. "No word of other casualties," the corporal confirmed.

Charlie looked bewildered. "What we do now, Ostin?"

"I want to get to the ranch fast," Jack said to Bagley. "I must ask you again. Can I borrow one of your cavalry mounts?"

Bagley scratched his head, uncertain. "Mr. Drumm, I'm in a pack of trouble already with the major. Them bangtails is U. S. Gov'mint property. If I was to let a civilian take one —"

"This is a matter of life and death!" Jack burst out. "Good God, Bagley, can't you see that —"

"Not so fast!" the corporal grumbled. He pulled at his lip. "Just let me think here a minute!"

"There's no time to think! Phoebe Larkin has been kidnapped! Even now she may be in Agustín's camp in the Mazatzals, subjected to God knows what tortures, indignities —"

"You was sweet on the gal," Bagley remarked. It was a statement, not a question. Jack Drumm stared at him.

"What do you know about my feelings for — for —"

"I know," the corporal said. "George Dunaway told me."

Exasperated, Jack said, "Are you going to lend me a horse or not?"

Bagley sighed, then whistled to a barrel-chested roan with a white star on the forehead.

"My own mount," he said, throwing a saddle blanket over the horse's back. "Take good care of Tom, Mr. Drumm. If anything was to happen to old Tom, I'd have to cut out your liver with a rusty knife." Drawing the cinch tight, he spoke from under the horse's belly. "You know why I'm trusting you with this here horse?"

Jack shook his head.

Bagley straightened, and contemplated him across the saddle.

"I finally figgered you for a natural man. Till now I took you for a stuffed shirt, as they say — river water in the veins, and didn't give shucks about anyone but yourself. But I guess I was wrong." He shoved a Spencer carbine into the saddle scabbard and tossed Jack Drumm a quick-loading cartridge box of patent design. "Seven-shot magazine — tube slides in through the buttplate. I'm charged with the damned carbine, too; bring it back along with the horse or Major Trimble'll kick my butt right into Leavenworth Prison."

Jack mounted the roan. Skittish at his neatly pressed suit and bowler hat, Tom danced for a moment,

193

snuffling and pawing the dust. He settled down when Jack pulled firmly on the reins.

"I'm going to ride directly to the ranch," he told Charlie. "You take the mule and wagon and come back through Prescott. I will cut straight across; down the Verde for a ways, then along Turkey Creek to the Agua Fria and the ranch."

"Keep your eye peeled, Mr. Drumm!" Bagley warned. "No telling where Agustín has got to by now! He may be heading for that country himself!"

Jack nodded. "And I want you to know, Corporal, I'll never forget what you have done for me this day!"

"Neither will Major Trimble," Bagley said glumly, "if'n he finds out! But it's in a good cause, I guess. I liked Miss Phoebe." He dug a toe in the dust. "I had me a gal, onct, back in St. Louis, at Jefferson Barracks. She was a lot like Miss Phoebe. She —" Embarrassed, he broke off.

Jack leaned from the saddle, shook hands, wheeled the horse, and clapped his heels into Tom's ribs.

"Good luck, Mr. Drumm!" Bagley called after him.

It was almost fifty miles from Bear Spring station of the A. and P. to the ranch. The roan had a long easy pace, but much of the country was forbidding and rubble-littered, the way hindered by patches of cactus and narrow canyons. He had no map, but from the position of the sun he calculated a generally southerly course and knew that sooner or later he would intersect Turkey Creek.

By late afternoon the sun dropped behind the ridges and a chill crept over the land. The sunset was glorious in these high elevations, streaks of pink and saffron and a blue that was almost gunmetal trailed streamers across the sky. Jack pulled the coat tighter about him, suddenly aware that he was hungry. He had not eaten since morning, and breakfast had been scanty.

At the bottom of a gloomy canyon was a small spring. He and the roan Tom both drank from it. Squatting nearby, he watched Tom wrench up tufts of grass from the borders of the spring. If only man could digest grass like a horse! Instead, he pulled off a handful of mesquite beans and chewed them. They were sweet, but a little floury, and he drank more water. Stretching his legs, he once more mounted the roan and headed south.

Riding in the twilight was difficult, but he kept stubbornly on. Once the horse shied, almost throwing him. A rattle sounded underfoot. Remembering, Jack muttered, "Ostin snake — sorry!"

A bit of moon rose, cup-shaped, as if to hold water. In Hampshire that meant rain, but here there was small prospect. The moon gave a little light, however, and they plodded on. Giant saguaros loomed high, the moon casting faint shadows of the many-armed figures. The moon drifted into a rack of clouds, feeble light dimming. In the distance a lone coyote howled, a high-pitched mournful keening that made Jack shiver, and not from the growing cold. In the small night breeze, desert bushes stirred, leaves rustling dryly.

195

For a while he dozed in the saddle. Suddenly he jerked erect, wondering where he was, what he was doing wandering in this strange desert. Tom moved easily under him, picking a dainty way through a waste studded with *pitahaya* and *cardon*. Jack stared upward at Polaris. They were still on their proper course. "Good horse!" he muttered, and rubbed the roan's warm neck.

Sometime before dawn, slipping into an almost drugged sleep, he staggered off the horse and threw the reins over Tom's head, Arizona style. Taking off the saddle and the sweat-rank blanket, he left Tom to graze while he cradled his head on the saddle and pulled the coarse stinking wool of the blanket about him. At dawn he awoke only when slanting shafts of sunlight crept over the ridges. He sat up, blinking, rubbing his reddened eyes. Lord, he was sore! He was not used to riding such distances, or sleeping among the rocks.

The roan, dangling reins tangled in a cholla cactus, rolled patient eyes at him.

"Good horse," Jack said again, and untangled the reins. Once more they started southward. In the distance he could see a vein of green that must be Turkey Creek.

The rising sun grew warm, then hot. At noon it had driven the chill from his bones, and he took off his coat and laid it over the saddle before him. His unsated hunger grew, possessed him. He felt faint, and wondered whether it was the heat or simply lack of food. Resting for a while in the shade of a desert ironwood, he thought longingly of Beulah Glore's hot

196

biscuits, smothered in sidemeat gravy. What was happening at the ranch? Was there any word of Phoebe Larkin? He saw a tiny mouse gamboling about the twisted roots of the ironwood, pausing only to stand on hind feet and nibble seeds. He remembered Charlie the Papago snaring mice to eat, and almost wished he had a bit of thread or twine. After all, mice were animals, mammals, the same as beef cattle or sheep, only smaller. He would clean them first, of course, and it would take several mouse haunches to make a mouthful, but —

He got painfully to his feet and put the bowler hat on his head. The brim was narrow but the headgear, however inappropriate in these wilds, offered some protection against the sun.

"Tom!" he called, looking about for the horse. But behind him something made a small snapping sound and he wheeled, frightened. The carbine was in the saddle scabbard; he was defenseless.

Nothing — no further sound. He stared into the thicket of greasewood where the noise had seemed to originate. "Who's there?" he called. His voice sounded dry and reedlike.

Again, nothing; no sound. The wind blew, the sun bore down. Tom ambled up and stood patiently by him. Jack snatched the car-bine from the scabbard, grasping it uncertainly. In the wilderness of scraggly bush he did not know where to aim.

On sudden impulse he picked up a stone and flung it into the bushes. Anything was better than waiting to be slaughtered.

197

"Who's there?" he called again.

He was sweating; the shirt was wet, and the breeze pressed it cold and clammy against his chest. As he stared into the bushes, clutching the Spencer nervously, he caught sight of a gray doglike animal loping from the greasewood and onto the stony slope. The coyote looked back at him, tongue lolling pinkly from its mouth.

He sighed with relief. What he had heard must have been the coyote, sleeping off an all-night hunt in the bushes. He and Tom had come on it unexpectedly, that was all. But he would not dismount again without the carbine. *Agustín may be heading for the same country* — that was what Corporal Jim Bagley had reminded him.

High and hazy, the Mazatzals now loomed on his left. He stared at them, narrowing his eyes against the sun, wondering where the Apache camp lay. Could Phoebe Larkin be up there, looking longingly down at the playa and freedom, or was she — was she —

He refused to think about it. Together man and beast plodded on. The roan was tired now also, and ambled slowly unless Jack urged him on. Finally reaching Turkey Creek, they watered in the sluggish pools. Remembering Beulah Glore's "poke salat," Jack chewed a handful of greens pulled from the muck. They tasted rank and medicinal, and nearly made him sick. Again he thought longingly of Eggie's omelets, Mrs. Glore's brown-crusted pies, the warm fragrant tortillas and rich *frijol* beans in the *cantina* at Prescott that night with Alonzo Meech.

198

Spitting out the shreds of grass, he rose, backside sore and chafed. Not too far down Turkey Creek, now, lay the junction of the Agua Fria, and the ranch. Straining his eyes into the distance, he saw dust devils whirling above the playa, tall spirals rising up and up, thousands of feet into the dry desert air. The wind was blowing hard. Looking at the towering columns, he saw something else, something that made him immediately apprehensive: blinks of light like small diamonds, sparks of brilliance punctuating the hazy distance. Watching, he saw one glimmer out. Almost immediately another flashed, as if in response, from the foothills of the Mazatzals. Were the Apaches out in force? Had other bands, encouraged by Agustín's rebellion, gone on the warpath against the white man? Perhaps the valley of the Agua Fria was already filled with them, looting, murdering. Perhaps Rancho Terco was finally overrun, perhaps even the Army was at last powerless to defend the valley. Climbing again onto the weary roan, he clapped his heels into the sweating ribs.

"Let's go, damn it! Hurry, Tom!"

When he splashed through the muddy pools of the Agua Fria just above the ranch the sun was low on the western horizon. Weary in the saddle, clothing worn and stained and face stubbled with beard, he hardly heard the challenge.

"Halt! Who goes there?"

Only half comprehending, he gazed slack-mouthed into the reeds while the horse stumbled on, splashing in the mud.

"Halt, I say!"

The roan ambled on; the cavalry picket fired. Jack Drumm's bowler hat flew from his head. Startled, now fully awake, he threw his hands in the air and yelled, "God damn it, stop shooting!"

The reeds parted, a bearded face poked through.

"Advance and be recognized! That's what I'm supposed to say, mister!"

Wrathfully Jack slipped from the saddle to pick up the punctured hat. It had cost him four pounds sixpence at Mason's in the Strand. "What in hell did you think I was? Did you ever see an Apache in a bowler hat?"

The picket stepped from the greenery, reloading his Springfield. "I seen a Sioux, onct, wearing a plug hat and a long-tail coat. Shot the hell out of Corporal Voss." He squinted. "Who the hell are you, anyway?"

He herded Jack Drumm toward the cavalry headquarters, a tent pitched in the ruins of the despoiled Rancho Terco. Sadly Jack stared about. Ramadas had been burned, the painfully built adobe pulled down until only the walls, to a height of about a yard, remained. The corral had been destroyed, the watchtower set afire. Now it was only a blackened skeleton watching over a landscape of discarded clothing, broken pots, a few books. Everything smelled of fire, of rapine, of death. Something glittered in the ashes. Stooping to pick it up, he saw it was the Apache knife that had pinned Agustín's last warning to a post.

Someone spoke his name. It was Ben Sprankle, followed by a gaggle of his children. "Mr. Drumm!"

"Hello, Ben."

Sprankle's face was worn and sooty, a bloody bandage was tied around his arm. "They come down on us at night," he said in a dull voice. "Guess we got a little careless. Anyway, they was on us in an instant, whooping and hollering. There must have been a hundred of 'em! They come over us like a wave, set fire to everything, run off our stock. It wasn't no good to stand and fight; they was everywhere! Sloat —" He broke off, eyes filling with tears, and bit at his lip.

Jack waited.

"Sloat — he told me to take the women and the kids and hide 'em in the reeds. The last I seen of him, he was in the middle of the fracas, swinging an empty gun. Then —"

Mrs. Sprankle put a comforting arm around her husband. "There now, Ben!"

"Miss Larkin," Jack said. "Did she — did she —"

Sprankle took a deep shuddering breath. "I guess they hit your diggings the same time they did our'n. They was all up and down the river. I heard screams from your place, but then it hushed up. Miss Phoebe ain't no place around. We searched both sides of the river but all we come up with was this." Fumbling in his pocket, he brought out the tiny derringer and handed it to Jack. Both barrels had been fired.

"I wanted to go after her," Sprankle said, "but the cavalry said no, said they'd take care of everything."

They stood silent together in a community of grief. Finally Sprankle said, "I guess the only one that ain't suffered from this was old Uncle Roscoe. He left here early in the morning day before yesterday. Said he was going on a little practice run to get himself in shape for a spell of prospecting in the Mazatzals. Went up that way —" He gestured toward the snow-covered peaks. "I hope them devils didn't run on him too. I dunno."

With difficulty Jack cleared his throat. "What about Charlie's family?"

Sprankle shrugged. "They must have had some kind of a preemonition. Skedaddled — at least I didn't see no sign of them during the fighting, and they ain't around now."

"Maybe they were the wisest — to leave this place, I mean. Run away."

"They can't drive *me* out!" Sprankle bristled. "This is my home, home for Edie and the kids! We ain't going to leave our *home!*"

George Dunaway slouched from the tent, where a lantern burned in the dusk, and an officer with gold leaves pored over a map. "It's you," he said. "Drumm."

"That's right."

"I thought you were on your way back to England — Hampshire, wasn't that it?"

"I got the word at Bear Spring," Jack said. "Corporal Bagley was kind enough to share a telegraph message about a raid along the Agua Fria. He said Phoebe was apparently kidnapped by Agustín."

"Seems to be the case." Dunaway pulled aside the tent flap and introduced Jack to Major Trimble. The major, a small trim man and obviously a West Pointer, shook hands.

202

"It must have been a raid in force," Jack said. "All the way down from Bear Spring I saw their mirrors, signaling."

Dunaway grunted. "Not their mirrors — ours." He pulled a tripod-mounted instrument from the rear of the tent. "New Army heliograph."

Proudly Major Trimble showed Jack the polished mirror, the shutter that was depressed to send telegraph-code messages of dots and dashes of reflected sunlight. "We've needed something like this for a long time!" he enthused. "The red bastards always seem to know where our forces are, where we're headed for, when we arrive. They're smart, but now we've got a tool to outsmart them, beat them at their own game! Now we can communicate over a range of fifty miles on a clear sunny day, concentrate our forces in a few hours to wipe them out!" He smashed a fist on the desk. "Obliterate them, destroy them!" His eyes shone.

"What are you going to do about Miss Larkin?" Jack asked.

"When they come down, as they eventually will have to do —"

"When they come down? Do you mean you're just going to wait for them?"

Major Trimble stiffened. George Dunaway cleared this throat, but the major silenced him with a curt wave of the hand.

"Mr. Drumm, we're doing all we can! We have an effective battle plan mapped out, and it does certainly not include sending U.S. troops helterskelter up into the Mazatzals. That is exactly what Agustín would like

— a chance to cut us up piecemeal. No, sir, we are deployed along the Agua Fria in an extensive skirmish line and there is no way out for the rascals but to come down and try to fight their way through our lines. That is when we will break them for once and for all!"

"But how long will that be?"

Major Trimble smiled a small savage smile. "When the snow up there starts getting deep, and the children are crying from cold and hunger. That is when they will come down, and we will be waiting for them with our new battery of Gatling guns."

Hopelessly Jack Drumm looked at Dunaway. Dunaway looked back, discouragement in his eyes.

"I told the major," Dunaway muttered, "I was willing to take a dozen men — including Jim Bagley, if I could get him back here from Bear Spring — and go up after her!"

Major Trimble shook his head. "I'm not going to have any dead heroes! We've already lost over a dozen men in this campaign, and General Crook himself is watching our operations with a keen eye! No, gentlemen — no heroics — just good sound tactical planning and organization."

Outside the tent, Jack and George Dunaway stood together in their discouragement.

"God damned little bastard!" George said through set teeth. "Threatened to court-martial me if I went anywhere without orders!"

Around them were pitched the shelter halves of B Company, together with a company of recently arrived infantry. Campfires glowed in the dusk, coffee boiled,

204

Jack caught a whiff of frying bacon and remembered his hunger. Someone sang a song called "Laura Lee" in a mournful baritone, and the setting sun glinted for a moment on the polished barrels of the new Gatlings the infantry had brought.

"When the snow starts getting deep!" Jack blurted. "How long will that be?"

"Two, three weeks anyway," George said, kicking at the dust. "That little tin soldier won't move until February at the earliest."

Together they sat on a bench partly consumed by the flames.

"Do — do you think there's any possibility she's still alive?" Jack asked, his voice trembling.

Dunaway shrugged. "Who the hell knows? Sprankle and the rest can't tell us anything — they were too busy saving their own butts! But from what I know of old Agustín, he's got her up in his camp in the Mazatzals." Taking a metal flask from his pocket, he drank, then handed it to Jack Drumm. "Bourbon. Good bourbon. None of that Old Popskull they sell at the Lucky Lady."

Jack shook his head. "I didn't think you were supposed to drink when you were on duty."

Dunaway snorted. "If I didn't drink sometimes I'd go crazy!"

"Major Trimble —"

"Screw Trimble!" Dunaway wiped his mouth, put the flask back in his pocket. "Yes, Phoebe's up there all right, and it's my guess she's alive. You know, up in the Dakotas once we were having a little dustup with some Oglalas we had cornered in a canyon. One of them stood up on a rock and pulled down his pants to show us his ass. That was their way of showing off. Kidnapping Phoebe — stealing a white woman right under our noses — that's probably Agustín's way of doing the same thing."

Behind them, boots crunched in the dust and ashes of the ruined ranch. George Dunaway stared moodily ahead, not caring if it was Major Trimble himself. Jack turned.

"Gentlemen," Alonzo Meech said. "Mr. Drumm!" Taking off his broad-brimmed hat, he sat amicably beside them on the charred bench.

"I guess," he said, "we're probably all three looking for the same female person."

CHAPTER
ELEVEN

The sergeant major came to summon Dunaway to the command post.

"What does Trimble want now?" George asked morosely.

The sergeant grinned. "I dunno, sir. But he was kind of snotty!"

Dunaway spat into the dust. "That's what they teach them at that mechanic's school on the Hudson — to be snotty with inferiors. It's part of the science of command."

"Are you coming, sir?"

"I'm coming." Dunaway turned to Jack Drumm.

"I guess it's pretty farfetched, but if — if you —"

He broke off.

"If I what?" Jack asked.

"Forget it." Dunaway shrugged. "It was just a wild hare of a thought." He got up and strode toward Major Trimble's lamplit tent. As he left he called to the sergeant major. "Maloy, see Mr. Drumm gets some beans and bacon and coffee, will you? He's likely hungry after that long ride."

Ravenous, Jack spooned beans into his mouth, chewed the bacon, burned his mouth with hot coffee full of grounds. Alonzo Meech sat beside him, watching. At last, uncomfortable under scrutiny, Jack laid down the spoon and looked at the detective. "What's wrong?"

Meech reached in a pocket and brought out a silk kerchief. It was the China silk, all vivid greens and blues, that Phoebe Larkin wore that first day Jack Drumm saw her step off the Prescott coach. In the still desert air he imagined — or knew — a faint perfume.

"I figured all along," Meech said, "someone was helping them two. Otherwise they couldn't have got away so slick. In Phoenix I almost had the cuffs on 'em. In Prescott I run 'em down to Mex Town, and they got away again. By asking around and handing out greenbacks, I was told they'd been smuggled back to what you call Rancho Terco here. And when I get here, flogging that damned mare all the way — she bit me twict — I find Miss Phoebe Buckner took by the Apaches."

"Phoebe *Larkin*," Jack muttered, spooning up the last of the beans.

"Buckner."

"That old man treated her cruelly. From what Phoebe told me I doubt he could even consummate the marriage. There are certainly grounds for a divorce, possibly even an annulment."

Meech folded the kerchief; the perfume, unmistakable, laced the evening air.

"I don't intend to quibble, Mr. Drumm. All I got to say is that you obstructed justice, aiding and abetting them two miscreants the way you did." He looked keenly at Jack. "Where's Mrs. Glore? I got a warrant for her too."

How much did Meech know? Not a great deal, Jack decided; Alonzo Meech was not the world's shrewdest detective, as he himself admitted. Meech did deserve credit, however, for persistence.

"Mrs. Glore," he said, "also is beyond your reach."

"Well —" The detective shrugged. "It was my mistake, I guess. I never thought you'd cross me the way you did. I took you for an honest law-abiding English gentleman, and that was a mistake."

Jack looked around at the campfires sprinkling the night. Most of the soldiers were stretched out in slumber, some only in underdrawers. By morning it would be near freezing, and they would welcome blankets. Somewhere a trooper sang softly against a muted plinking of banjo. A crescent moon crept over the ragged outline of the Mazatzals.

"I guess," he admitted, "it wasn't the first time a beautiful woman addled a man's judgment."

"I'll give you that," the detective sighed. He handed the kerchief to Jack Drumm. "You might as well take this thing. I know you was in love with her — it stuck out all over you, like warts. I ain't exactly a sentimental man, but maybe — well, since you ain't never going to see her again, it could be a keepsake."

Jack was moved; there was a lump in his throat. Gently he took the kerchief, touched the glossy silk. Perhaps, at one time, Phoebe Larkin had tied it about her waist. He recalled the ballad, the one called "The

209

Girdle," that he had sung to himself the day he drove into Prescott for supplies:

> A narrow compass, and yet there dwelt
> All that's good and all that's fair.
> Give me but what this ribbon bound,
> Take all the rest the sun goes round.

"Eh?" he asked suddenly.

Meech peered at him in the gloom. "You ain't listening to me, Mr. Drumm!"

"I'm sorry! I was thinking about something else."

"I said," Meech repeated, "it don't make no difference now."

"What doesn't make any difference?"

"Her," Meech said. "Miss Larkin, whatever you want to call her. She's probably dead. In any case, I'm told I got to give up the hunt." He took off his hat, ran a hand through thin gray locks. "First customer I ever lost! Oh, some took me a little time! How-somever, I always caught up with 'em. But the home office finally called me off. I'm person non grotto — spent too much money, too much time, got no results. The Buckner family cut off the money — said they didn't want to spend all the old man's legacy hunting down the females that robbed and shot him."

"Legacy?"

Meech nodded, put his hat back on. "Phineas Buckner died two weeks ago. Oh, his passing didn't have nothing to do with Phoebe or Mrs. Glore! The old bastard fell down a stairway and broke his neck. So it's

210

kind of 'come see come saw.' That's French for it don't make no never mind now anyway!"

Phoebe and Mrs. Glore free from pursuit, from arraignment, from conviction! It was ironic! After all these months of playing hare and hounds, Beulah was safe in Hampshire, or soon would be, and Phoebe —

"I'm going back to Philadelphia," Meech concluded. He looked around, sniffed the night air, cast a speculative eye on the moon. "You know, this Arizona Territory ain't a bad place! Someday, when they put me out to pasture, I might just take my savings and buy me a little shack in Tucson or Yuma. In Philadelphia the old bones aches during the winter, but out here I feel like I was forty again!"

"I thank you," Jack murmured, "for giving me her kerchief."

Meech rose, flapped his coattails. "Soon's my butt heals, I'll sell that ugly old mare to a glue factory and buy me a ticket home on the A. and P. I don't guess I'll be up to sitting for a week on the cars just yet." He shook hands with Jack Drumm. "You give me a lot of trouble, Mr. Drumm, but can we part friends?"

"We can," Jack said.

The sergeant major brought him a blanket. "Lieutenant Dunaway said you'd need this, Mr. Drumm."

Wrapping himself in the coarse wool, Jack lay down next to the wall of the ruined adobe. The moon rose higher. Slanting shafts of yellow light shone through the blackened roof beams. He lay quietly for a long time, silk kerchief wadded in his hand. After a while he slept.

He dreamed, inevitably, of Phoebe — of poor lost Phoebe, poor ravished Phoebe, poor — dead Phoebe Larkin.

At dawn he awoke, disturbed by a returning cavalry patrol. George Dunaway, wrapped in a blanket beside him, stirred sleepily and called to the fresh-faced young lieutenant. "Find anything, Lucius?"

Lucius reined up and looked at them. "Didn't expect to," he grumbled. "Nothing but a lot of hoof tracks where they ran all those horses up into the mountains."

Propped on an elbow, Jack watched the young lieutenant clamber wearily from his mount and go into the tent to report.

"The Apaches eat horses, I know that," he observed. "With all that horsemeat, they may be a long time coming down."

"I don't know," Dunaway said. He sat up, wrapping his arms around his knees, and watched the dawn flush over the Mazatzals. "Maybe they're getting second thoughts about horses. They're poor horsemen — a Sioux would laugh himself silly seeing an Apache trying to get on a horse — but don't ever underestimate Agustín's smarts. I wouldn't put it past him to be planning some kind of mounted attack along the river. An Apache can go on foot all day, that's true, but it takes a lot of time. With Agustín's people on horses, good horses, the Apache problem in the Territory can balloon into something that'll take the whole damned Army of the Potomac to settle!"

Eating from a tin mess kit, Jack stared down the deserted wagon road. The news of heavy raids along the

Agua Fria had once again paralyzed commerce between Phoenix and Prescott. Agustín was still in the Mazatzals, watching the road from the lofty distance. *When the snow up there starts getting deep!* Remembrance of Trimble's smug words stung him. He flung the un-eaten food away; it was Army food, exactly as George Dunaway once described it — sour bacon and rusty beans.

"Mr. Drumm!"

Startled, he turned. Uncle Roscoe beamed at him, whiskered face split in a grin. He pumped Jack Drumm's hand.

"They told me you come back! Lord, ain't I glad to see you! Sad circumstances, I guess — the young lady that was visiting you was took off by the Apaches, I hear — but it's an ill wind that blows nobody any good, or however they say it."

"Any luck with the Gypsy Dancer Mine?" Jack asked.

The old man turned his burro loose to graze and squatted beside Jack in the shade of a smoke tree.

"I got her narrowed down," he confided. He pointed to the wrinkled slopes of the mountains. "See them twin peaks up there — kind of lookin' like a woman's tits? The Gypsy Dancer lays right between 'em, like a pendant around a female's neck. This time I didn't really go out for a long stay — just had me a few biscuits and a canteen of water — but when I go back up there —"

Something hit Jack Drumm hard.

213

"Listen," he said. He gripped the old man's skinny forearm. "Listen to me! How would you like to go up there right now?"

Uncle Roscoe's watery blue eyes blinked. He pulled away, saying plaintively, "God damn it, you're busting my arm bone!"

"I'm sorry," Jack apologized. "I didn't mean to hurt you! But I want to make you a business proposition. You know the Mazatzals better than anyone, even Major Trimble and his cavalry."

Uncle Roscoe bit off a chunk of tobacco. "When them soldiers was running around in didies," he confided, "I was climbing those mountains. Why, didn't I never tell you? Me and Agustín was blood brothers! Onct I had me an Apache wife! It was back in —"

"Never mind!" Jack said. "Not now, anyway! Do you think you could find Agustín's camp for me?"

Uncle Roscoe's jaws worked steadily.

"I'll give you five hundred dollars cash if you'll guide me into the Mazatzals and put me in the way of finding Agustín!"

The old man shook his head. "You better wrap cold cloths around your head! I think you got sunstroke!"

"Never mind that! Will you do it?"

"The mountaintop is swarming with Apaches! They'll cut out your gizzard and pass it around for horsy-doovers!"

"Are you afraid?"

Uncle Roscoe swore, kicked the dust. "Hell no — I ain't afraid! Them's my blood-brothers, and I don't take kindly to the way they been treated by the

214

gov'mint! But Agustín ain't going to put no welcome mat out for *you!*" He peered keenly at Jack Drumm. "It's that female, ain't it — that red-haired Miss Larkin? I never seen her — she left Rancho Terco before you took me in — but I guess she was a looker!"

"That's neither here nor there," Jack said. "All I'm asking is whether you'll guide me up there!"

The old man rubbed his chin, chewed, spat. He looked at his burro, Pansy, grazing peacefully among the cavalry mounts.

"For a thousand dollars?" Jack prodded.

"God damn it, Mr. Drumm, it ain't the money! You took me in when I was sick, bled me, fed me, emptied my slop jar! I ain't never paid you back for that, and I guess there ain't any amount of money that'd settle my bill proper. But what in Tophet you aim to do onct you get up there?"

Jack took a deep breath. "I don't know," he confessed. "But if Phoebe Larkin is alive, I will do whatever I can to rescue her. Maybe I can ransom her. Maybe I can —"

"Not to speak blunt," the old man snorted, "but you're a God damned fool, Mr. Drumm! You're askin' to be kilt, maybe roasted over a slow fire! You started up Rancho Terco here, along the river, in the middle of what's holy ground to Agustín and his people. You fit 'em right down to the ground, tooth and nail — scragged a few, too. When they catch you up there in Gu Nakya —"

"What's that?"

"Gu Nakya? That's where Agustín used to hole up in the old days. That's where some of his folks is buried, only they don't bury 'em, of course — they just burn down the brush hut the feller lived in. Gu Nakya is over the top of the mountain, looking down that steep drop to the other side."

"Will you take me to Gu Nakya?"

Uncle Roscoe sighed. "All right, if you're so damned anxious to lose your liver and lights! Soon's I pack up a few more supplies, I intended to head up that way anyhow. This time I got the Gypsy Dancer dead in my sights. But you sure you don't want to change your mind?"

"Dead sure! I am firm in my decision."

Borrowing dried meat, hard cheese, and some tea and biscuits from the Sprankles, Jack told George Dunaway what he planned to do. Dunaway pushed back his hat and stared.

"You mean it?"

"I do indeed."

"Only yesterday I was thinking 'What if Drumm went up there, tried to find Phoebe?' It was a wild hare of an idea — I said so at the time — but now —" Dunaway fumbled for Jack's hand, gripped it hard. "Once," he muttered, "I beat the tar out of you in a fight. Remember?"

"I do."

"I used a few Arizona tricks on you, things you never saw before, and I flattened you. But I'm bound to admit you're a better man, Jack. While I sit here on my butt, scared of a court-martial, you — you —"

216

Dunaway took a pad of paper from his pocket, scribbled quickly. "Here," he said. "You'll need this."

"What is it?"

"A pass through our pickets." Dunaway gestured toward the foothills of the Mazatzals. "They'll stop you when you get up there. No civilians allowed." He grinned wryly. "When Major Trimble finds out, it'll be my butt in small pieces! But it's the least I can do." He shook hands with Jack Drumm. "If — if you ever see Phoebe again, tell her I — I —" He broke off. "I guess I loved her," he said awkwardly. "Hard to tell, in a way, since I never had experience with the real thing. But —" He turned on his heel, walking rapidly away.

On the flanks of the Mazatzals, far above the river, they paused for breath and to rest Jack's roan mount and the heavily laden Pansy. Though it was still winter, the sun bore heavily down. The playa below shimmered in the heat. Uncle Roscoe sat in the shade of a rocky ledge and drank from a canteen. His face was flushed with effort, and the dirty shirt was black with sweat under the armpits and across his meager chest.

"Hard going," Jack wheezed, squatting beside him.

Uncle Roscoe hooted. "You ain't seen any hard going yet!" He nodded skyward. "Wait till we get up there!"

Below them, the new M-7 heliographs winked in the sun. They were stationed, as the major had said, all up and down the river, a chain of rapid communication, making Agustín's situation difficult. If he risked a raid at one point, it was likely that troops quickly summoned from another would cut off his retreat into Gu Nakya.

Still winded, Jack clambered onto Tom. Uncle Roscoe prodded Pansy with a stick and they moved forward again, forward and upward. A rattler sunning on a flat rock watched them with dusty hooded eyes. The old prospector glanced at the snake, moved slightly aside, estimating the serpent's striking range, and said, "He don't mean us no harm, and I don't mean him none. That's the way to get along in the Territory. Wisht the gov'mint and the Apaches had the same policy."

At noon they stopped for a quick meal of dried meat and iron-hard biscuits. Uncle Roscoe, tattered hat over his face, took a nap. Jack Drumm was whittling with the Apache knife when a corporal, followed by two soldiers, stepped from the bushes. The soldiers trained Springfield rifles; the corporal waved a revolver menacingly.

"What you people doing up here?"

Uncle Roscoe sat bolt upright.

"What in hell you mean, what are us people doing up here? This is a free country, ain't it? What in Tophet you yellowlegs doing up here so God damn far from your mammy? Why, I —"

"Be quiet," Jack said. Under the watchful eye of the corporal he took the paper from his pocket. "We have a pass," he explained.

The corporal examined the paper. "I didn't hear nothing about any passes being issued."

"Do you recognize Lieutenant Dunaway's signature?"

The man scratched his stubbled chin. "That's his signature all right — he give me a three-day pass last week at Fort Whipple. But —"

Jack took the pass and put it again in his shirt pocket. "Then let us go on. We have a long way to travel."

"I ain't sure!" the corporal protested. "Where you two going, anyway?"

"That's for us to know and you to find out," Uncle Roscoe snapped. "Come on, Pansy."

"All right, then! I was only intending to give you some good advice." The corporal gestured toward the mountaintop. "Up there the Apaches are swarming like bees! They say Agustín's been joined by more hostiles that's bolted the reservation. I don't know what your business is, you fellers, but don't say I didn't warn you!"

"Thank you," Jack said. "If you'll tell your men to put down those rifles, we'll pass on through."

Late in the afternoon, several thousand feet above the playa, they paused, winded and staggering with fatigue. Pansy, sides heaving, stood stiff-legged under her burden as if fearing relaxation of her legs would result in complete collapse. Tom, the roan, limped badly with a stone-bruised foot. Uncle Roscoe took off his hat and fanned himself; a blue vein in his temple pumped. Voice hoarse but exultant, he pointed to the twin crags above them. "There's where she lies, the Gypsy Dancer! God, I spent most of my life lookin' for her! Now I can practically *spit* on her!"

The sun was sliding down the western wall of the sky and the air was cooler. Above them Jack could see scattered patches of snow. The flora, too, had changed. There were junipers, and an occasional pine tree. Different birds fluttered about in the undergrowth; chickadees and nuthatches, they were called.

"I'm glad you're near the Gypsy Dancer," he panted, "but you're going to take me to Gu Nakya — remember?"

Roscoe swallowed a long draft of water; the knob of Adam's apple bobbed up and down in his lean throat.

"That's right," he agreed, corking the flask. "I ain't one to forget a promise! Now this here is the plan." He pointed upward. "Behind that peak, sloping down to the other side, lies Gu Nakya. I don't doubt but what some scout seen us already, and wonders what in hell we're up to. We best hunker down right here for the night, get a little rest. When the moon comes up so's we can see a little, we'll go on up. Mebbe they won't ketch sight of us till we're pretty well up on 'em. By sunup we'll be on top, and then —"

He broke off, the words slurring oddly.

"And then —" he repeated.

Again he broke off, looking at Jack Drumm with a worried expression. "I — I feel kind of queer," he muttered.

Concerned, Jack squatted beside him. "Are you ill?"

The old prospector shook his head. "Dunno! It don't seem like sick, exactly, but —" With Jack's help he got to his feet, swaying, fumbling with a gnarled hand at his throat. "A little dizzy, seems like, but —"

220

Suddenly he collapsed, bandy legs folding under him. Alarmed, Jack let him gently down, pillowing Roscoe's head with his coat. When the old man struggled, Jack forced him to lie still.

"Don't exert yourself!" he urged. "Lie quietly for a few minutes and you'll feel better! It's — it's probably the altitude."

Even in the fading light he could see that the old man's face was red and perspiring; even more than red, the wattled cheeks took on a purplish tinge. Roscoe's lips moved clumsily.

"Dizzy — it's just a little — dizzy —"

"That's all it is," Jack soothed. "And it will pass."

A wind rose, a chill wind laced with the breath of the upper snows. The sun, a red ball veiled in smoky haze, balanced on the ragged western ridges, then sank. In a nearby bush an owl hooted, something rustled.

"There she is," Roscoe said suddenly, with great clarity.

"What?" Jack asked. "What do you mean?"

The old man's skinny chest heaved with the effort of breathing. He made an effort to raise a withered arm to point. The muscles only trembled a little; his hand fell back to his side.

"There. Up there! See, in the sun?"

Jack looked toward the twin crags. Caught by the rays of the setting sun, they glowed like fine gold.

"I — I see her," he murmured.

"She's there!" Roscoe insisted. "She's there, waiting!" He tried to sit up. "I'm coming!" he cried. "God damn it, wait for me! I'm coming!"

The fit climaxed, the old man stopped, frozen into immobility by the bursting of some great blood vessel. When Jack caught him in his arms, Uncle Roscoe was already dead.

He laid the old prospector down, drawing his coat over the waxen face, now drained of blood. Pansy ambled up and stared at the still form. She looked questioningly at Jack Drumm, made a small whickering sound.

"He's dead," Jack told her. "Uncle Roscoe is dead, Pansy."

Without his coat, he was cold. He shivered in the chilling air. The sun was well gone, now. Over the Gypsy Dancer shone a faint silver glow. Soon the moon would rise.

He muttered a few remembered words over the still form, then piled rocks over the body. Tearing off branches of juniper, he fashioned a rude cross, laced together with vines, and propped it at the head of the grave.

"*Requiescat,*" he muttered, "*in pace, amicus meus.*"

Cold, weary, and apprehensive, he took Tom's reins and started again up the rocky slope, slipping and falling in the rubble, bruising his knees and his hand. He had hardly started, however, when strong arms pinioned him from behind. He was thrown violently to the ground. The roan whinnied in fear as shadowy forms surrounded them, pulling at the bridle. Dazed by the fall, Jack lay flat, staring at the lean form bending over him.

222

There was not much light but there could be no mistaking the savage visage. His captor was the *sobrino*, Agustín's nephew. His captor was the youth who had been captured at the Second Battle of the Agua Fria, and whom Jack Drumm had freed to carry a defiant message to his uncle.

CHAPTER
TWELVE

For days they kept him in a brush hut. It was dark and cold, though winter sun filtered through. Twice a day a guard brought a tin plate filled with stew — from the faintly sweetish taste Jack guessed the meat was horseflesh. At night he slept under captured cavalry blankets, and was warm enough. Though they did not bind his hands, always there were guards lounging about the hut, bandy-legged silent little men with repeating rifles and sullen stares.

When one brought in his food, Jack tried to speak to him.

"I came here to talk to Agustín," he said, speaking slowly and carefully. "Will you take me to him?"

The man sat cross-legged near the low door of the hut, watching him eat. A Springfield rifle, probably captured also from the cavalry, lay across his knees.

"Do you speak English?"

Only the sullen stare; the eyes were flat and opaque, like those of a snake.

"Do you speak Spanish, then?" Jack tried hard to remember. "Let me see! ¿Que va usted a hacer con — well, conmigo?"

Still no response, only the heavy-lidded stare.

"Is there a white woman here? A woman with red hair — *cabello rojo, como cobre* — like copper?"

Seeing the plate empty, the man rose and snatched it away. When Jack shouted at him, he paused for a moment, silhouetted in the light through the doorway.

"Damn it all, I'm tired of sitting here in this hut like a rabbit in a hutch!" Frustrated, he rubbed his limbs. "Can't you let me out of here for a bit? I won't try to get away! I just want to walk a little — stretch my arms and legs!"

The man did not appear to understand. But that afternoon one of the other guards stuck his head in and motioned.

"Thank you," Jack said. "*Gracias!* That's very thoughtful of you."

A watchful captor on each side, he was allowed to stroll through Gu Nakya, Agustín's stronghold. First reports had indicated that only about fifty Apaches had run away from the Verde River reservation. Yet there were many more here, including women and children. Other bands had joined the rebellious chieftain.

Though the sun shone brightly in the thin atmosphere, the air was cold and biting. A chill wind tossed the branches of junipers and stunted pines, and drifts of snow lay about. In a sun-warmed depression among the rocks women ground something between flat rocks — probably mesquite beans or sunflower seeds — to make Apache bread. A small boy left his mother and followed Jack about, eating a fruit of the *nopal*, the "Indian fig." The fruit was spiny with thorns; not for a moment taking his black eyes from the prisoner, the child picked off the needles and continued to eat.

In the middle of Gu Nakya was a brush hut larger than the others, with a pennon of some sort floating over it. Apparently it was a ceremonial structure, perhaps Agustín's headquarters. Warriors gathered about it, playing cards with a greasy deck. As Jack watched, a band of horsemen, riding awkwardly as Dunaway said the Apaches did, cantered toward the flag and dismounted as if reporting. It was then that he saw the pennon was his own Union Jack, the glorious old red flag, hanging over an Apache jacal.

Furious, he started toward the hut. One of his captors struck him on the shoulder with the barrel of his rifle and motioned him back.

"That's my flag!" Jack protested. He scowled at the man. "*Bandera!* Mine! Do you understand?"

Roughly they pushed him back into his hut. The next day he was not allowed out. Sullen, he sat cross-legged all day, marking the passage of time by the tracery of sunlight crawling across the dirt floor. When they let him out again, he was more circumspect. As he walked, feeling the juices flow in his cramped limbs, he stared hungrily about, trying to find some sign, some bit of evidence, that Phoebe Larkin was in the hostile camp. Men came and went, parleys were held in the big hut, his flag snapped in the breeze as if not knowing its disgrace. People watched him shamble about with little interest, though the small boy eating figs still dogged his heels.

226

"A woman," he said to his guards. "A pretty woman —" Was Phoebe pretty by Apache standards? Probably not. "A tall lady, taller than you —" He gestured. "With red hair." Searching, he found in his pocket a few bits of horehound candy he kept for the Sloat children. He handed some to the guards. "Have you seen her?"

They held the candy in leathery palms, sniffed. One touched his tongue to it, nodded with satisfaction. The others sucked on theirs, and appeared more favorably disposed toward him. But still they would not speak, though by now he was sure some of them understood English.

It was frustrating, as well as nerve-racking, to be kept like a prize capon in a pen, fed, exercised, maintained in prime condition for — what? He did not know. If they wanted his death, surely the *sobrino* would have slain him when the scouting party first stumbled on him. Perhaps the only thing that now maintained a semblance of his sanity was the possibility of Phoebe Larkin still existing somewhere in the rabbit warren of brush huts dotting the rocky bowl of Gu Nakya. As time went on, even that small possibility dwindled.

One night he awoke trembling and perspiring from a bad dream. Usually, in spite of captivity, he slept well enough. This night, however, he tossed and rolled and muttered strange words. The camp was silent; over the hut floated a shadowy thing with a soft feathery flutter. An owl, undoubtedly — a great owl. That, he remembered from Uncle Roscoe's reminiscences, meant death; at least, to an Apache it meant death.

227

Suddenly, bitterly, he knew Phoebe Larkin had perished. No doubt about it — the consciousness fastened an iron hand over his heart. They had killed her, of course. A white woman had been seized; that was enough to show Agustín's defiance of the Army. Phoebe Larkin would be an inconvenience in this rude camp. He hoped she had died quickly, mercifully. But why was *he* still alive? He fell into a troubled sleep, waking late and then only when a stolid-faced guard shook him by the shoulder.

"You — come."

Stumbling into the winter sunshine, rubbing his eyes, he saw the youth who had captured him — Agustín's nephew — waiting. In spite of the chill, the *sobrino* wore only a thin cotton shirt and a breechcloth. He carried a ceremonial lance, and regarded Jack Drumm with an obsidian stare.

"I am Nacho," he murmured.

Jack pulled the remnants of his best woolen suit about him. "Nacho, eh?"

"I am Nacho. You come with me."

"As I remember it, you didn't speak any English when you were tied to that chair down at my ranch along the Agua Fria. As a matter of fact you didn't say anything — just sat there like a carved Buddha!"

Nacho shook his head. "I not know Buddha." He pointed toward the great hut. "You go there. He — *mi tio* — wait."

Inside, the hut was dark and smoky. A fire burned low. In the corners of the structure lay earthenware ollas, scattered furs and blankets, boxes of Springfield ammunition from a looted wagon train. As Jack's eyes became accustomed to the smoky darkness, he saw warriors with painted faces sitting in a ring. A man dropped wood on the fire, kicked it into flame. Fiery tongues leaped up. Sitting on a dais was Agustín himself, Agustín the renegade, the scourge of the Agua Fria. The chieftain wore the high leather hat; twinkling flames reflected from the bits of glass and tin adorning the crown.

When they had first brought him to the camp as a prisoner, Jack Drumm had been very frightened. After a while, unable to maintain the intensity of great fear, fear had turned into despondency, at last almost indifference. Now, standing alone before Agustín himself, he felt fear again. Though the air was cold — the small fire did little to warm the hut — beads of perspiration broke out on his forehead. Fear pervaded his loins also, as if they were filled with an enervating fluid.

"My uncle talk to you," Nacho said, indicating the dais.

In one hand Agustín held a rattle, ornamented with feathers and shells. Around his neck hung the sack of hoddentin, sacred hoddentin, his personal medicine. Sitting cross-legged on the dais, there was great majesty about him. He was broad-chested, large by Apache standards, shiny black hair only slightly tinged with gray. The hawklike nose had been broken in some forgotten fight. Though askew, it gave him a faint resemblance to a woodcut of an ancient Roman senator Jack recalled from a book in his father's library at

Clarendon Hall. For a long time Agustín stared unblinking at Jack Drumm, measuring him. Then he spoke.

"Eh?" Jack asked. "What did he say?" His lips were dry, throat parched. His voice sounded strange and husky.

Nacho lingered behind him. "He say — he give you that scar on your face — in a fight."

Jack's fingers moved toward the jagged scar traversing the cheek and ending on his upper lip. The cicatrix seemed to tremble, burn.

"Yes," he admitted. "He did! But he also lost one of his warriors! I buried him near the river, with a stake at his head and his medicine sack hanging from it."

It was sheer bravado. Yet, having said it, he felt better. Nacho translated. Agustín spoke.

"That is so. It was Eskimin you killed. He was old, and not a very good fighter." In a voice high-pitched for such a powerfully built man, Agustín went into a long discourse. Pausing, he looked at his nephew and imperially waved the rattle.

"He says he not know why he lets you live. Maybe, my uncle thinks, it is because he wants to look you. Before — night — everything fighting, all mixed up. But now you prisoner. You stand here, he looks, everybody looks, see what kind of man you are, how — how —"

"Yes?"

Nacho shrugged, a gesture almost Oriental. "How you look when you going to die."

230

The flush of panic swept through him again but Jack willed himself to resist it.

"Let him take a good look at me," he cried. "He will see how an Englishman faces death!"

Agustín nodded, as if terminating some private thought. Leaning forward, he shook the rattle in imprecation. His voice was rancorous, and from time to time the circle of elders grunted approval. Jack stood his ground, willing himself not to flinch even when the feathered rattle danced near his face.

"He say, my uncle say," Nacho translated, "you come on his land, along the river, and make camp. He say you stay there, fight his people, kill some. He say he try make you go away, write you —" The youth fumbled for words.

"Letter?" Jack muttered through dry lips.

"I write letter for him. But you do not leave when he asks you."

Outside the hut the wind howled, but inside the heat became stifling. Jack wiped his face with a dirty handkerchief, dabbed at his forehead. A man sitting close to him pulled curiously at the fabric of Jack's trousers, and he jumped. He remembered his brother Andrew's stories about India, how Andrew had once been caught in a crowd of hostile Punjabis and faced them down. He could do no less.

"More people come, camp along the river where our gods live. The horse-soldiers come too, to protect them." Agustín's voice rose to a singsong wail, reciting Apache grievances, describing how his people had been maltreated, cheated, herded onto reservations like

231

animals, when they had once owned all the Territory and the lands beyond.

"Tell him —" Jack interrupted, but was silenced by a hatchetlike sweep of Agustín's brown hand. The chief stood up; the circle of elders chanted a Greek chorus to his lament.

"This world and the sun were made by the gods, by our gods. It ought to be left as it always was. No man has any business to divide it up, to say the Tinneh go here and the Tinneh there, and the white man will take everything else. We have been here for a long time. The gods made us out of clay and water and baked us in the fire of the sun and put us here to stay. Who made the white people?"

Why was Agustín telling him all this? Jack had a prickly feeling at the back of his neck.

"The Tinneh and the earth are the same. The measure of the land and the measure of our bodies is the same. We always lived here until you came, you white people. Maybe you think the gods sent you here to do with us what you want. If we thought that was what the gods wanted we would bow our heads and obey. But the gods did not send you!" Agustín clenched his fists at the smoke-blackened roof of the hut. "*They did not send you!*"

Even through the imperfect screen of Nacho's translation the words carried a towering emotional impact. The words were frustrated; they were tortured and despairing, the words of a powerful man whose magic has unaccountably waned. The old men were

232

moved, also. They wailed, some covered their faces with blankets.

Agustín opened his eyes, the knotted fists slowly relaxed. As if recovering from a spell, he looked about him. His bare chest heaved wetly. He seemed smaller, physically smaller. Breathing heavily, he wiped sweating hands on his cotton pants. The feathered rattle fell to the dirt floor.

"Tell him —" Jack said.

No one paid any attention to him. They were watching Agustín. The chorus wailed, and the sound was a dirge. Someone in the circle started what sounded like a protest, but the rest quickly cut him off and looked again to their leader.

"Tell him," Jack insisted again, "tell him I do not come to fight him any more! If the land was his, it is his again. I do not want his land. All I want is — I want the white woman, the woman with the long red hair. I will die if that is what Agustín's gods want, but first he must tell me what happened to the white woman. If she is alive, I want to talk to her. If she is dead — if she has been killed — I want to go where she lies and tell her I am sorry. Will Agustín —" He turned to the elders. "Will anyone tell me about the white woman?"

Agustín made an impatient gesture.

"He does not know anything about a white woman," Nacho translated.

If he were going to die anyway, he might as well speak his mind. "We are different people," Jack said. "We do not see things the same way. But there can be honor among men who fight each other, like the

233

Tinneh and the white men. So I say — anyone who lies is not an honorable man."

Agustín's eyes glittered. "Who is talking about honor? A white man! The white men steal and kill and lie all the time! They give my people sick beef, and tell Two Star Crook we are making trouble! White men are devils, all of them!" He flung something at Jack Drumm. Startled, Jack caught it. It was the Apache knife, the one that had pinned Agustín's threatening note to the hitching post, the scrawled note commanding Jack to leave Rancho Terco.

"My uncle says enough talk now," Nacho murmured.

The elders drew back to the far recesses of the hut. Someone kicked out the fire and dredged the embers away. The great hut was only dimly lit by winter sun filtering through the brush of its construction. Jack looked down at the fine-honed steel.

"You are brave, you talk loud outside!" Nacho said. "My uncle wants to find out if you are brave inside, where no one can see!"

Jack weighed the knife in his hand. So this was it, this was the end. When he and Eggie were in Galati, near Bucharest, he had once seen two gypsies fight with knives in a café. He knew nothing of such fighting, remembering only the slain man, stomach slashed open, life spilling from him like oats from a torn sack. He took a deep trembling breath, and hoped his trembling did not show. The knife betrayed him. A reflected glow shimmered on the mud-daubed wall as his hand trembled also.

"I do not know how to fight this way," he muttered.

Nacho did not speak, did not translate his words. It was too late for words. Agustín smiled a hard-lipped smile. The single utterance, almost spat, could mean only one thing.

"Fight!"

The chief stepped like a cat into the cleared circle, holding the knife low, cutting edge uppermost, motioning in a gesture like a snake's forked tongue darting in and out.

"Fight!"

Surely if Agustín wanted to dispose of Jack Drumm all he had to do was signal one of the braves! They would drag him into the open and hack him to death with knives and hatches, not wasting bullets.

"Fight!" Agustín's face contorted with scorn. In a half crouch he darted forward; the menacing knife sliced through the stuff of Jack's coat sleeve and drew blood. Involuntarily Jack drew back, and someone in the circle of elders tittered.

"All right!" he cried. "Damn it all, if that's what you want, you'll get it!"

It was not bravado this time. He was angry, annoyed, humiliated in a way no Englishman could countenance. He tore off the hampering coat, unbuttoned his shirt, and held out his own knife in a reasonable facsimile of the gypsy in the Romanian café.

The fight, if so it was called, did not last long. Agustín circled relentlessly, darting in and out and pinking him whenever and wherever he chose. The chief had been born to the knife, the hatchet, the gun. Grinning, he taunted his opponent. The elders shouted jeers and catcalls, much the same as the spectators at the Boxing Club when one of Jem Mace's opponents made a poor showing. Jack was in excellent physical condition, trim and hard-muscled; never in his life had he felt so quick, so alert, so conditioned by the arduous labor at Rancho Terco. Yet these things did not avail. He simply did not know how to fight with a knife.

Sweating and winded, he threw his pale body against Agustín's swarthy one. Knife wrists locked, bodies strained against each other. Lungs laboring, sweat rolling from his brow, he managed to get his heel behind Agustín's naked calf and pushed the chief backward in a hock-trip. But Agustín quickly recovered, only for a moment staggering in lost equilibrium and then gliding forward again. But he spoke to Jack Drumm, a single word. It was an odd thing to say — *Inju*. Jack remembered that word — old Charlie used it a lot. *Inju*. Good!

The elders applauded too, with appreciation of skill even in a white man. Only the *sobrino*, Nacho, remained impassive. From the corner of his eye Jack saw the young man standing somberly in the shadows, arms folded. But Agustín darted snakelike toward him again and he retreated, stepping backward, hoping to let the chief tire himself in the attack. Perhaps something would happen. Agustín might stumble, fall —

The end came quickly. Jack's booted foot caught. He toppled and fell, knife flying from his hand. Perhaps he had tripped on one of the wooden ammunition cases. Perhaps one of the elders, impatient at delay of the final

236

bloodletting, had stuck out a moccasined foot. In any case, details were unimportant. Half stunned, he lay flat, the Apache atop him, bare knees on his chest and knife poised.

Had it been foredestined? Had Clarendon Hall, the public schools, Cambridge, Glasgow, the Grand Tour — all these — were they only preparation to die under a savage knife in the Arizona Territory? Fascinated, he watched the blade poised in midair. The world disappeared, Agustín disappeared, there was only the knife — and John Peter Christian Drumm.

He found himself trying to think of a prayer, a plea to a God whom he would soon meet, but could think of nothing. Nothing, that is, except Phoebe Larkin. He saw again her pale face burned by the sun, the high-piled red hair. He saw the sprinkle of freckles across the bridge of her nose, the cerulean depths of her eyes. He ought to be commending his soul to an Anglican deity, but there was Phoebe Larkin, smiling at him, eyes wet with tears! Was she there, across the Styx waiting to welcome him with tender arms? Or was she —

Suddenly he knew he could not die in the brush hut under Agustín's knife. He knew Phoebe was alive, and he must go to her. Gathering his muscles, tensing his back, he heaved himself into the air, at the same time shouting to the limit of his lungs. He did not know what he yelled; "God and St. George!" would have been a nice touch. But he shouted, and heaved, and rolled and scrambled to his knees. Agustín, caught unawares, tumbled off him. Jack Drumm sprang like an Indian tiger, reaching for the throat as the tiger did.

Together they rolled on the dusty floor, Agustín's hands vainly trying to break the iron grip on his throat. But Nacho fell quickly on Jack Drumm also, breaking his grip, aiding his uncle. That was unfair, but there it was. Savages knew nothing of fair play. Finally pinioned, Jack stood panting in the middle of the circle, Nacho and some of the elders holding his arms.

Agustín faced him, one hand rubbing a bruised throat. He too was sweating, caked with dust. The bare chest heaved; the leather hat, sign of chieftaincy, had been knocked off. He looked at Jack Drumm. There was no triumph in his stare; it seemed compounded of a strange mixture of emotions — sadness, perhaps, and yet a certain satisfaction.

"*Inju,*" he said again.

Picking up the beaded leather hat, he held it a moment in his hands. In a corner of the hut the fire still flickered. Agustín dropped the hat into the flames, watching as tongues of flame licked at the oiled headgear.

No one spoke. The elders watched, waited, Nacho did not speak. There was only Agustín, chief of the Tonto Apaches, gazing abstractedly into the fire while the leather curled, blackened, burned. He touched the charred remains of the hat with his toe; they fell into ash. He sighed. Jack Drumm realized it was the first time he had heard an aborigine make that sound. It had always seemed a white man's device.

238

Suddenly Agustín squared his shoulders. Not paying any attention to the spectators, he raised the deerhide hanging over the doorway of the hut and stalked outside. In single file the elders, and Nacho, followed. In the winter sun waited the others; warriors, a few women and children. Golden light of late afternoon streamed through the dwarfed trees, dappled the rocks, lit the patches of snow. Smoke from cooking fires drifted through the branches of the pines and junipers. From a brush corral a stolen horse whinnied. The people, his Tinneh, watched Agustín. But he did not look at them.

With the easy lope of the trailwise Apache he passed the waiting faces, taking a path through the trees, toward the sun, toward the east. For a moment Jack Drumm, winded and perspiring, glimpsed him among the trees. Then he was gone.

Jack turned to Nacho. The youth was staring at the ground, scratching a cabalistic pattern in the dust with a stick. Jack looked at the camp people. They were still watching the trees where Agustín had disappeared. One woman drew a blanket over her head. A child whimpered, and the mother put a gentle hand over its mouth. Nothing broke the silence except the call of a jay, the mourning of the chill wind.

"We go now," Nacho murmured.

Jack blinked in the fading sunlight. His arm bled where Agustín had cut him, and he dabbed at the wound with a dirty handkerchief.

Nacho pointed toward the huts. "We go this way."

239

Limping behind Nacho, Jack was aware he had twisted his ankle during the fight. In the aftermath of the struggle he began to tremble. Now that immediate danger was gone, he shook like one of the quaking aspens indigenous to the mountains. With clumsy fingers he wrapped the handkerchief around the wound in his arm and pulled it tight.

"*Aqui*," Nacho said. "Here. This is the place."

They stood before a low brush shelter, so cradled among giant rocks it appeared almost a natural part of the landscape.

"You go in," Nacho gestured.

Was this some kind of trick? But there appeared to be no deceit in Nacho's eyes.

"Go in," Nacho repeated, and walked away. He joined the rest under the trees; they sat on the rocks, and did not talk to one another, yet seemed united in common feeling.

Puzzled, he pulled aside the deerhide and stepped within. For a moment he stared blindly, eyes unaccustomed to the darkness.

"Jack?"

He blinked.

"Jack?"

Suddenly she was in his arms, clasping him tightly, head pressed hard against his chest, crying and laughing at the same time.

"I knew you'd come!"

It was Phoebe Larkin.

240

CHAPTER
THIRTEEN

Holding her in his arms, body warm and soft against his, he paused for a moment, listening.

"What is it?"

"I don't know," he muttered. "I don't know." He shook his head. "Something queer is going on tonight in the camp."

"What do you mean?"

He told her about the big brush hut, about the fight, about the way Agustín walked, silent and erect, toward the east, and how the people seemed to mourn.

"Listen," he said, "even now —"

Together they peered through the chinks in the hut where the mud plastering had fallen away. The sun had fallen quickly behind the screen of trees, and it was twilight. A huge fire blazed in the clearing. Around it Agustín's people — the Tinneh — were ranged. Someone harangued them in the sibilant Apache tongue. A meeting was taking place.

"What are they doing?" Phoebe whispered.

"I don't know."

"What will they do with us, Jack?"

"I don't know that either," he admitted.

She shuddered, pushing a strand of hair back from her face. He saw her face dimly, very pale, in the gloom of the hut.

"They came so quick, that night along the river! I was cleaning some wild celery. All of a sudden there they were, swarming all over the place like — like bees! I shot one — I always carried the derringer in my — bosom. But one of them grabbed me and tied me up and threw me over a horse. Mr. Sloat came running, then, and tried to help me, but —" Her voice trailed away in a half sob.

"No need to talk of it now," Jack comforted, patting her shoulder.

He went to the doorway, pulled aside the deerskin flap. After a moment he slipped outside. When he returned his face was puzzled.

"There's no one out there. I mean — no guard!"

"What does that signify?"

"Our situation appears to have changed in some way."

He could see the spark of hope in her eyes.

"Maybe — maybe they're going to let us go!"

"Hardly likely! And there's no one so unpredictable as an Apache. If we tried to get out of here, they'd cut our throats, quickly."

"What must we do then?"

In distress she clung to him. The red hair, loose and flowing, lay silkily against his cheek, the ripe swell of her thigh pressed against the hard muscles of his own. Voice trembling, but not from fear, he muttered, "Wait, I guess."

"I suppose I should be scared. I was, till you came. Now I'm not anymore. Maybe they'll kill us, Jack, but — but somehow I'm happy! Happy you came, happy we're together, even in a scary situation like this!"

His arm girdled her slender waist in the poet's narrow compass. *All that's good and all that's fair.* At the meeting in the clearing someone pounded a drum; the pulse in his ears thudded in time to the savage beat.

"Phoebe," he said thickly. "Phoebe, I —" He touched her hair, feeling pleasure as the coppery strands sifted through his calloused fingers.

"What is it, Jack?"

He carried her to the pile of skins in a corner of the hut and they sank down clasped together in ecstasy that was strange and wondrous to John Peter Christian Drumm. He hoped it was wonderful to Phoebe Larkin also, and finally believed on good evidence that it was.

Afterward they lay for a long time in each other's arms. Moon-light, light from a winter moon, shone fitfully through cracks in the brush hut. The air grew cold but they were warm in their nearness. The meeting of the Tinneh was still going on. The voices, the drum, came to them only faintly.

"Do you love me, Jack?"

Unbidden in his mind came a quick image of Cornelia Newton-Barrett. He ought, of course, to feel very guilty, but somehow he did not; that troubled him. To cover his confusion, he equivocated.

"Do you love *me?*"

As always, she was quick and forthright in her answer.

243

"It seems like I always have, and I know I always will! How could it be any other way? When the Prescott stage came into your place along the river, arrows sticking out all over it, and I saw you standing there, something — something inside of me trembled. Oh, I couldn't give it much thought right then — Mr. Meech was hot on our trail — but a shiver went through me, and I said to myself, 'This is it, Phoebe Larkin! This is it — the real thing — and now you're on the run and won't probably ever see him again.'"

Reminded, he told her, "You need not worry any longer about Mr. Meech; he has given up the pursuit. It seems old Buckner fell down the stairs and broke his neck. His relatives have balked at spending any more money to catch you — you and Beulah Glore."

"He didn't!"

"He did, indeed."

She rose on an elbow to face him. "I can hardly believe it! I mean, to have been chased so long —" She sighed. "Still, I feel sorry for poor Mr. Buckner. He was lonely, I suppose, but he didn't know how to love anyone." For a long moment she was silent. Then she said, "It's — what do you call it? Ironic — yes, that's the word! It's ironic that I don't have to worry about Mr. Meech anymore, but now I've got to worry about — about —" She wept, burying her face against his shoulder. "About — about us! I don't mind dying so much, but I don't want to lose *you!*"

In the face of her love he hated himself for his lack of equal frankness. The words of the song came to him: *All that's good and all that's fair*. He made the plunge.

244

"Yes, God damn it! Yes, indeed — I *do* love you, Phoebe! I loved you from that first instant, only I was too damned cold — what was it you said? Cold as Mose's toe? I was too damned glacial and British to admit my own feelings! So I was very polite and reserved, though inside I felt something churning, but I made myself believe it was the damned wild corn I ate that day! I *did* love you, and I *do* love you, and I will never stop loving you!" He paused. "Ah — by the way, who was Mose?"

"Mose who?"

"The one who had the cold toe."

In spite of the danger, she giggled. "*I* don't know! It was just something Uncle Buell used to say!" She was thoughtful for a moment, then asked hesitatingly, "Am I as pretty as Cornelia, Jack?"

Somehow or other, he could not remember exactly how Cornelia Newton-Barrett looked. Blond, certainly — stately, with brown eyes. He did, however, remember exactly how Cornelia's ogress mother looked, and winced. But Cousin Lionel had always gotten along well with Cornelia's mother. In fact, Lionel had been one of Cornelia's unsuccessful suitors. Yes, that was right! He felt relieved. Probably when he heard the news, Lionel would take up where he had left off when Jack Drumm entered Cornelia's picture. Probably Lionel would even become Lord Fifield; the thought did not distress him.

Phoebe gave his arm a hard pinch. "What were you dreaming about? I was talking to you!"

"Yes," he said. "Yes, indeed. You are *much* prettier than Cornelia! She cannot hold a candle to you, Phoebe Larkin, and I am the luckiest man in the world to have discovered you, here in the Arizona Territory, and being captured by Apaches is a small price to pay for being here with you, in this brush hut, no matter what happens tomorrow — or ever!"

Not caring about tomorrow, they lay again in each other's arms until it was tomorrow. Sometime during the night the firelit meeting came to a conclusion. The voices departed, the drums stilled, finally there was only moonlit silence. Jack went to the doorway and looked out. There were no guards, no restraints. In the lime-white rays of the moon the camp at Gu Nakya slumbered. The fire the Tinneh had built was now a bed of coals. A scrawny dog, bone in its mouth, hurried past him and was lost in the shadows. From far down the mountain came the frantic yips and yaps of coyotes on the hunt. Though Jack could not see the Tinneh sentinels, he knew that on the parapets of rock overlooking the valley they were scanning the night, watchful for attack. He went back into the hut and lay again beside her.

"What is it, Jack?"

"Nothing."

"What time can it be?"

"Near dawn, I think." He kissed her ear. "Now go to sleep. Whatever is to happen, you will need your rest."

"I am not afraid," she said, and slept with her head in the crook of his arm. He lay silent, thinking of Eggleston and Beulah Glore, safe on the cars of the

Atlantic and Pacific. By this time they were certainly in New York City, perhaps even on the high seas. He would not, however, exchange his situation for theirs. He was happy, almost irresponsibly happy, in a way he did not know Englishmen were supposed to be happy. It seemed very improper, yet there it was. The whole thing was so right, so utterly right; even, perhaps, preordained. After a while he slept, also, and did not wake till there sounded a scratching at the hide-covered doorway. Instantly roused, he sat up.

"Who is it?"

The deerskin flap was pulled aside. Early morning sun bathed the rude interior of the hut. He blinked, rubbing his eyes.

"Who's there?"

It was Nacho — the *sobrino* — Agustín's nephew. Blanket thrown over his lean shoulders against the morning chill, he squatted inside the doorway. Around his neck was the precious sack of hoddentin, the sacred meal, that his uncle had previously worn.

He pointed to Phoebe Larkin. "You send her away."

"But —"

"Send her away! We talk. A man does not talk important things before his women!" Nacho gestured; one of the old women of the camp entered the hut and took Phoebe by the arm.

"Where are you taking her?" Jack demanded.

"The Red Hair Woman will not be hurt," Nacho promised. "They give her food —" He looked at Phoebe's scanty attire. "They give her food, and clothes to wear."

247

"I think it's all right," he said. "Go with the woman, Phoebe."

"I will," she said. "I'm not afraid, Jack."

Though giving him a last uneasy look, she obeyed. Nacho watched her go.

"We talk now."

"As you wish."

The young man took out the scratching stick the Tinneh men carried and poked at his head, apparently at a loss as to how to begin. After a while, not looking at Jack Drumm, he muttered, "Words! English words! I don't have many to say what I want. But I try."

"I will understand," Jack promised.

"My uncle," Nacho began, "raise me from a little boy. He was a warrior. But when white men cheated him he took his men and went away from the Verde River place — the — the —"

"The reservation," Jack prompted.

"Yes. That is what they call it. But it was a thing to keep animals in, that reservation. So he lead the Tinneh away, and started to fight again, as we did in the old days. But things did not go right. My uncle had bad medicine. Too many soldiers came along the river. We fought them — we fought you too, Ostin —"

Jack remembered Uncle Roscoe's words. *Ostin is Apache talk for "Lord." Anything they respect or fear they call Ostin — the bear, snakes, lightning.*

"We fought you too. My uncle said you were a brave man, stay along the river when it was his sacred place, his medicine place, and he wanted you to go away. He

248

thought you a good man, too, let me go back to Gu Nakya — no kill."

Tentatively, respectfully, Nacho's slender fingers fumbled at the hoddentin sack around his neck.

"We went down and stole a lot of horses. Always, the Tinneh walked before, but we thought maybe horses, riding horses, would make a difference. We ride horses, the way the soldiers do, and ride back to the mountain before the soldiers could catch us." He shrugged. "But now they have mirror-talk, same as us. Always there were soldiers ready when we came. So that did not work either."

He got up to pace the dirt floor of the hut, strong brown legs knotting in muscles as he walked.

"My uncle knew it was no good. He led the Tinneh up on the mountain just to die. It was no good to fight anymore. But he had the Red Hair Woman. He told me, he said that Englishman along the river, that white man I cut in the face with my knife, he come after the Red Hair Woman. My uncle said that. My uncle believed that. And he said, my uncle said — when he comes, I want to talk to him and see if he is brave and good like I think."

"But — why? Why did he not just kill me when he had the chance?"

Annoyed to be interrupted with a difficult task, Nacho made an impatient gesture.

"You came! My uncle looked at you, talked to you. He fought you with knives, and you not afraid to die. So he was satisfied. He took his lucky hat, his chief's hat, and burned it. He walked away, to the big rock in the east, and —"

Jack Drumm had never seen an Indian weep. Certainly Nacho did not weep. But there was a glint in his somber eye. For a moment, it seemed his voice caught, broke.

"So he died. Because he had bad luck, he did not want to live anymore."

Jack was moved. "But why — I mean — why am I —"

"Ostin Drumm," Nacho said, "my uncle told me you are a brave man, a fair man, a smart man. He said you would lead us down the mountain, speak for us to that Gold Leaf Trimble. My uncle said that Trimble was a bad man, an evil man, a man who understood only blood, a man who killed Tinneh women and babies at Big Canyon to get those gold leaves on his shoulders. Now we know Trimble has these new guns, these shiny guns, that shoot faster than a hundred men. We are scared of those guns, scared that when we come down to the river to surrender Trimble will shoot even the old people and the sick people with those guns and —" Nacho wiped one palm across the other in an eloquent gesture. "Wipe us out — women and children, everybody!"

He paused, his voice trembling with passion. "Ostin, the Tinneh do not beg! If Gold Leaf Trimble tries to shoot us with those shiny guns we will all die like Tinneh! But if you come with us down the mountain, go first to talk to Trimble, tell him we are giving up our

250

guns and will go to that Verde River place and learn how to be farmers and herdsmen —"

Afterward, Jack realized the young man could not have been so eloquent. Nacho's limited English was not equal to the task. Later he realized that much of what he remembered was supplied by Nacho's eloquent gestures. Much came also from Jack's own interpretation of an awkward phrase here, a misused word there.

"It is not the men," Nacho added. "We know how to die. But the women and children should not die."

Remembering how Indians weighed their words, deliberating a long time before speaking, Jack sat cross-legged in the hut, hands on knees, half naked, staring at the bright rectangle of sunlight in the open doorway. Nacho did not speak either. *Ostin*, Jack was thinking. *I am Ostin Drumm.* Somehow he was prouder of that title than he would ever have been of the title of Lord Fifield, Lord Fifield of Clarendon Hall, in Hampshire.

Nacho, he knew, was thinking also; thinking of a free and wild way of life that was vanishing. The Tinneh had been beaten. They would go back to the Verde River reservation. Hoes would be thrust into their hands, and rakes and shovels. The government, that mysterious force far to the east, would make of them farmers, herdsmen, mechanics. Maybe it was all for the best; surely it was the best for the citizens of the Arizona Territory, and perhaps best for the Tinneh too, in the long run. But something would be lost, something wild and free and soaring, like the eagle — Ostin Eagle. Agustín knew that, and died rather than lose it. Now the *sobrino* — Nacho — knew it too, and was ready to take the Tinneh into exile. He wanted Jack Drumm to help.

"I will do it," Jack promised. "It is an honor that you give me."

At dawn the next morning the Tinneh went down the mountain on their journey of surrender. Most, particularly the old men and women and children, rode horses — the stolen horses, the unavailing horses. They rode awkwardly, as Apaches did.

The journey was rough. Many would not have been able to make it on foot. There were wounded, too. Jack Drumm, with his small knowledge of medicine, did what he could, bandaging, lancing infected wounds, improvising a travoislike litter for a gangrenous man who suffered, but only lay silent and tight-lipped in the litter.

Nacho, chosen head of the vanquished Tinneh, led the way. Jack Drumm trotted beside him on Tom, the borrowed Spencer carbine in his saddle scabbard. Folded in his pocket was the precious Union Jack, also returned to him. It was ragged and dirty, and displayed several bullet holes. Behind them rode Phoebe Larkin in an Apache dress sewn from deerhide. She rode easily, expertly. "Why, of course!" she said in response to Jack Drumm's inquiry. "Of course I can ride! My uncle Buell taught me when I was a little girl in Pocahontas County!"

At the bend of the rocky trail Nacho reined up and stared toward the plume of white smoke above Gu

Nakya. When they left, the Tinneh had set afire the brush huts. *When someone dies*, Jack remembered, *they set the whole village afire and move away. They don't want to be reminded.*

Gold Leaf Trimble was certainly aware of their coming. Up and down the sierra winked the shafts of reflected sunlight from the new M-7 heliograph. At noon the band paused for water from a spring, ate a little dried meat from their scanty stores, and *pinole*, parched cornmeal soaked in water to make a thin gruel.

Sometime in the afternoon the wounded man in the litter died, as uncomplainingly as he had borne his wounds. They placed the body in a cairn of rocks. The women gathered around and wailed in unison, comforted the wife of the dead man. Then the column moved on, faster, hoping to reach the Agua Fria by dusk.

An orange ball glowing in a purplish haze, the sun was setting behind the ragged ridges as they approached the cavalry outposts.

"Wait here," Jack instructed. "I will ride down and tell them we have women and children, and some wounded, that we are coming in under parole to surrender."

Nacho gave him a long fathomless look. Finally he nodded. "*Inju.* All right."

Jack rode into the twilight, the roan stepping daintily among the rocks, pretending to shy and be startled when a partridge boomed out of a thicket.

"Easy, now," Jack muttered, patting the horse's arched neck. "Easy, Tom!"

Where are they? he wondered. *Where are the cavalry pickets? This is where Uncle Roscoe and I met them before.*

In the canyon with its steep sides he could see nothing but the trail directly ahead. Where were they? Surely Trimble knew they were coming. He reined in Tom, looking about. Could it be — an ambush?

"Trimble!" he shouted. "Dunaway! George Dunaway! It's me — Jack Drumm!"

Someone turned the crank of a Gatling gun and fire spat from the shadows of the canyon. Splinters of rock flew from the slablike walls, dust stung his nostrils, slugs screamed down the canyon, ricocheting from wall to wall.

"God damn it!" he yelled. "Stop it! Stop the shooting! It's me — Jack Drumm!"

Tom reared, pranced in a tight caracole, and threw him to the ground. He must have hit his head on a rocky ledge because brilliant yellow and red and green lights flashed behind his eyes, the world turned upside down, his ears rang. The Gatling gun cranked on, now joined by others; the canyon was filled with smoke and fire and deadly rolling thunder. He was showered with needlelike fragments of lead.

"Stop it!" he screamed. "God, stop the shooting!"

Gasping for breath, unsteady on his legs, half blinded from the stone dust and lead fragments, he groped along the canyon wall toward the guns.

"Stop it, I tell you! It's Drumm, Jack Drumm! Stop the shooting!"

254

The hungry chattering of the Gatlings paused, stuttered, paused again. For a moment the silence in the narrow canyon was oppressive. Then he heard George Dunaway's voice raised in anger.

"God damn it, stay away from that gun!"

"But Major Trimble said —"

Dunaway's words, most of them, were unprintable. "I don't care what Major Trimble said! Stand clear of that gun or I'll put a bullet through your fat skull!"

"George?" Jack called. "Dunaway?"

Through the dust and smoke came George Dunaway, revolver in one hand, the other clutching for support as he clambered among the rocks.

"Drumm! Is that you?" He shoved the revolver back in the holster and put an arm under Jack's elbow. "Here — let me help you! Are you hurt?"

Jack shook his head, gasped, "I don't think so!" He waved his arm toward the mouth of the canyon, now almost shrouded in night. "The Tinneh are back there! They're waiting to come in, to surrender!"

"The who?"

"Agustín's people! I rode down with them! They — they want to surrender!"

Dunaway was quickly professional. "How many of them? Are they armed?"

He was too tired, too recently released from the terror of the guns, to do anything but sit down on a flat rock. "Don't worry!" His lungs labored for air; he wheezed, coughed, holding his throat. "Don't worry about anything. I'll vouch for them."

For a long time he sat on the rock, Phoebe Larkin beside him, watching the defeated Tinneh ride by. The soldiers had lit torches; in the flickering light each warrior, as he passed by, raised a hand in salute to Jack Drumm, muttered something. Dunaway watched them, and shook his head.

"Beats anything I ever saw," he murmured, pushing the battered felt hat far back on his head. "We didn't have to fight them — they just came to us!" He chuckled. "No blood and brains spattered all over the rocks! Old Hardbutt Trimble will be real disappointed!"

As the Indians passed, Dunaway kept a tally in a notebook. "What is it they're saying?"

Jack knew. Each passing brave held up his hand, palm out, and called "Ostin." *Ostin Tinneh. Lord. Lord Drumm. Lord Apache.*

"They are saying good-bye," he told Dunaway.

"To you?"

He nodded. "To me, I suppose — and to a way of life. This is the end for them."

The end for them, he thought. *And a beginning for me and Phoebe Larkin.*

Wire communication was fast improving in the Territory. It did not take long for the word of the capture of Agustín's rebellious band to spread. Freed from the Apache menace, people rode out from Prescott in wagons to see the camp where the captive savages waited for the long journey back to the Verde River reservation.

256

Almost immediately wagon traffic had resumed on the road. The vehicles of the California and Arizona Stage Line made their runs between Phoenix and the capital. Quickly the story spread, also, of Jack Drumm's role as intermediary in the capture, and of how he had rescued the Red Hair Lady. Stuff of a legend was in the making, and it embarrassed him.

Sam Valentine wrung his hand, thanking him in the name of the Arizona Legislature. Ike Coogan grinned toothlessly and handed him a chew of Wedding Cake, allowing as how he'd better start now to carry his own tobacco, like a real Arizony *hombre*. Charlie the Papago brought his whole family to see the famous man. The children made garlands of desert flowers to hang around Jack's neck while he turned beet-red, prevented from flight only by Phoebe's arm linked with his. Perhaps the only unhappy person, with the exception of Nacho's people, was Major Henry Trimble, who — according to George Dunaway — was searching War Department regulations to see if there was something illegal in a civilian interfering with a military operation in the field.

Jack and Phoebe sat together in the shade of a ramada, the one structure of Rancho Terco that had not been destroyed. A carnival air prevailed. The Firemen's Brass Band and Silver Cornet Quartet had come out from Prescott with several barrels of beer in the back of their wagon; the settlement along the Agua Fria had a holiday air. Families strolled about, children played in the reeds and splashed in the river, the more daring citizens approached the Apache camp and stared at the subjugated foe, sullen in captivity but resigned. An issue of prime government beef had ameliorated their discomfort somewhat, and over greasewood fires sizzled whole sides.

"This place has changed since I — since we — came here," Jack mused.

Phoebe laid her cheek against his hand. "We have changed too, Jack."

Yes, he thought. *I have changed, certainly.* He could hardly remember the plump young man in sporting dress who wandered through the Territory only a few months ago, fowling piece under his arm and his nose buried in *The Traveler's Guide to the Far West*. Now that young man, dimly remembered, seemed a caricature, a foppish and absurd figure.

"When I first came here on the stage that day," Phoebe reminisced, "I was a foolish and a flighty young woman. I had my excuses, I suppose; after all, I *was* being pursued by the law for murder, or so I thought. By now —" She fell silent, staring into the purple distances.

"Now?"

She turned, looking into his eyes with that cerulean gaze. "I — I suppose, now, you will want to go home."

"Home?" For a moment he was puzzled. "Hampshire, I suppose you mean. Clarendon Hall."

Her gaze was steady, asking nothing. "That is what I mean."

He smiled. "I want our child — our first child — to be born in the Arizona Territory. Does that answer the question in your mind, Phoebe Larkin — soon to be

Phoebe Drumm?" Taking the carefully folded Union Jack from his pocket, he walked to the river. Cutting a stout reed, he fastened the flag to it. The United States flag fluttered over Major Trimble's command post, next to the ruined adobe. Jack drove the improvised staff into the ground next to the Stars and Stripes, propped it with a few rocks, and stepped back to admire the effect. It was then he heard Phoebe's shriek.

Shaken, he ran to the ramada. Alonzo Meech was smiling like a hoary crocodile, one cuff snapped to Phoebe's slender wrist and the other to his own. Jack stopped, bewildered, looking from Phoebe to the detective.

"What — what is this? Meech, you told me —"

The detective grinned. "Just to kind of round things off, Mr. Drumm! *Veni, vidi, vicious!* That's Latin for 'I caught up with her at last.' It's my little joke, kind of." Chuckling, he unlocked the bracelets and stuffed them in a capacious pocket. "Maybe it's a technicality, and it don't make any difference now, but I can say I *did* actual put the cuffs on Miss Phoebe! My record stands. I ain't never yet lost a customer!"

George Dunaway, too, found them sitting hand in hand under the ramada.

"Tomorrow," he said, "I'm taking B Company and escorting Nacho and his people to the Verde River reservation."

Jack looked toward Major Henry Trimble's tent.

"How is *he* taking all this?"

Dunaway grinned. "General Crook's sending Trimble to the Dakotas to fight Sioux! I'm commanding at Fort

Whipple, at least until they write orders for some Washington coffee-cooler to come out here and take over."

"I thought you were going to Australia," Phoebe said.

Dunaway looked sheepish. "Hell — excuse me, ma'am — but soldiering's my business, always has been. They don't need soldiers in Australia. I guess I'll just string along here, put in my thirty years, then retire and sit in the sun till the Big Bugler blows Taps. It's a rough life at times, but on the whole it isn't too bad — especially with old Trimble a thousand miles to the north of me!"

He shook hands with Jack Drumm, bowed awkwardly to Phoebe. "No, you don't, George!" Phoebe protested. She threw her arms about Dunaway, kissed him hard on the cheek.

"Good luck, George, in whatever you do," Jack called after him.

Dunaway paused in his rapid retreat, rubbing his cheek, the grizzled face an unaccustomed pink.

"I guess," he said, "the first boy ought to be called John Peter Christian Drumm, after his daddy. But you might give some thought to naming the next one George. George isn't a half-bad name for a boy."

Phoebe laughed. "It is surely not, George! Next to Jack, it is my favorite!"

When the moon rose over the Mazatzals they continued to sit under the ramada, listening to the night sounds, seeing the dying fires of the Apache camp. After a while Jack sighed, kissed her, pulled her close to him.

"It is time for bed," he whispered. "And in the morning I intend to get up early and start making adobe blocks for our new home."

Bibliography

1. Davis, Britton. *The Truth About Geronimo*. New Haven, Conn.: Yale University Press, 1929.
2. Summerhayes, Martha. *Vanished Arizona*. Philadelphia, Pa., 1908.
3. Hodge, Hiram C. *Arizona As It Is*. Boulder, Colo.: Johnson Publishing Co., 1877.
4. Bourke, John G. *On the Border with Crook*. New York: Charles Scribner's Sons, 1891.
5. — *An Apache Campaign in the Sierra Madre*. New York: Charles Scribner's Sons, 1886.
6. Harris, Foster. *The Look of the Old West*. New York: Viking Press, 1955.